CAUGHT IN A Bad Fauxmance

ELLE GONZALEZ ROSE

joy revolution

CONTENT NOTE: mentions the death of a parent

Text copyright © 2023 by Elle Gonzalez Rose
Jacket art copyright © 2023 by Cannaday Chapman

All rights reserved. Published in the United States by Joy Revolution, an imprint of Random House Children's Books, a division of Penguin Random House LLC, New York.

Joy Revolution is a registered trademark and the colophon is a trademark of Penguin Random House LLC.

GetUnderlined.com

Educators and librarians, for a variety of teaching tools, visit us at RHTeachersLibrarians.com

Library of Congress Cataloging-in-Publication Data is aavailable upon request.
ISBN 978-0-593-64579-6 (hardcover)—ISBN 978-0-593-64580-2 (lib. bdg.)—
ISBN 978-0-593-64582-6 (tr. pbk.)—ISBN 978-0-593-64581-9 (ebook)—
ISBN 978-0-593-70998-6 (int'l. ed.)

The text of this book is set in 12-point Baskerville MT.
Interior design by Ken Crossland

Printed in the United States of America
10 9 8 7 6 5 4 3 2 1
First Edition

For Daddy, who always knew I was a writer

CHAPTER ONE

Thirty minutes in the backseat together and my sister wants to kill me—a new record.

"Devin." Maya snaps her manicured fingers in my face when I ignore her. "Move over."

It's the third time she's made that demand since we piled into the car. Any other day I would pack up my drawing tablet and laptop and give her free rein over the backseat, but I'm holding my ground this time.

I push her hand away. "No, I'm working."

"No, you're not," she scoffs. "You've been looking at your phone this whole time. Your tablet isn't even on."

Up in the peaceful driver's seat, Dad sighs while Andy tries and fails to hold back a snort. We should've seen this coming when we let Andy call shotgun. It made sense at the time—shoving our six-foot-three stepbrother into the cramped backseat of our Honda Civic wouldn't have been fair—but Maya hates long drives, and my tablet takes up all the extra leg space. It was a recipe for disaster.

"I'm doing research," I reply indignantly.

I turn my attention back to the profile I was scouring, only for Maya to snatch the phone out of my hand. She tucks it right into the one place she knows I'm not willing to go: her bra. "Social media stalking your classmates doesn't count as research."

Scoping out the competition absolutely counts as research. "Yes, it does."

She gives me a deadpan look.

Okay fine, it doesn't.

Not that I'd ever admit it to her, but Maya's right. If I want any chance of not shooting my barely existent art career in the foot, I *should* be working on my application for the Cardarelli mentorship. Every spring semester, one CalArts freshman is whisked away to undergrad stardom by Professor Lila Cardarelli, an animator with so many accolades under her belt she needs a separate Wikipedia page to list them all.

Professor Cardarelli's protégés are basically gods, according to my roommate, my advisor, and just about everyone else at CalArts. You give up any semblance of free time in exchange for shadowing one of the most iconic names in animation. Internships at Pixar and Disney are essentially guaranteed once you've got a recommendation letter from Lila Cardarelli, who has the Disney family on speed dial. No one has any clue how Cardarelli picks her mentees, but it's the same application every year. Standard background information, and one enormously daunting assignment: attach *one* piece that you feel best expresses who you are as an artist.

Which sounds easy enough, except I barely have any idea who I am as a person, let alone an artist.

My first semester of almost-adulthood was less than stellar. Being surrounded by people who have been creating since they could hold a pencil and can produce gallery-worthy art in their sleep isn't exactly encouraging when you can barely grasp the basics of color theory. Especially when you're like me, someone who didn't consider animation as a profession until their junior year of high school. Six months ago, I thought I'd be in my element—living the cool, aloof LA art school kid life I'd seen in movies. Instead, I spent the past four months hardly ever leaving my dorm room just so I could keep up with all the homework. I've been in the land of eternal sunshine for three months and I'm even paler than when I arrived, and I've spent more time with the vending machine on my floor than my roommate.

So, yeah, I could really use a win right now.

The application isn't actually due until the first day of spring semester, and while procrastination has never done me any favors, I can't focus on productivity when my innocent phone is being held captive in my sister's gross, sweaty clutches.

"C'mon, give it back," I whine, nudging my knee against Maya's.

"Nope." She smacks her bubblegum and waves a finger at my tablet. "Pack it up or get drawing."

I can explain to her for the hundredth time that that's not how my artistic process works, or I can play dirty.

"Dad, Maya stole my phone."

"Give your brother his phone back," Dad mumbles, squinting at a sign about road closures.

Maya's glare would turn me to stone if I wasn't so used to being on the receiving end of her rage. Whoever said twins have a special psychic bond lied. The last time Maya and I were on the same page was when we sent Mami into labor ten weeks before our due date. We've been menaces since the day we were born.

We stare each other down, unblinking and unrelenting, until she lunges at me. On instinct, I curl around my tablet, protecting it from her wrath. She goes for the cord connecting it to my laptop instead, ready to yank it free, when Dad springs into action.

"Hey!" he shouts, startling all of us, even Andy, into total silence. "Watch it around the tablet," he warns, focusing back on the road once Maya retreats to her side of the car.

She begrudgingly hands me back my phone, sticking her tongue out at Dad when he's distracted by a Prius that gets too close to us. "Sometimes I think you love that thing more than you love either of us."

"With how much I paid for it, yes, I do," Dad replies.

Guilt settles too comfortably in the pit of my stomach. It's no secret that my tablet's price tag was more than we should've spent, but Dad had insisted we splurge on the CalArts recommended model instead of the used three-generations-old one I'd found on eBay. It was for a special occasion—an eighteenth birthday and "congrats on getting into art school" gift rolled into one—but bills like ours don't leave room for five-hundred-dollar special occasions, as Maya, the golden child who abandoned her grand plan to move to New York and study cosmetology for the more affordable option of staying home and commuting to Florida State, loves to remind me.

Case in point: this entire trip. We haven't been to our cabin in Lake Andreas for four years, but Dad begrudgingly kept up with the payments for the sake of nostalgia. Swinging the extra couple hundred bucks a month felt worthwhile when there was still a slim chance we'd spend another summer or winter break at the lake. Especially after we gave up our childhood home to find a place big enough for Andy and his mom, Isabel, to move in last year.

With two college tuitions, a new mortgage, and unpaid medical bills that have been sitting on the kitchen counter for what feels like eons to keep up with, nostalgia doesn't make the cut anymore. As much as it might suck, avoiding lifelong debt outweighs sentimentality.

That's the part none of the therapists warned us about— grief is hell on your bank account.

Not that I'm not grateful for our "special occasions." The tablet makes me feel more like a serious artist than the now-infected nose ring I let my roommate Marcus talk me into because "all artists have cool piercings." And at least we're getting a chance to say goodbye to the cabin. Christmases since our last trip to Lake Andreas have been . . . weird. We rarely even acknowledge holidays anymore. Christmas is just a day. Sometimes we sit around an undecorated pine tree in the living room and exchange gifts, but the first year we didn't even do that. It must be odd for Andy and Isabel, walking into a family that acts like one of the biggest holidays in the world doesn't exist.

Which is why I pinched myself when Dad suggested this

trip in the first place. He always made vague promises that next year we'd do something different, and now he's finally delivering. One last nostalgic, and very strictly budgeted, Christmas in Lake Andreas before our cabin heads onto the market.

With my phone back in my pocket and Maya in full-on sulking mode, I finally return to my tablet. Instead of doing work like I promised myself, I let my gaze wander over to her when I'm sure she's not looking.

She's been on edge since I came home two days ago. Not that she's usually a happy-go-lucky person—snark has always been her brand—but she's especially huffy lately. Every time I deign to mention any of the three Cs—California, CalArts, or Cardarelli—she either scoffs, rolls her eyes, or leaves the room when we don't switch to a new topic. Yesterday she snapped at me for taking too long to get a glass of water. Maya's had problems with controlling her anger since we were old enough to talk, and I'm still not able to tell whether she's mad at me, our family, or the world at large. But I do know that the Devin Báez Reunion Tour is going terribly so far.

A four-hour road trip no longer feels like the right place to work on finding who I am as an artist. The application isn't due for another month, and not pissing off my sister is higher priority right now. Especially if I want to make it back to CalArts with all of my limbs, and electronics, intact.

Once my tablet is tucked away, Maya stretches herself out like a cat in the sun. She doesn't grace me with a smile or even the basic decency of eye contact, but her shoulders slacken, and her frown softens. That's Maya for "thank you."

Three hours and two bathroom breaks later, Dad takes the exit for Lake Andreas and lowers the volume on his trusty road trip mixtape. "Nearly there," he says, and rolls down our windows.

Andy leaps up, hanging his head out of his window like a golden retriever. I unbuckle my seat belt when Dad isn't looking, sliding in beside Maya to peek at the familiar welcome sign.

LAKE ANDREAS: THE HAPPIEST PLACE IN FLORIDA

The sign is frayed and has yellowed at the edges, but it warms my jaded little heart.

The car slows down as highways turn into one-way streets, giving us time to take in the scenery. Oak trees sprawl as far as the eye can see, shielding the rustic wooden cabins along the side of the street from view. Tire swings and Little Free Libraries on every corner. Bikes and paddleboards abandoned on front lawns and the smell of saltwater and sunscreen in the air.

Pure magic.

I lean out my window as we pull onto the main strip, ready to *ooh* and *aah* over all the places Maya and I would terrorize as kids, except . . .

They're gone.

Well, not all of them. The deli that gave me and Dad food poisoning is still around. The shops on Fulton Drive are still painted pastel pinks, blues, and greens, but their windows are shuttered and doors barred, lining the street like rotten gumdrops. The entire block, like the welcome sign, feels frayed and yellowed at the edges. The abandoned shops haven't even been replaced by a Starbucks or a Chipotle, or one of those business-casual places that charge $16 for salad. They're just empty. Sad, forgotten shells of a town that once meant so much to us.

"Huh," Maya murmurs as Dad parks in front of what was once a pretty decent Thai restaurant. "Was the lake always this depressing?"

Dad takes off his Florida State cap, his hair in sweaty disarray. "I don't think so."

"Me neither," I reply. I know kids see the world through rose-tinted glasses and all that jazz, but this is *definitely* not our Lake Andreas. At least not the one we remember. Even if my memories are kinder than reality, there's no way Mami would've let us spend our Christmases in a ghost town every year when we could've skipped the four-hour drive from Tallahassee and stayed home.

"Probably just an off year." Dad slips his cap back on and turns off the car, gesturing for us to follow him as he steps out.

Most of our favorite places have bit the dust. The Winter Wonderland miniature village—complete with fake snow and a Ferris wheel made of chocolate—in the front window of the candy store has been replaced with a foreclosure notice and cobwebs. Our favorite bakery, Loafin' Around, looks like it's been boarded up for months. A hunger pang rips through my empty stomach at the thought of never having their sundried tomato and rosemary focaccia again.

Sam's Superior Souvenirs is hanging in, though. And so are their signature I GOT CRABS IN LAKE ANDREAS shirts. Wonderful.

The streets somehow feel emptier than they look, with only the distant sound of seagulls and the echo of our footsteps for company. The kind of empty that feels ominous even in broad daylight. I stick close to Maya as Dad leads us toward the grocery store at the end of the block.

"Watch it," she hisses when I accidentally step on the back of her chancla. Forget playing nice—if an ax murderer decides to come after us, I'm using her as a shield.

I fall back, lingering beside Andy instead. He's a foot taller and lifts weights heavier than me during football practice. No way I can force him into being my unwilling shield. So, I guess this is the end of me. Can't say this is how I thought I'd go.

We make it to the grocery store without coming across any other signs of life. Not even the usual swarm of blood-hungry mosquitoes. I'm half expecting the store to be abandoned, but when the bell over the door announces our arrival, we're greeted by a familiar face.

"Well, I'll be damned," Old Bob says with a slap to his knee.

Well, *I'll* be damned. The candy shop didn't survive, but Old Bob did.

It's a relief, really. Old Bob is a Lake Andreas staple, welcoming families with open arms and hard candy year after year. Once upon a time, he'd been the mayor of this place, winning two consecutive landslide elections before passing the mayoral torch to his wife, Janine, and opening up the General Store. He's the kind of person who always remembered our birthdays and what sports we were into and whether we preferred soft serve or Popsicles. And one of the few locals who actually looked forward to visitors like us coming around to wreak havoc on their usually quiet community, never minding the extra noise and bigger crowds. He always said folks like us kept life at the lake exciting.

"Tony Báez, come 'ere you bastard." It's not until he's pulling Dad in for a hug that I remember we don't actually know Old Bob's real name. It had been a joke at the time, but it suits him. He looks like a Bob, and he *is* old. Five-year-old Devin and Maya were on to something.

"It's been a while . . ." Dad hesitates, slapping his hand down on Old Bob's shoulder. "My friend." Nice save.

Old Bob settles back down on his stool behind the front counter. "What brings the Báezes to our neck of the woods?" He stiffens suddenly, eyes narrowing. "You passing through on the way to that new water park across the lake?"

Andy's eyes light up. "There's a water park?!"

Old Bob bristles, nodding sternly. "Allegheny Park. Thing's been taking up most of our usual business. Everyone wants to stay over in Hillsdale these days. Something about a state-of-the-art waterslide."

That explains the tumbleweeds. The opposite end of the lake, better known as Hillsdale, was usually for the more upscale "round of golf before lunch at the country club" types, but maybe some money-hungry developers decided to cash in on the Lake Andreas crowd and create more budget-friendly options.

Well, at least we won't have to wait in line at the kayak rental stand . . . if it's still around.

"How's the family been?" Old Bob continues, back in good spirits. "Think I can talk Ximena into letting me sneak a piece of that tres leches cake again this year?"

Without missing a beat, Dad pulls out the shopping list Isabel left on the kitchen counter that morning, handing it to Maya. "Think you guys can handle grabbing everything? We've got some catching up to do."

Maya and I nod, dragging Andy away as Dad turns back to Old Bob. This is the part we're not supposed to see. The smiles that turn into frowns. The *I'm so sorry*s and *I had no idea*s. A bitter reminder that this town isn't the only thing that's changed. I put as much distance as I can between us and the counter, heading toward the far corner of the store. Nothing says happy holidays like avoiding your dad's practiced spiel about how your mom died.

Once we're safely hidden between the produce and fish bait aisles, Maya carefully tears the shopping list down the middle, handing me the lengthier half. "Meet you up front in ten?"

Andy and I nod, grabbing a basket from a stack beside the apples before heading to the opposite end of the store. All we've managed to grab is ice cream and pasta sauce when we're brought to a complete halt in the cereal aisle.

"Just pick one already!" I shout after Andy puts back the box he was holding for the hundredth time.

"I'm trying!" He carefully picks up a family-size box of Count Chocula, looking at it longingly before shaking his head and setting it back down. "Do you think we can get two?"

"No." I hold up our half of the list, pointing to the bright red total Isabel marked at the bottom of the page, and the price tags on the shelves. "Not in the budget."

"Stupid budget," Andy grumbles under his breath as he picks the Count Chocula back up.

"I'm going to the next aisle. Meet me when you're done."

Andy doesn't respond, turning his full attention to a box of Honey Nut Cheerios. I should've known better than to get between him and sugar. For a seventeen-year-old linebacker, he has the diet of a picky toddler. Grabbing our basket, I head to the next aisle.

Miraculously, there's another sign of human life. A guy around my age, tall with taut shoulders and a jaw that could cut me in half. He doesn't strike me as the Lake Andreas type; he's decked out in designer sneakers and a name-brand hoodie. Not the usual Crocs and Hawaiian shirt crowd. I can't quite make out his face, but even with what little I can see, there's no denying that he's startlingly handsome.

Guys like him don't exist in places like this. Lake Andreas is for families who want a break from the oppressive Florida humidity but can only afford to go somewhere with a light breeze. Not for hot guys who wear designer sneakers to go grocery shopping. Though a cute new local in town does have a very Hallmark movie ring to it. The charming lumberjack to my jaded big-city businessman. Or maybe I'm the lumberjack in this situation? I *do* wear a lot of plaid. . . .

One second I'm admiring Hot Guy's forearm as he reaches for a gallon of milk, and the next I'm tripping over my shoelaces. Story of my life.

The jar in my basket shatters the second I hit the ground,

splattering pasta sauce and glass across the floor while the ice cream rolls down the aisle. What're the odds that Hot Guy didn't notice any of that?

"Oh my God, are you okay?"

Great.

I gingerly push up onto my elbows before I can embarrass myself any more. No broken bones, but my dignity has seen better days.

Hot Guy delicately navigates around the sea of broken glass, coming to stand beside me. "Are you all right?" he asks again.

His voice is as strangely familiar as the acoustic song blaring through the store's speakers. I hold a hand over my eyes, squinting to make out his face against the harsh fluorescent lighting. He leans down, his face slowly coming into view. My mouth goes dry as I reach two very important conclusions in a matter of seconds.

One: Hot Guy's face is as hot as the rest of him.

Two: I know him.

"Devin?" Julian Seo-Cooke chokes out, brows shooting up to his hairline.

Awesome, our awful next-door neighbors are still around.

"Julian," I reply through gritted teeth, wishing I'd stuck through Andy's indecisiveness in the cereal aisle.

Julian shakes off his obvious surprise, standing back up and offering his hand. My first instinct is to flip him off and go about the rest of my day, but I look down at the mess of sauce-stained cans and boxes, groan, and take the help. I brush some of the sauce off my stained shirt, grateful that I've never cared much about my fashion choices.

"Haven't seen you around in a while," he says after I'm on my feet again.

"Yeah, well, my mom died. So we didn't feel like going kayaking."

He frowns, shifting his gaze down to his sneakers. "Right . . . I'm sorry."

"It's fine," I say, more to myself than to Julian, while I chase down my runaway ice cream.

"You're bleeding."

I blink, finally turning to face him. I don't let myself look for long—prolonged eye contact with him can't be good for my health—but I'm surprised by the person I see. There's no doubt that it's Julian. He still has that mole above his right eyebrow, the scar cut through his upper lip from when I tripped him when we were ten, and the thick, dark hair blown every which way but flat. But something's different. Or was his jaw always that sharp? And his shoulders so broad?

The thrill I'd felt at the idea of a cute boy in town morphs into disgust. That's what I get for not keeping my hormones in check. I flinch as I look away from him, as if I've spent too long staring at the sun. "It's pasta sauce."

Julian points to my left arm, the one that's dripping sauce down to my wrist. "No, your arm. It's actually bleeding."

I look back down at my arm, trying to shake off the image of this very new Julian. Between the chunks of tomato and freckled brown skin is a shallow, rough-edged wound just above my elbow.

"Oh. Right." I pull down my rolled-up sleeve, applying as much pressure as I can with my nondominant hand. It's not until I press that the pain surges all at once, ripping through my arm like a current.

Julian takes a hesitant step toward me. "Let me—"

"No! I mean, it's fine. I'm fine." I lunge for my basket at the same time as Julian, our heads colliding with a *thwack*.

"Hey, I found the perfect— Whoa. What happened to you?" Andy stills at the front of the aisle, box of Froot Loops in hand.

"Nothing. Let's go." I push through the pain in my head and arm to kick the basket toward Andy, but all he does is stare at it.

"I can carry that up to the counter for you," Julian offers while rubbing the red mark forming on his blemish-free forehead.

I nudge the basket out of his reach when he goes to pick it up. "No, really, that's—"

"Thanks!" Andy interrupts, throwing his Froot Loops into the basket and kicking everything over to Julian.

I inhale sharply, glaring daggers at Andy. Okay, stay calm, he doesn't know any better. How is he supposed to know that the Seo-Cookes are to be avoided at all costs? It's not like Julian, or any of the Seo-Cookes, look like the Disney villains they really are. We walk to the front counter in silence, Dad and Old Bob's conversation faltering when they catch sight of me in all my sauce-covered glory.

Maya nearly walks right into Julian, looking up from her phone at the last second. She freezes in place, one of her curls twisted around her index finger, her mouth hanging open in shock. If Julian is fazed by the uncomfortable silence, he doesn't let it show. He sets our basket down on the counter along with a five-dollar bill for his gallon of milk. He doesn't bother waiting for change before backing away slowly.

"Nice seeing you all." He gives us a stiff wave and exits the store. Old Bob chuckles under his breath as he watches us pull our jaws off the floor.

Maya's the first to snap back to reality. "He's still here?"

"Oh, they're all still here. Came up a few days ago," Old Bob answers. "One of the last few families to stick around."

"Am I missing something?" Andy asks, scratching his head.

Old Bob gives him a hearty belly laugh and leans across the counter. "Your stepfolks and the Seo-Cookes have history."

That's putting things lightly. Then again, it's hard to sum up over a decade of spite.

"Speaking of the Seo-Cookes . . ." Old Bob trails off, hopping down from his stool and hobbling over to a closet behind the front counter.

There's a collective inhale between me, Maya, and Dad as Old Bob unleashes the hideous creature that's haunted us for years.

"Spill detected," the robot announces, its unnerving googly eyes wiggling around as it makes its way out from behind the counter and toward the dairy aisle.

"Paul dropped it off last week. Latest model—hasn't even hit the market yet," Bob says with a grin. He watches proudly while we stand there in horror as the robot makes its way to the mess I left behind, slurping up the pasta sauce and glass in a matter of seconds.

Spill-e: Paul Cooke's greatest invention, and my family's worst nightmare.

"Spill eliminated," Spill-e announces once the mess is cleaned up, returning dutifully to its charging dock behind the counter.

Old Bob gives Spill-e a round of applause before turning back to our groceries. "Incredible, those things."

"Right," Dad spits out. We're lucky he didn't try to punch it square between the googly eyes. It wouldn't be the first time.

Maya starts shoving our groceries down the conveyer belt. "We need to go."

Dad and I nod. Now's not the time to monologue to Old Bob about Spill-e's salacious backstory, so we focus on helping Maya unload the last of our things while Andy looks on in dazed confusion. We shove things into Old Bob's hands faster than he can scan them, all of our groceries bagged in three minutes flat.

We're halfway to the exit when Old Bob snaps his fingers, ushering us back over. His eyes are wide as he reaches for a flyer from the stack behind him. "If you'll be sticking around for a bit, you should sign up for the Winter Games." He slaps the flyer down onto the counter, pushing it toward us. "Hasn't been much of a competition lately. A little Seo-Cooke versus Báez action could be the shake-up this place needs."

The flyer is as lively as the town that lives in my memories, cheerful snowmen and dancing elves welcoming one and all to compete in the annual Lake Andreas Winter Games. Or, better known to us as the Lawgies. Because "Winter Games" was too complex for a pair of five-year-olds to remember.

These games are as sore a subject as the Seo-Cookes themselves. Years of second-place medals and dirty tricks flash through my mind as Dad snatches the flyer and stuffs it into one of our bags.

"Sign-ups are next week," Old Bob explains. "We haven't gotten much interest these past few years, so we decided to push the date out, to try to lure in some of the New Year's Eve crowd."

"We'll think about it." Dad hoists our bags into his arms, mumbling a hurried goodbye before ushering us out of the store.

"Glad to have y'all back!" Old Bob calls out as we bustle toward the entrance. "Hasn't been the same without ya."

That I can believe. Who would've thought our greatest family legacy would be our rivalry with the assholes next door?

We hustle back to the car, checking over our shoulders for any signs of Julian, his siblings, or his parents. "Was the rest of the pack with him?" Maya whispers to me.

"I didn't see anyone."

She breathes a sigh of relief, slowing down to a fast walk instead of a jog. "We're probably safe, then. We would've been able to smell Stella's hair spray by now. And Henry's impossible to miss. Like a mountain troll."

"Who are we talking about?" Andy asks, visibly annoyed.

"They're a family that we don't exactly get along with," Dad answers diplomatically.

"We hate them," Maya interjects.

Dad shakes his head, opening the trunk and tossing in the groceries more haphazardly than anyone with a carton of eggs should. "*Hate* is a strong word."

"Am I wrong?"

His silence speaks volumes.

Maya claps her hands once we're back in the safety of the car, waiting until she has Andy's undivided attention before continuing. "Let me break it down for you. The Seo-Cookes are basically evil incarnate."

Dad eyes her in the rearview mirror. "Cuídate," he hisses—his go-to phrase for when she needs to check herself.

She rolls her eyes but heeds the warning. "Fine. They're loaded, obnoxious, and annoying as hell." She pauses, turning to Dad with a critical look. He nods in approval, waving his hand for her to continue. "Every year they manage to find new and cruel ways to torture us. Kicking sand in our eyes, sabotaging our kayaks, stealing our swimsuits whenever we use the communal showers at the pool."

"One time they dumped a bucket of earthworms on me." I pause for dramatic effect. A chill runs down my spine at the cold, slimy memory. I still can't use a communal shower without feeling like someone's out to get me. "So, we threw pies in their faces."

"I didn't endorse that prank, for the record," Dad cuts in.

"You helped us bake the pies."

Once again, Dad remains silent, not even bothering to hide his amusement this time.

Andy frowns. "So, you don't like this family because of something that happened when you were kids?"

Boiling down a decade of anger and resentment to "something that happened when we were kids" makes the matter seem petty. But the Seo-Cookes were never just rivals. They were bullies, all of them. Well, not their mom, but *especially* their blowhard dad. Paul Cooke: entrepreneur extraordinaire—which, no joke, is how he describes himself on his business card. We used to have one on our fridge, with a minor alteration. Paul Cooke: asshat extraordinaire.

"We don't like them because they suck," Maya insists, which doesn't really help us seem less petty.

"They do suck," Dad whispers under his breath, throwing the car into gear.

We tear down Fulton Drive fast and furious. There are no cars on the road and the fear of running into the Seo-Cookes again is still running high, so we're willing to make risky exceptions. The lake comes into view, calm and gleaming in the afternoon sun. We finally spot other familiar faces—an older couple that has an unhealthy obsession with fishing and the family of four that always wears the type of bald eagle camo T-shirts that make me nervous. If I look closely enough, I can make out the outline of the Seo-Cookes' three-car garage through the thicket of trees. I slump back against my seat, body heavy with the burden of what running into Julian means.

"Oh my God, are you bleeding?" Maya shifts as far to the opposite end of the backseat as she can, keeping her white cotton shorts out of harm's way.

I look down at my mess of a left arm with a sigh. In all the chaos of trying to get out of the grocery store ASAP, I'd forgotten that I didn't make it out without injury. Blood dribbles down my forearm, staining the sleeve of my shirt and the stretch of the backseat we'd been arguing over two hours ago.

Well, at least our last trip to Lake Andreas won't be boring.

CHAPTER TWO

Our cabin, like most of what we've seen of Lake Andreas so far, is nothing like what we remembered. We pause as we take in the gray, shabby home that makes me want to sneeze before I'm even out of the car.

"It just needs a fresh coat of paint," Dad says, breaking the uncomfortable silence. One of the windows' shutters creaks menacingly as we approach with caution.

"And an exorcism," Maya mumbles, jumping when the screen door suddenly slams open.

Dad waves her off, whistling a tune under his breath as he gestures for us to get out of the car. He's unusually cheerful for someone whose son is bleeding in the backseat.

The front steps buckle ominously under my weight. I skip the last few by jumping to the safety of the landing, prepared to warn the others to tread lightly when a crash does that for me.

"I swear I didn't mean to!" Andy shouts as he pulls his foot out of the hole he created in the first step.

Dad's good mood deflates as he helps Andy shake off the scraps of wood sticking to his gym socks.

The cabin's interior hasn't fared much better than the exterior. The nostalgic smell of Christmas morning cinnamon buns and nightly hot chocolates is long gone, replaced by an overwhelming stench of mildew and stale air. The cabin's been empty since our last trip four years ago, with the exception of a family from Maine that Dad rented it to. They lasted six months before skipping out on the rent and disappearing to who knows where. Dad headed up that weekend to make sure they didn't leave the place trashed. The cabin was intact, but whatever damage they did was enough to make him swear off renting for good.

"Those are new," I mumble as I take in the unsettling number of animal heads mounted over the fireplace.

"You can blame the Maine family," Dad says as he lugs two armfuls of bags into the foyer.

"Creepy," Andy says as he runs a finger along a buck's dusty antler.

"Very," Isabel echoes, stepping out from the kitchen. "Don't leave me here alone again. Those eyes have been following me since I got here." She points to the mountain lion at the center of the pack, forever mid-roar.

Dad apologizes with a hello kiss and a slap to her butt that makes her giggle and us groan. We love Isabel, but watching Dad act like a horny teenager will never not be weird.

"Dios mío, nene!" Isabel exclaims once she gets a look at me. She pulls herself out of Dad's arms to force me onto the couch so she can examine the wound more closely. "¿Que pasó?" She stiffens for half a second. "Did your dad try to fight one of those supermarket robots again?"

"No," Dad replies indignantly before coming to sit down beside me. One hand rests on my shoulder while the other holds up my sleeve so Isabel can dab the dried blood with a paper towel. "We had a little run-in at the grocery store."

"With what, a bear?" She gestures for Andy to grab her purse from the dining table.

"Worse," Maya mutters, throwing herself onto the couch. "Our neighbors."

Isabel pulls out a bottle of peroxide and a sleeve of cotton pads from her bottomless purse. "From that big house over there?" She juts her chin in the direction of the Seo-Cookes' cabin. My protests are swallowed by a hiss as Isabel tightens her grip on my arm, pressing a peroxide-soaked pad to the cut.

Maya drops the suitcase in her hand, whipping around to face Isabel. "You saw them?!"

She nods, cocking her head toward the dining table this time. "They dropped that off on the porch about an hour ago."

There's a bottle of champagne on the table, wrapped up in a bright red bow.

Those assholes.

"We don't accept gifts from the enemy." Grabbing the bottle, Maya heads straight for the kitchen.

"Whoa, whoa, whoa." Isabel abandons my half-bandaged wound to slide in front of Maya, grabbing the bottle back. "This stuff is worth fifty dollars."

"Of course it is," Maya sneers with narrowed eyes.

"All right, what's going on?" Isabel crosses her arms, keeping the champagne close to her chest. "Did we walk into a cult town or something?"

"Apparently, the neighbors are evil," Andy explains for us, pushing past his mom to grab a bag of Doritos from the kitchen cabinet.

Isabel eyes me and Maya warily, pulling a small gold card off the champagne bottle. "'A little welcome back gift for our favorite neighbors,'" she reads aloud, the ornate Seo-Cooke monogram embossed on the back of the card.

Maya yanks the card out of Isabel's hand, scrutinizing it before tossing it aside. "They must be spying on us. How else would they know we're here?"

"They probably heard me pull up when I got here," Isabel replies. "This place is so deserted, they could hear us sneeze if they tried hard enough."

Maya isn't swayed, crossing the room to close the blinds.

Isabel reexamines the champagne, running a finger along the glossy label with a pleased grin. "Doesn't seem very evil to me."

It's easy to fall for a Seo-Cooke trap. That was our biggest mistake, our first trip here. The Seo-Cookes showed up on our doorstep hours after we'd arrived with two bottles of Merlot and the good juice boxes to welcome us to the neighborhood. Dad and Mami let them in without hesitation, grateful that there was another family with kids around the same age as us. We slotted easily into each other's lives. Playdates in the afternoon at our place and wine (for the parents) and cheese (for the kids) on the Seo-Cookes' back deck in the evening. Maya and I fell hard for Stella, Henry, and Julian. It was impossible not to when they came bearing fancy monster trucks, special edition Barbies, and an endless supply of marshmallow-filled chocolate snack cakes.

"What's so bad about these guys?" Isabel tucks the champagne under her arm and returns to the couch to finish bandaging my wound. "Did they toilet paper the house or something?"

They have. Twice. Though we did the same thing to them. Also twice.

Maya's preoccupied with closing all the curtains, so Dad taps in to help catch Isabel up to speed. "Do you remember that man I told you about? The one who invented Spill-e?"

Isabel nods slowly. "And?"

With a disgruntled frown, Dad jabs his thumb in the direction of the Seo-Cookes' cabin. "That's him."

Her jaw drops in silent shock. Yeah, that was the reaction we were looking for.

Long before Maya and I came along, Dad was the family creative. He may have traded his middle-school dream of becoming a comic book artist for an engineering degree and a stable paycheck, but that didn't stop him from exploring other outlets. Rigging the coffee machine to turn itself off, saving Mami from dozens of burnt cups of coffee. Combining his alarm clock with a motion sensor so it wouldn't stop blaring until he was up and out of bed. A wired basket contraption that brought our mail straight from the slot to the kitchen table. Just because he wasn't creating art on a page anymore didn't mean he couldn't at all.

Our first year at the lake, Dad spent weeks working

on a Christmas gift for Mami. Having twin five-year-olds meant our house was in a perpetual state of disaster. It was a miracle Maya and I never managed to wreck Suck-o, the Roomba he modified to be able to both vacuum and mop messes—a feat Roomba's actual makers hadn't figured out yet. Giving us the naming rights on the machine meant we were willing to avoid it in our path of destruction. We'd even given Suck-o our own Devin and Maya touch, adding a pair of googly eyes before we officially gave it to Mami on Christmas morning.

Mr. Cooke was intrigued by Suck-o the minute he saw it mop up the beer he'd spilled in our kitchen. Dad happily answered all of Mr. Cooke's questions, going on for hours about how Suck-o worked, how he'd come up with the design, and how he planned to perfect it—reduce noise, increase battery life, upgrade the cleaning tech until it was able to mop up messes the OG Roomba wouldn't dare try to tackle.

"Wanna make a bet?" Mr. Cooke asked after Suck-o slurped up a graham cracker I'd dropped.

It seemed innocent enough. Dad and Mami were still waffling about whether to enter the games. Sign-ups had long passed, but Old Bob had offered to make an exception for us if we decided to join. Mr. Cooke proposed an offer they couldn't refuse. If we won, he'd give Mami the high-end espresso machine she'd been eyeing since our first playdate at the Seo-Cookes'. If we lost, he'd get Suck-o. At the time, it seemed like a no-brainer. Appliance for appliance, fair and square.

In the end, it came down to an egg toss. After ten perfect passes, the egg I'd gingerly tossed to Mami shattered in her

hands. We were disappointed, but not enough to be sore los-
ers. So we handed off Suck-o without complaint.

Six months later, Spill-e hit the market.

"*That's* the robot guy?" Isabel chokes out, glancing down
at the champagne in betrayal.

We nod solemnly. The wound of the Spill-e incident
formed into a scab we've been picking at for years. Mr.
Cooke planted a seed that would grow over the years into
fully bloomed hatred. We watched bitterly as the Seo-
Cookes' cabin expanded along with their wallets. Spill-e was
the big break Mr. Cooke needed, the cash grab that catapulted him and Cooke Corp from a struggling startup to a
Forbes-worthy empire. It was impossible to escape him—the
shiny new success story in Florida's Latino community. For
months, all we'd hear about on the local Spanish-language
news station was how Paul Cooke, a half-Cuban businessman from Miami, had catapulted to stardom.

All because of what he took from us.

Dad confronted him about Spill-e the following year, but
there was nothing we could do. He'd insisted that the version on the market was far beyond what Dad had created—
improved and upgraded past what Dad could do. The model
we handed over wasn't patented, and you can't sue someone
over a stolen idea. Not unless you want to drown in legal fees
to get an official "Sorry, sucks for you." There were no loop-
holes or smoking guns we could use to our advantage. He'd
won that bet. Fair and square.

So we found new games to play.

It's easy to hate someone when you're six years old. We
knew the Seo-Cookes got a pool and a swing set because of

something they hijacked from Dad. That was enough for us to go to war. Maya was born with a short temper, and I've always been a petty little shit.

Fights in the sandbox turned into backhanded compliments and vicious insults as we grew older but never wiser. Our parents stood by as they watched their kids find new and contrived ways to annoy the hell out of each other, playing their own, subtler hating game behind the scenes. They kept up appearances around the community, attending happy hours and local mixers with saccharine smiles, letting their friends think this family feud was something they let us kids indulge in to pass the time. Our parents would joke, laugh, and exchange shortbread recipes like they weren't the ones handing us the tools to tear each other apart.

In total, our friendship with the Seo-Cookes lasted a month. The resulting rivalry has lasted a decade.

Every year, we picked our loathing back up where we left off. Hating the Seo-Cookes was second nature here, as much a part of our routine as eating tres leches cake and going swimming after dark.

Maya snaps her fingers after she pulls the last of the curtains shut. "We should build a catapult."

"What?" Andy asks around a mouthful of Doritos.

"A catapult, or a really big slingshot." She grabs a notepad from the dining table. "Something we can use to lob garbage at them."

Andy perches himself a safe distance away, craning his neck to peek over Maya's shoulder. Dad hovers behind her, using his engineering expertise to guide her in the right direction.

"Isn't this a bit extreme?" Isabel asks from her place across the room.

"No," all three of us answer together.

Maya scribbles at top speed, her tongue peeking out of the corner of her mouth. "Maybe there's a way we could use this in the Lawgies," she muses, tapping the pencil to her lower lip. "Depends on what events they go with this year, but we could figure something out."

Our relationship with the Seo-Cookes evolved over the years, but one thing has always stayed the same: the bet. Like clockwork, we'd head down to the visitors center for sign-ups, Mr. Cooke would make some snide comment to Dad about how we wouldn't stand a chance, and we'd wind up with yet another wager on our hands. None of the prizes were as valuable as Suck-o had been. After the Spill-e incident, Dad's creative drive faded. The fear of being tricked a second time, or never making anything as successful as Suck-o, was too deep for him to shake off. There were meager consolation prizes. A new toaster or a pair of slippers. One time we agreed to clean the leaves out of the Seo-Cookes' gutter if we lost. That was an especially annoying defeat.

"Okay, slow down." Isabel waves her arms. "The log what now?"

At least Andy has accepted that he's never going to understand what's happening here. Having to explain ourselves every five minutes is going to take every ounce of fun out of brainstorming weapons of mass annoyance.

"Lake Andreas Winter Games. L-A-W-G. Lawgies," I say slowly enough for her to follow. As eager as I am to get back to plotting, I can still acknowledge that a five-year-old's naming convention doesn't make much sense. "It's this thing the town hosts every year to raise money for the community. They use the entrance fees on stuff like repairs or to help out local businesses," I explain while Dad snags the pencil from Maya to make some tweaks to her blueprint. "It's a full day of events. Sack races, puzzles, softball tournaments, how-much-of-this-food-can-you-eat-in-thirty-seconds competitions. That kind of thing. You get points for how well you place in each event, and the team with the most points wins."

This piques her interest. "Do you get something if you win?"

Glory. Power. The knowledge that you've finally beat the Seo-Cookes. "A plastic gold medal. And a gift card to the souvenir shop."

The Seo-Cookes must have enough gift cards to cover their entire house in I GOT CRABS AT LAKE ANDREAS T-shirts by now.

"And your face on the Wall of Champions at the visitors center," Maya adds.

How could I forget the rows and rows of stiff Seo-Cooke smiles that Mami glared at every time we went to the visitors center? That was what mattered the most to her, more than the bets and the useless prizes. Proof that we'd finally beaten them at their own game.

Every year she'd wake us up early on the day of the games to practice our poses and smiles in the mirror. Every year we came home biting back frowns and tears.

Isabel nods slowly. "Right . . . And we need a catapult for this because . . . ?"

"Because the Seo-Cookes cheat every time!" Maya interjects, slamming her fist down on the table hard enough to topple the decorative bowl of fruit.

Well, we're 99.9 percent sure they were cheating. Even if we started the day off with a significant lead, the Seo-Cookes always found a way to creep up on us. Magically, they'd leap to first place after pulling off mental and physical feats that would make Einstein and Houdini sweat. And yet we'd still train until our tiny knuckles bled year after year. All for second, third, and sometimes fourth place.

Dad suddenly looks up, tossing the pencil and rushing toward the back door. "There should be some plywood in the shed out back."

Isabel stops him in his tracks. "Oh no." She rests her index finger on Dad's chest, making him go rigid. "You said this was going to be a peaceful family vacation. I didn't cash in all of my PTO to come up to the boonies and play Bob the Builder. No games, and no waging war on the neighbors."

Maya launches out of her seat, coming to stand beside Dad. "But the games are a tradition." It's a low blow, pulling the tradition card on someone who's always been so careful about treading the delicate line of life before and after Mami. Especially now, *here*, in a home full of lost traditions.

But the Seo-Cookes bring out the worst in us.

Isabel softens, biting her lip as she looks from Maya to Dad. "Look, I know that there's a lot of tension here, but holding grudges doesn't do any good, right?"

No one responds. The lack of support makes her pivot,

shifting to face Dad specifically. "What if we made our own traditions?" she suggests to him, wearing the smile I know he can never say no to. "Ones that don't involve revenge."

Miraculously, Dad doesn't buckle. "We have a long history with them. That's not something you let go of easily."

Isabel bristles, eyes flicking from Dad to us and back. A smirk plays at her lips as she leans in to whisper something in Dad's ear that makes him fold like a house of cards.

"Isabel's right. We've wasted enough of our time on them. This trip is supposed to be about family, so let's focus on us instead of them."

Gross. I can hear Maya gag as Dad and Isabel seal their pact with a kiss.

"We could work on DIY projects together," Isabel says with a smile. "Spruce up the cabin a bit before it goes on the market."

That sounds more like free labor than fun family bonding if you ask me, but Dad nods enthusiastically while Isabel rushes off to grab cups for our traitorous champagne.

"Your mom was always saying we should give this place some TLC," Dad says while Isabel's gone.

Yeesh. Guess Maya's not the only one dealing low blows tonight. Playing the Mom card is a dirty move, Dad.

He's not wrong, though. Every trip, Mami found something new to add to the never-ending list of repairs she wanted to make next time around. Switching up the backsplash in the kitchen, or painting the living room, or sanding the wood on the back deck. But being here is about having fun. Paddleboarding to the middle of the lake to watch the sunset, and staying up all night crafting the perfect s'more, and falling asleep while sketching in the backyard. Not home improvement.

Before we can protest, Isabel returns with a stack of red Solo cups. She waves one of them under my nose, winking as she pours me an extra generous serving of champagne. My attempts to decline are ignored, earning me dirty looks from Dad until I shut up and take the peace offering. Maya clucks her tongue in disapproval, swirling her own untouched cup.

Isabel sets the bottle aside and raises her cup in a toast. "To new traditions."

"To new traditions," I mumble half-heartedly as I knock my cup against Maya's, who is as bitterly disinterested as I am.

"New traditions my ass," Maya says out of the corner of her mouth, loud enough for only me to hear.

I nod in agreement, taking a slow, careful sip. Dad and Isabel sing the champagne's praises while Andy finishes his drink in one gulp, but I can't stomach another sip.

It tastes like admitting defeat.

CHAPTER THREE

Dad and Isabel don't waste time kicking off our "new traditions." And it doesn't take long for us to find out that a weak front step is the least of the cabin's issues. Our lackluster champagne celebration came to a crashing halt after a piece of the ceiling in my and Andy's room broke off and nearly knocked him unconscious. Isabel bandaged yet another wound, and Dad started poking around the cabin for any other "surprises."

Chances are we won't get any bites if we try to sell the cabin in its current state. If we did, there's no way we'd break even, let alone make a profit. No one wants a cabin with a hole in the ceiling, possums in the crawl space, and a bat infestation in the attic. Our Lifetime movie vacation about rediscovering the joy of Christmas has turned into an HGTV *Extreme Makeover: Home Edition* special.

Considering the amount of heavy lifting we're going

to be doing around the house, I can't put off working on my piece for the Cardarelli mentorship anymore. At least not if I want to submit the application in time. Something tells me "too exhausted from helping your family de-bat the attic" isn't on the list of acceptable excuses for a deadline extension.

As soon as we finish breakfast the following morning, Dad hands us paint rollers and announces our first home renovation project: a fresh coat of paint. We all work in silence, occasionally singing along to the "painting vibes" playlist Maya spent more time curating than actually painting. The world is calm . . . until Henry steps outside.

Henry Seo-Cooke is hard to ignore. At a whopping six foot five, Henry is so big his shadow could swallow all five-foot-three of me whole. Maya once called him "a brainless country ham," and truer words have never been spoken.

At some point since our last winter here, the Seo-Cookes bought a Jet Ski, which makes Henry *impossible* to ignore.

Our peaceful afternoon of home improvement goes sideways the minute Henry decides to take the Jet Ski out for a spin. Between the sound of the engine and him grunting and panting during breaks, I haven't been able to hear myself think for the past hour and a half. Which is probably for the best. I may not be able to hear my thoughts, but I know they're not nice.

"He's gotta be getting tired by now, right?" I ask after Henry's fifth lap around the lake. The Seo-Cookes' place is so massive, the rest of them probably can't even hear his one-man show.

Maya shrugs, peeking out the window at where Henry has

stalled on the water to tighten the strap on his Apple Watch. "He's a cornerback—he probably has energy for days."

Anyone who's come into contact with the Seo-Cookes knows that Henry's destined for football stardom. His dad would tell anyone who would listen, and even people who wouldn't, that scouts were stopping by Henry's games his freshman year of high school. Now that he's fulfilled his dad's prophecy and become Florida State's most promising sophomore recruit, Maya *really* can't avoid him.

It's annoying, but not surprising, that the boasting wasn't just talk.

"That's it!" Dad snaps when Henry and the Jet Ski from hell return to our end of the lake.

"Well, that was quick," I whisper to Maya as Dad storms off to the kitchen.

"Knew it." Maya tosses her roller aside, splattering Eggshell Breeze all over my jeans. She ignores my grumbled protest and holds her palm up to my face. "Pay up."

We figured it wouldn't take long for Dad to crack, but I'd made the mistake of thinking he'd last until the end of the week. "Fine," I mutter, pulling out my wallet and slapping a twenty into her hand. That's what I get for underestimating the Seo-Cookes' ability to annoy us.

Dad comes back into the living room with a notepad and a phonebook that looks as old as me. He slams it onto the dining table, a cloud of dust sending him into a sneezing fit. "What's the name of that couple who used to live behind the Mexican restaurant on Irving?" he asks once he gets his sneezing back under control.

"The Khans?"

"That's the one." He rewards me with a high five before flipping to the KH section of the phonebook.

Isabel pulls out one of the earplugs she'd wisely thought to pack. "What're you doing?"

"The other neighbors have got to be hearing this too. If enough of us file complaints at the visitors center, the bastards will get a fine." He doesn't look up from the phonebook until Isabel clears her throat, deflating at the look on her face. "Or a polite warning."

"I don't think we have other neighbors," I point out.

At least not on our side of the lake. The locals, wisely, invested in cabins that're farther from Fulton Drive and, by default, the noise. Besides the Seo-Cookes, our only immediate neighbor is the mushroom growing on the roof of the empty cabin to our left.

The brief silence is broken by Henry screaming at the top of his lungs. Dad's grip on the pencil tightens enough that I'm sure it's going to snap, but Isabel comes to the rescue.

"We deserve a break," she announces, shouting over the noise. "How about lunch on me? Screw the budget."

We haven't even finished priming the walls yet, but I'm not going to turn down a chance to get out of the house.

Dad scowls when the engine revs yet again. He throws the pencil down and stomps across the room, grabbing his coat off the rack in the entryway. "I need a drink."

We quickly bustle out of the house. Maya stalls in the driveway, double-checking that Dad and Isabel are occupied with finding a place to go. She carefully creeps over to the Seo-Cookes' dock, grabbing the messy pile of stuff Henry left behind. She tosses the pile—a T-shirt, sneakers, his phone, and a Gucci fanny pack—into a bush on the side of their house before racing back to us.

"Nice," I whisper, rewarding her with a subtle high five.

"Still got it, baby," she replies with a grin.

According to Google, our favorite haunt—the Italian restaurant that served meatballs the size of your head—went out of business last year. Guess that makes sense, considering they were selling ten-pound platters of those monster meatballs for five bucks. By the time we make it to the only restaurant in Lake Andreas that's both open and serves alcohol, Dad's not the only one who needs a drink. It took thirty minutes of idling in the car just to find a place that wasn't over an hour away.

The Swordfish Bar and Grill isn't a place we've been to before, and I can quickly see why. There's an unsettling layer of grime covering every surface—from doorknobs to tabletops—and a hazy, lingering scent of cigarette smoke despite the SMOKERS CAN GO TO HELL sign on the front door.

But it has half-priced margaritas and that's enough for Dad.

"See, peace and quiet," Isabel says once we're settled at our booth.

I wouldn't describe a place with such a threatening vibe as peaceful, but it is quiet. I can make out three men lingering by the bar, and there are a few occupied tables on the opposite end of the room, but the place is so dimly lit I can't tell if any of the faces are familiar, or friendly.

The quiet doesn't last long, though. Now that we don't have to shout to be heard, we can get back to what we do best: bickering.

"Hot wings are obviously superior," Maya argues when the topic of appetizers comes up.

"No, they're not!" Andy replies, going red in the face. "At least with a chicken tender you don't have to eat around the bone."

I'm prepared to present my argument for mozzarella sticks when Maya leans across the table to punch Andy in the arm. He narrowly dodges the blow, pulling me into the line of fire instead. Maya's fist lands right on top of the wound from yesterday's pasta sauce incident, the dulled pain re-igniting on impact.

"What the hell?!" I snap through gritted teeth. The pain is even stronger than it was yesterday, the sting stretching down to my fingertips.

"Take it easy on the innocent bystanders," Isabel warns. She takes a sip of her mango margarita before rolling up my sleeve to assess the damage. A drop of blood creeps beneath the lining of the bandage and trickles down my arm. She does what she can to stop the light bleeding with a napkin before sending me off to the bathroom to clean up. At this rate, I'll run out of shirts that aren't stained with blood or sauce by the end of the week.

I set my phone on the edge of the sink and pinch my sleeve with my chin, nose scrunched up in concentration as I struggle to unfurl the fresh bandage Isabel gave me. The pain starts to come in waves, each more intense than the last. I curse like a sailor at full volume, focusing on as many color-ful ways to say *shit* to distract myself from the pain.

My phone starts to vibrate every few seconds, almost sending it off the lip of the sink. I'm prepared to text back whoever it is to shut up and let me concentrate when I catch a glimpse of the most recent message, the seventeenth in a series from Maya.

GET BACK OVER HERE NOW!!!!!

If this is about the hot wing debate, I'm going to kill her.

I slap the new bandage on lopsided and wrinkled before opening the text thread. They're all too frantic for me to figure out why she needs me to come back so badly. The barely functional overhead lights flicker as someone else enters the bathroom, my phone the only source of light for a moment. It buzzes again, the screen shifting down to the latest message.

RED ALERT THEY'RE HERE!!!

Oh sh—

"Hey," Julian says.

I whip around to face him, letting out an undignified squeak when he takes a step toward me. The sink digs into my lower spine as I press myself as far back as I can. "Hi." I don't dare move a muscle.

When it came to pranks, Stella and Henry were the ringleaders. Once she was old enough, Stella became the mastermind and Henry the muscle. Julian was somewhere in between, too timid to be the brain and too weak-willed to be the brawn. He was always more of a distraction, never the main event, luring us out of our safety zone with promises of candy or a chance to get back at one of his siblings. Knowing the Seo-Cooke playbook, Julian's probably waiting for the perfect moment to blind me with Silly String so Henry can jump out of one of the stalls and dunk my head in the toilet as payback for hiding his stuff. Doesn't matter that I didn't do it myself, so long as someone pays.

Instead, the silence stretches on, and I start to scan the room for a weapon or a way out. I'm considering the merits of sacrificing my phone by throwing it at Julian's head when he finally speaks up again.

He nods toward my rolled-up sleeve. "Is your arm okay?"

"It's just a scratch."

"Awesome." His eyes widen. "I mean, it's not awesome that you got cut with glass. Awesome that you're not really hurt."

"Right . . ." I nod slowly, feeling more uncomfortable with each passing second. I don't like closed, locked spaces, I don't like Julian, and I especially don't like closed, locked spaces with Julian.

What little I can see of him in the glow of the single working light bulb floors me as much as it did in the grocery store. Full lips and fuller hair. Skin so smooth he must have skipped the acne phase of puberty. There should be a law against awful people being this attractive.

"I like the nose ring," Julian says with pinkened cheeks and a sheepish smile, like we're old friends catching up over coffee.

"It's infected."

"Oh . . . That sucks." His smile falters, his cheeks nearly the same shade as his maroon lacrosse polo. "It doesn't look like it's infected, if that makes you feel any better."

"It doesn't."

My reply leaves Julian flustered enough that I can attempt to escape.

"I . . . I actually . . . I . . . uh—" While Julian's busy tripping over his words and avoiding my eyes, I bolt past him.

I rush through the maze of tables and chairs as quickly as I can, checking over my shoulder to make sure Julian isn't following me. There's no sign of him when I'm a few feet from our booth, turning back around seconds before walking right into the worst Seo-Cooke.

"The man himself!" Mr. Cooke slaps me on the back so hard I hiccup.

Maya looks ready to kill, breaking her glare long enough to give me a sympathetic shrug. At least she tried to warn me. Dad, on the other hand, is flashing the brightest megawatt smile he can, continuing their conversation as soon as I slide into our booth.

"Dev is a freshman at CalArts," he says far louder than he has to, clearly trying to one-up Mr. Cooke. "Top of his class already!"

Not exactly, but sure.

"CalArts, very impressive." Mr. Cooke gives me the world's stiffest fist bump. "Julian's headed off to Princeton next fall. Thank God for affirmative action, am I right?" he says with a hearty chuckle.

Well, that confirms it. The only thing that's changed about Mr. Cooke is his hairline.

"Me and the boys were having some drinks at the club last weekend and my buddy who works down at the realty office mentioned you were thinking about putting your place up for sale?"

Mr. Cooke knowing this much about our financial situation is unnerving, yet not surprising. There may not be many people in Lake Andreas left, but they're still as up in each other's business as ever. Telling one person a secret means you've told half the town. One year, Mami headed home early to fix a tooth she'd chipped on a stale cookie, and everyone and their mother showed up on our front porch to wish her well.

Dad stiffens, his back ramrod straight. "We've floated around the idea," he replies with a noncommittal shrug. "The kids are in college now or close to it, so doesn't make total sense to hold on to the cabin anymore."

Mr. Cooke nods and rubs his chin thoughtfully—or nefariously, depending on how you look at it. "Of course. Shame, though. He mentioned how close you were to paying off that mortgage too."

That catches us off guard, our entire table biting back a gawk or a gasp. Is *anything* considered private in this town?

"If you're interested in selling, I'd love to chat." Mr. Cooke pulls out his wallet, setting a business card down in front of our hot wings. "I've had my eye on one of the boats over at the marina in Hillsdale. Trouble is we don't have much room left with the deck expansion, so I've been looking into . . . other options."

Oh my God, this man wants to bulldoze our cabin and make it into a garage for his boat. That's next-level evil. Like I said before, Disney villain evil.

"That's good to know." Dad does an impressive job of not looking like he wants to punch Mr. Cooke in the face. He flicks the business card against his palm before tucking it into the breast pocket of his shirt. I'm sure it'll join the other one we have pinned to our fridge. Maybe we'll adjust it to "Home Destroyer Extraordinaire" this time. "But we're still not confident we want to sell."

Last I checked, we were *very* confident we wanted to sell. So confident that he and Isabel are siccing me and Maya up against the possums on Monday. But Mr. Cooke doesn't need to know that. He can find out when his new neighbors move in.

Mr. Cooke holds up his hands, beginning to back away slowly. "Well, if you change your mind." A wicked smile plays at his lips as he lowers his hands. "Unless you want to have some fun, for old times' sake."

"What do you mean?" Dad should know better than to let a Seo-Cooke draw him in with promises they'll never keep. But even I'm hanging on the edge of my seat.

"You should sign up for the games, if you're feeling up to it. It'd be nice to put up more of a fight for once." His laugh makes my skin crawl. "We could make things interesting. Like we used to." He quirks an eyebrow, and the tension in the room skyrockets. "You win, I pay off that last bit of your mortgage. Shouldn't be all *that* much, right? Considering how much you paid for it."

My stomach churns at the fact that he doesn't consider thousands of dollars that much money.

"And if I win, you let me buy it off of you." He holds his palm up in front of Dad for a shake. "Fair and square."

Nothing about this sounds fair or square. We'd sooner give up our car than let Mr. Cooke bulldoze a home that's meant so much to us. A place that, even when it's falling apart, holds so many memories of Mami that destroying it would mean destroying a piece of her too. No way in hell.

"You're on," Dad replies, slapping his hand into Mr. Cooke's outstretched one before we can even process what's happened.

What the *fuck*?!

"Atta boy!" Mr. Cooke exclaims, lifting his beer up in a silent toast. "Welcome back, Báezes."

Dad holds up his beer with a grin, nudging Isabel until she lifts her margarita too. The gesture brings Mr. Cooke back to our table, his smile morphing into a frown. "And I heard the news about Ximena. Such a vibrant woman, an awful loss." He pats Dad on the back before shifting his gaze to Isabel. "Good to see you landed on your feet, though." And with a cheeky wink, he finally walks away.

God he's the worst.

Isabel shakes her head, sneering as she watches Mr. Cooke finish off his beer and throw down some cash at the bar, beckoning for a dejected-looking Julian to follow him. "Que pendejo."

Not for the first time, I wish I'd listened to Mami and practiced speaking Spanish more often. I've run out of words in English to call Mr. Cooke an asshole.

Maya takes an angry swig of her Diet Coke. "Believe us now?"

Andy's still too shocked to respond, his mouth, full of chicken, hanging ajar. Isabel nods soberly, running her finger along the salted rim of her margarita.

It's not until Mr. Cooke has finally left that Dad drops the fake smile, realizing what he's agreed to. "I . . . I didn't mean to say yes. We don't have to sign up. We can—"

"We should do it," Isabel interrupts, her jaw set as she knocks back the last of her drink.

She sure changed her tune quick. "Seriously?"

Isabel nods before gesturing to a waiter to bring another round for her and Dad. Order placed, she holds up her nearly empty glass in yet another toast.

My hand stills while everyone else's rises. Maya nudges her shoulder against mine, jutting her chin toward my glass.

"C'mon," she urges.

For a flash of a second, it feels like old times. When Christmas was something worth celebrating. When there wasn't this weird tension between me and Maya, and all that mattered was us, what snacks we had in the pantry, and practicing our smiles for the Hall of Champions portrait. A time when we were a team.

Maya shoots me a wink when I finally lift up my Diet Coke. Isabel proudly leads the charge.

"To new traditions. And kicking ass."

We clink our glasses more eagerly than we did last night, drinks downed and hearts racing as we huddle together with cunning smiles. Over the thrill of the fight to come. This isn't the winter break I had in mind, but then again, I also didn't picture our childhood cabin getting turned into a boat garage. And it's not going to. Not if we have anything to say about it.

CHAPTER FOUR

Maya throws herself headfirst into our training. Self-care projects are her coping mechanism—for both grief and rage. Whenever she needs to calm herself down, she storms off to her room to knit, paint her nails, or practice outlandish makeup looks. Anything to keep her hands busy for a few hours. After Mami died, she spent four months learning how to make wigs with a sewing machine. From there, she moved on to learning how to create her own lip gloss.

It was a very depressing but fashionable year.

Without a social life to keep her busy, and the cabin's god-awful Wi-Fi, Maya has nothing but time. Her first draft of our schedule is a color-coded manifesto, combining strength, conditioning, and endurance training into a workout program that even Dwayne "The Rock" Johnson would groan at. Before anyone could think to confiscate her debit card, she ordered a megaphone, whistle, and three types of protein powder. She even went the extra mile to make a memory exercise regimen for Andy. Thankfully, the logic side of the games has always been our strong suit. It's what makes us so good at arguing—we remember everything.

Foolishly, I'd thought we'd have the rest of the weekend before sacrificing our freedom to our training overlord. I'm not big on sleeping in, but waking up at six a.m. every day of your winter break would make even the most straitlaced teenager weep. Thankfully, Maya doesn't come looking for us at the crack of dawn on day one.

I'm camped out at the kitchen table with my sketchbook and a plate of semi-burnt pancakes when she storms into the room dressed in her finest athleisure, her hair parted down the middle into two Dutch braids.

She stops in her tracks to glare at me. "What're you doing?"

"Working."

My tablet has earned a special kind of sneer from her, but she scowls at my sketchbook all the same. It's been months since I last touched it, dust clinging to the rings holding it together. My tablet may be my pride and joy, but if I want to snap myself out of this creative slump and finish my application in time, something needs to give. Maybe returning to my roots is the answer.

"Why aren't you dressed?"

I peer down at my sushi-patterned pajama pants. "I am dressed?"

"I mean dressed for today's drills," she replies with an eye roll. "We've already lost an hour because my alarm didn't go off."

Thank God for that. We're lucky her megaphone won't be delivered until Monday, or else she wouldn't have been as kind about this morning's wake-up call.

"And where's Andy?" She looks over her shoulder, as if someone as large as him could hide his presence for this long.

I take a sip of coffee before replying. I'll need all the caffeine I can get before this inevitable bloodbath begins. "Still sleeping."

Getting Andy out of bed during the school year was a James Bond–level mission that tested everybody's patience. We're lucky if he gets up before noon on weekends. Maya growls through gritted teeth, lunging for something in the cabinet beneath the sink before stomping back toward our bedroom.

Turns out she didn't need her megaphone. Banging a wooden spoon against the bottom of a frying pan works just fine. She's lucky Dad and Isabel are out buying home-improvement supplies. Pot banging is usually off-limits.

Andy comes tumbling into the kitchen seconds later, half asleep and nearly tripping over himself as Maya forces him down into the chair across from me.

"Wha' time's it?" Andy mumbles as he struggles to keep his head up.

"Time to wake up." She taps the spoon on the top of his head, emitting a hollow knock. "Eat, get dressed, and be ready in twenty. Or else."

Neither of us bothers to ask what "or else" entails. Once she's walked off to her room, I push my plate of half-finished pancakes toward Andy. He needs the fuel more than I do.

"Thanks, dude," he mumbles in reply before his jaw un-hinges like a snake to devour a pancake in two wolfish bites.

I give him a thumbs-up before heading to our room. Get-ting changed into sweatpants and a ratty T-shirt doesn't take long, so I go back to the kitchen to be productive with the little time I have left. While Andy pokes through the fridge and goes into feral animal mode, I search my sketchbook for inspiration.

Sketches of Mami on the front porch, Dad playing the bongos we got him for Christmas, and Maya dancing in her room. Reminders of what I love most about art—something I often forget now that it's a measure of my worth. That I can capture moments, thoughts, feelings in ways that keep them alive forever. That I can tell stories that don't require words. These pieces aren't about skill. They're about the people I want to remember.

There was a time when Maya used to love watching me draw. She'd peek over my shoulder every time she walked by, asking for copies of her favorite pieces to hang up in her locker. When she stopped sneaking peeks, I assumed she'd gotten bored watching me work on the same handful of drawings for my portfolio. Soon enough, I moved on to new projects, but she still kept her distance. And I still haven't found the right thing to say to bring her back.

The last thing I was working on was a sketch of her, twist-ing around to tell me a secret, her hair tied up with a purple silk scarf. One of the last few moments of peace last summer, before I left for California.

Before she iced me out.

The sketch is far from finished, but it might be a good

option for my application. A nod to my humble beginnings. *The Devin Báez Story: From chalk drawings of his twin sister on the playground to drowning in student loan debt at one of the best art schools in the country.*

Knowing she was the centerpiece of my application will definitely win me some brownie points with Maya. There's nothing she loves more than being the center of attention. Maybe I could give her the drawing once it's done. Nothing is usually allowed to leave my sketchbook. Anything I use in here has to be photocopied, no originals. It's always been just for me, for the works close to my heart. Ripping out one of these pages would be like tearing off the top layer of my skin.

But I'd do it for her.

"Is that me?" Maya's voice is warm against my neck, while her hand on my shoulder is damp and ice cold.

The touch makes me jump, accidentally spilling a few drops of coffee onto the edge of the page. The droplet smudges sketch-Maya's bronze skin, turning the sharp curve of her wrist dull and shapeless.

"Maybe," I reply as I delicately dab the other drops of coffee. "I was thinking of using it for my mentorship application."

She sets a water gun down on the table, a safe distance from the sketchbook after I shoot her a warning glare. That explains the cold hands. With her arms crossed, she takes in the sketch with a critical eye, all the admiration she once had for me and my work long gone. "You made my head too big."

"Your head *is* big," I reply. Her grumbled reply is too quiet for me to make out over the sound of Andy snorting.

"Oh, that reminds me," Andy announces excitedly. "I found another place for you to add to your California list." He tosses his phone to me, the browser open to an overwhelmingly long menu. I cradle the phone close to my chest, out of Maya's view. The mention of one of the forbidden Cs makes her roll her eyes to the back of her head. "It's this restaurant that has over a *hundred* different pizza toppings."

My carefully curated list of galleries, beaches, and hole-in-the-walls quickly turned into a list of restaurants Andy wants to go to when everyone comes to visit me for spring break. With all the time I've spent struggling to stay above water in my classes, I haven't even opened it since move-in day, let alone crossed anything off. Not flunking takes priority over sightseeing, unfortunately. Still, I can't find it in me to be annoyed that my list has been hijacked. Not when Andy's the only person in this family who's shown any enthusiasm about California. Dad's understandably concerned about how his son, who can barely boil water without getting hurt, is now living alone across the country. And Maya, well . . .

"Time's up," she snaps. "Out to the backyard."

Andy and I drop the subject, but I add the restaurant to my list anyway. The least he deserves for putting up with us is a pizza with an obscene amount of toppings.

"Now!" Maya barks when we don't immediately move.

It doesn't matter that Andy hasn't put on a shirt yet, when she lifts the water gun and aims it at us, we get up and go. She doesn't lower her weapon until the door has closed behind us, snapping her fingers and gesturing for me to follow her to the shed on the opposite end of the yard. I hold the door open while she sorts through broken power tools and tinker projects Dad abandoned after the Suck-o incident.

"What does this have to do with the Lawgies?" I ask after she shoves a dozen pool noodles into my arms.

"Ask no questions, young one," Maya muses as she hoists a traffic cone over her shoulder. Where the hell did we even get that from?

"We'll start with two laps around the woods," she announces once she's gotten everything she needs. "Then we'll meet here and—"

The sight in front of us makes her stop: Stella, decked out in a lime-green bikini and chugging an iced coffee, talking to Andy.

Stella freezes once she catches sight of us, quickly patting Andy on the arm before rushing back into her house.

Maya sprints over to Andy, instantly recognizing the love-sickness on his face. "Don't even think about it," she warns, slapping his arm. "She's off-limits."

Andy's dazed expression turns into one of confusion. "I only said hi?"

Maya narrows her eyes. "You like her. It's written all over your face."

It is. Stella is attractive, like the rest of her family, and Andy's a hopeless simp. He may be as loyal as a golden retriever, but I wouldn't be surprised if the Seo-Cookes found a way to talk him over to the dark side.

"Her dipshit brothers are off-limits too," I add. No telling how far they'd stoop to get one of our own to turn against us.

Maya gives me a nod of approval before shifting to the

more important task at hand. She claps her hands before Andy can protest, taking off into the woods for our first lap.

"Can I at least put on a shirt?" Andy calls out to her before breaking into a jog.

"Too late, already started," she replies without turning back.

Andy groans, casting one last look at the Seo-Cookes' backyard before taking off at full speed. Which leaves me, the slowest runner in our family, to trail behind. Catching up to either of them is next to impossible for someone as athletically challenged as me, but I put in a decent effort. I make it a whole twenty feet before a stitch starts forming in my side.

According to Maya, one lap through the woods should take fifteen minutes. It takes me thirty. Running for more than five minutes is too much to ask of my body, so I slow down to a jog. By the time I cross our backyard for my second lap, I'm down to a fast walk. Maya and Andy are so far ahead I can't even hear their footsteps anymore, or Maya shouting at me to go faster. Once she's done with her own laps, she'll come looking for me.

In the meantime, I enjoy the solitude. I'm taking my time walking along the lake's edge when the sound of a branch snapping near the trees makes me jump. My heart races as my knees lock into a runner's stance, prepared to bolt whenever Maya jumps out to force me to start sprinting again. But she doesn't pop out of the woodwork. Nothing does.

Cautiously, I edge toward the woods, realizing too late that I should've brought a weapon. For all I know, the ringleader of the crawl-space possums could be luring me in, prepared to take me out and lay its claim over the cabin once and for all.

What I find is a lot worse than the possum king.

"Jesus, calm down!" Julian hisses, lunging forward and covering my mouth when I gear up to scream.

I bite down on Julian's pinky finger hard enough for him to let me go, nearly slipping on the damp grass as I push him as hard as I can. "What is wrong with you?" I spit, getting rid of the sweat his palm left behind on my tongue.

Julian ignores me, clutching his reddened pinky to his chest. "Did you have to bite me?"

"Hello, you just lunged at me in the middle of the woods, so yes I had to bite you."

"Fine, I'm sorry." He holds his hands up in surrender. "Stella said she saw you guys earlier, and I wanted to catch you before you went inside."

I cross my arms, protecting my rapidly beating heart. "So you decided to scare the hell out of me?"

"I was trying to be quiet."

"You can be quiet without being a creep," I scoff, ignoring the way Julian glares at me. "What're you even doing here, anyway? Shouldn't you be reciting Latin backward, or something equally obnoxious?"

Julian rolls his eyes. "I want to talk to you, dumbass."

"About what, *dumbass*?"

He takes a deep breath, calming himself before replying. "You ran away from me in the bathroom."

"Yeah, because you cornered me in a dark, empty room. Excuse me for panicking." I try to put an end to the conversation by walking away, but Julian grabs my arm before I can get very far. I briefly consider walking him toward the edge of the nearby dock, close enough to push him into the lake once his guard's down. It's a beautiful mental image, but sabotage never goes well for me, even up against the least feisty Seo-Cooke.

"I only did it because I want to talk to you," he explains, sounding unusually earnest, but I still don't trust it.

I let out a humorless laugh and yank my arm out of his grip. "What could you possibly want to talk to me about?" I know there aren't many other people our age at the lake this year, but I can't imagine Julian's so desperate for conversation that he'd come crawling to me.

Julian stays quiet, biting his lip and shoving his hands into his pockets. I start a countdown in my head. I'll give him to ten to spit out whatever he has to say.

I make it to five before I realize I don't care enough to make it to ten.

"Wait, wait, wait," Julian pleads when I start walking away again, running ahead and standing in front of me. "Can you please just hear me out for five minutes?"

He holds his arm out to block my path. I scowl, trying to get around his left side, but he beats me to it. As always, the Seo-Cookes prove that they're the most frustrating people on the planet.

"You have one minute," I warn, prepared to start counting out loud this time when Julian blurts out one succinct sentence.

"I need you to pretend to be my boyfriend."

Hell has officially frozen over.

I start to laugh. Hard. So hard that I double over, clutching my stomach as tears well in the corners of my eyes. This is the funniest thing I've heard all year. Just the thought—me and Julian, holding hands and gazing lovingly at one another—sends me into another fit of laughter.

"Holy shit, I can't breathe," I choke out in between laughs, finally straightening myself out and fanning my flushed cheeks.

"It's not a joke."

Julian says something else, but I don't bother listening—I'm too busy trying to catch my breath. He mutters something to himself before taking my wrist and dragging me farther into the woods.

"What are you doing?" I plant my feet as best I can in the damp grass.

"Going somewhere more private since everyone probably heard your hyena cackle."

I stop laughing, ripping my arm out of Julian's hold for a second time. "I don't want to go somewhere private with you."

"Can you please just trust me on this?" he pleads.

"You've never given me any reason to trust you."

Julian holds his fist to his mouth, muffling a scream. "Fine." He steps back, holding his arms out at his sides. "I have nothing in my hands." He reaches into his pockets, pulling them inside out, letting his keys and wallet fall to the ground. "Nothing in my pockets." He takes off his sneakers, tossing one to the left and the other to the right. Birds squawk as they fly off their perches, but nothing new emerges. "Stella and Henry aren't waiting to jump you." He slaps his hands back down to his sides. "Believe me now?"

I don't want to believe him. If I do, it means this absurd idea might be something more than a twisted prank. I'll probably regret giving in to my curiosity, but . . .

I nod slowly and let Julian lead the way. We only go a few feet deeper into the woods, out of view of our houses. I map out an escape route along the way in case Julian tries to attack. I may even throw in a kick to the balls. Y'know, just to be safe.

Julian trails off to grab his sneakers while I lean up against a nearby tree. I reach into my pocket, breathing a sigh of relief when my fingers close around my keys. I do have a weapon.

"Explain," I demand once Julian has put his shoes back on.

"It's . . . kind of a long story," he mumbles, swiping at the dirt on his sole.

"Well, then get started, because the clock's ticking." I tap my imaginary watch.

Julian glares at me. He takes a deep breath, linking his fingers calmly. "I . . . have this ex-boyfriend . . ."

"Okay," I reply slowly. "And?"

He runs a hand through his hair, his bangs sticking up in a tuft that should look ridiculous but is somehow effortlessly cool. "He lives on the other side of the lake. Moved there two years ago. We were together for a hot second last summer, which was a *very* stupid move on my part." He pauses to roll his eyes, and I keep any insults to myself. "He's been blowing up my phone since the second we got here. Apparently 'no' wasn't enough to convince him I'm not interested in getting back together. But he kept pushing until I panicked and said I was seeing someone new, and now he's asking to meet him, so . . ." He throws his hands up into the air. "Here we are."

I gave Julian too much credit. He's an absolute dumbass if he thinks I'm going to believe any of that. "Nope," I reply, popping the *p* for emphasis. "Not interested. Bye."

I start marching back toward my cabin, but Julian follows me like a lost puppy. "C'mon, please? I wouldn't be asking if I wasn't desperate."

"If you're so desperate, find someone else to play your fake lover."

"I *can't* find anyone else, that's the point."

Julian goes to reach for my arm again, but I hold my finger up in warning. "Touch me again and you're losing a finger."

He holds his arms up beside his head. "Listen, if I could find literally anybody else, I would. I don't know if you've noticed, but I don't exactly have many options for fake boyfriends around here." He gestures toward the abandoned cabin to our left. The mushroom has started growing fur.

I rack my brain for any other potential fake boyfriends. I would offer up Andy as a sacrifice, but he's obnoxiously heterosexual. "What about the family that owns the souvenir shop? The Martinezes? They have two kids."

Julian gives me a deadpan look. "One is seven and the other is in his twenties."

"Perfect, if the older one's loaded, maybe you can get a sugar daddy situation out of it." I pause, tapping my chin in thought. "Actually, that would look fishy. You're too loaded for a sugar daddy."

"Ha ha," he replies dryly. "Come *on*. It's a one-time thing,

I swear. His dad's hosting a mixer at the Hillsdale Country Club tomorrow. All we'd have to do is say hi, eat the free food, and then you never have to see him, or stand within five feet of me again."

I'm not what many would call cunning, but that sounds like a pretty half-assed plan to me. "And what's in it for me?" I ask out of curiosity. "Besides free food."

He shrugs. "You'd be helping me."

Wow, what a compelling argument. He nearly had me there for a second. "You don't deserve my help."

Before I know it, he's in front of me again, beads of sweat trickling down his forehead. "Please, Devin. I—"

A shadow washes over him, his hands beginning to tremble when Maya presses the barrel of her water gun against the small of his back.

"Hands up," she orders into his ear. Julian quickly obliges, tremoring at the sound of her voice. Any confidence he had left has been stripped away by a girl who is five-one and armed with a super soaker.

Maya steps in front of him, standing firmly between the two of us. She keeps her weapon aimed square at his chest, nodding her head toward the Seo-Cookes' half of the yard. "If you ever try to corner one of us like that again, I'm unloading on your ass. Now go."

He hesitates for half a second, hands still shaking as he lowers them back down.

"I said go!"

Julian bolts so quickly he trips over himself, his sneakers slapping wetly against the dew-slick grass. Watching him scramble to get up is worth the brief panic of being alone with him. The sight sends me into another laughing fit, tears brimming in the corner of my eyes.

"I needed that." I wipe the backs of my hands across my eyes. "Thanks for bailing me out. I thought he was . . ."

I trail off when I notice Maya's wicked smile. Her eyes are trained on the Seo-Cookes' back door, her fingers so tight around the water gun her knuckles go pale. She turns to face me, her smile evolving into a Cheshire cat grin. The fire in her eyes makes my heart race and my forehead uncomfortably clammy.

"You just hit the freaking jackpot."

CHAPTER FIVE

Full disrespect to Maya, her ideas are terrible. Notoriously terrible. The last time she forced me into one, we were permanently banned from our high school's costume contest for bringing a live snake to class and causing "mass hysteria." In our defense, though, her Britney Spears costume would've easily taken first place if we hadn't been disqualified for breaking the "no live animals on school premises" rule in the Code of Conduct packet no one reads.

Before I can ask Maya what she means, she takes off toward the cabin, calling out for me to follow. I'm already winded from the lap, so I don't run after her like she wants me to. Still, I'm flushed and panting for breath once I catch up to her. Andy, finished with his second lap and downing a Gatorade, doesn't pay attention to me or my wheezing as I trudge past him.

Maya pulls me into her bedroom, making sure to lock

the door. "So . . ." She raises one of her perfectly sculpted eyebrows. "Julian needs a fake boyfriend?"

"You were there for that whole conversation and didn't bother to rescue me earlier?" I rub a hand over my wrist, still warm from the sting of Julian's touch.

She rolls her eyes, brushing off my concern to sit down at her desk. "Because I was intrigued. Duh."

"What was intriguing about an obvious trap?"

"I don't think it was a trap." Maya opens the notebook on her desk, flipping past her training notes and potential insults for Henry's new haircut and turning to a fresh page. "But I *do* think he's desperate."

Maya may be more emotionally intelligent than I am, but I don't think a Seo-Cooke would ever be desperate enough to do what Julian's proposing. Just because he isn't a mastermind doesn't mean we can trust him.

"Which means you have leverage," Maya explains, holding up her notebook. Written at the top of the page in hot-pink gel pen is *DEVIN & JULIAN*.

"I do?" Being someone's unfortunate choice for a fake boyfriend doesn't sound like leverage to me.

"*We* do," she clarifies. "If Julian's as desperate as he sounds, he'll give you whatever you want."

"So we ask for money?"

She whacks me over the head with the notebook. "No, you idiot. You ask to hang out at his house."

"I *what*?!" I choke on my own spit as I struggle to get the words out.

"Keep it down," she hisses, staying quiet for a second to confirm Andy didn't overhear. The only sound besides the buzzing of mosquitoes is the creak of the shower coming to life. "Getting inside the Seo-Cookes' house is like getting into a gold mine. Do you know what kind of dirt you could find in there?"

"What? Like that their dad is embezzling money? That seems sorta out of our league."

Maya looks like she's seconds away from strangling me. "You could find proof that they're going to cheat at the games. Or how they've gotten away with it before." Her voice is calm and composed, the tone she puts on for job interviews.

Proving that the Seo-Cookes are cheating is easier said than done. The games weren't supposed to be as high stakes as what we turned them into. There was never a rule book or a guide, just Old Bob's judgment and an element of good faith. We'd need something tangible, concrete. Blueprints on how to rig an egg toss, or the answer sheet to one of the logic puzzles.

"Is that the kind of thing they'd have lying around?" I'm not in the business of cheating, but I know you'd want to cover your tracks. Especially with an enemy in your midst.

"Probably not. Which is why you'd have to go looking for it. If we can't prove that they're cheating, then we can at least figure out what they're planning. Keep an eye on them."

I'm flattered that she thinks I'm stealthy enough to pull off a mission like that. But for once she thinks too highly of me. "Shouldn't we just try to win the games fair and square?"

"Why? They never have."

Now shouldn't be the time for me to have a moral superiority complex, I know. Not when our cabin is on the line. But there's a reason we never stooped to their level. We always wanted to win on our own, to show them that we don't need lies and tricks to come in first.

We always played it safe and paid the price.

"Let's say I did find proof that they're cheating—what next? We send it to Old Bob and have them disqualified?"

"That's exactly what we do," Maya replies. "They're out, we win by default, and the cabin is ours. End of story."

"Technically, the bet didn't say anything about being disqualified. Mr. Cooke could bring in an army of lawyers if he wanted to prove us wrong."

She rolls her eyes, flopping back down onto her desk chair. "Then we find out what they're planning and try to stop them. Make it an even fight for once."

"And if we get caught?"

She shrugs and blows a raspberry. "Then nothing. Going through someone's stuff doesn't count as cheating. Neither does eavesdropping. Worst-case scenario, they throw rotten eggs at you or something."

That sounds like a very unpleasant worst-case scenario for me, but I brush past it and focus on my other concerns. "And you expect Dad to be okay with all of this?"

"We wouldn't tell Dad," she replies casually. "He can't tell a lie to save his life, and Andy, God bless him, has the IQ of a walnut. We're better off leaving them and Isabel in the dark for now."

Letting them believe that I might *actually* be dating someone like Julian Seo-Cooke feels worse than lying straight to their faces.

"I don't know . . ." Thinking about the amount of lies

I'd have to keep up with makes me break into a sweat. "I'm supposed to be working on my mentorship application, and—" I wince before I can finish that thought, gearing up to apologize for bringing up a sore subject, when she cuts me off instead.

"I'll do your chores for you," she says, any annoyance over me bringing up one of the forbidden Cs gone. "You can work on your piece for your application, and I'll fight the bats in the attic, or whatever other torture Dad has planned for us."

That stops my protests right in their tracks.

"Except don't use that sketch of me," she adds, her nose wrinkled in disapproval. Her eyes shift to the floor, avoiding mine. "You can do better."

Maya always stays true to her word. Across all the deals we've made, she's never double-crossed me. I'd thought that sketch could be a new beginning for us, but maybe this could be one too. A chance to be a team again.

"And all I have to do is convince Julian to let me go over to his house a few times?" I ask, checking for any fine print.

She nods, holding out her hand for me to shake. "Promise."

I still hesitate. Shifting down to the edge of the bed, I walk myself through the reasons I shouldn't do this.

1. I'd have to pretend to *like* Julian.
2. I'm a shit liar.
3. Spending that much time with the Seo-Cookes will probably spike my blood pressure.

When I open my mouth, Maya leans forward, cutting me off as she rests her hands on my knees, her face inches from mine. "Don't you want to win?"

Of course I want to win. All we've ever wanted is to win, to show them up and rub it in their faces the way they have for years.

"You know I do."

"Devin." Her hands slip into mine, the edges of her nails digging into my skin, but I don't flinch. "This is how we win."

The thrill of getting even lights something in me as wicked as Maya's smile. It silences the nerves nestled in the pit of my stomach, all the *what-ifs* and *but hows* giving way to the *what could bes*. Me and Maya side by side, plotting and talking and laughing like we used to. Us with Dad and Isabel and Andy, smiling as we accept our gold medals and gift cards. Our portrait in the visitors center for everyone to see. Our cabin, still so alive with memories of Mami, staying with us. With our family.

There are a thousand ways this could go wrong. Our plans are never foolproof and this one's no exception. But in that moment, holding my sister's hands and dreaming of a future where we finally come first, it's impossible not to feel invincible.

I squeeze her hands back and swallow every rational thought that screams at me to focus on the safe route that we know.

"Okay," I reply.

Because maybe a little bit of risk is all we need to win.

CHAPTER SIX

Having Maya on my side is a very valuable asset. There's no way I would've decided to help Julian without an ulterior motive, but if I had, it would've been hell to keep that secret on my own.

Maya and I carefully construct a message to Julian asking him to meet tomorrow afternoon. Before I can sell my soul, I need to know more about what I'm getting into and convince him to give me what I need in return. A quick search through Julian's social media doesn't give us much relevant info. We learn that he's captain of the lacrosse team and the tennis team, and he founded the Everly Prep Asian Student Association. And can speak four languages. Just imagining what his schedule must be like makes me dizzy.

Julian agrees to meet me at Dixon's, the infamous deli

that gave me and Dad food poisoning. It's the one place I know no one in my family will come within ten feet of. Even Isabel and Andy know all about the food poisoning saga.

Maya makes up an excuse for me when I head out, telling the others I'm taking reference pictures of the lake for a painting class next semester. My suggestion that we say I'm on a hike was quickly shot down. She made a good point. Why would I—someone who almost failed gym twice—go on a hike of my own volition?

Once I've safely escaped our cabin, I throw on a baseball cap, lift the hood of my sweatshirt, and power walk as quickly as I can. The sun clings to my black ensemble, beating down on me even when I manage to find some patches of shade. I'm dripping sweat, seconds from collapsing, when Dixon's finally comes into view. It's the first time I've ever been happy to see the godforsaken place. I jog the last bit of the way, bursting into the deliciously air-conditioned entryway with a sigh of relief.

No sign of Julian yet.

"You gonna order?" a voice barks from behind the counter.

Patience is not a part of the customer service philosophy at Dixon's. If you don't order within thirty seconds, you might as well leave. The owners, elderly brothers that five-year-old Devin and Maya dubbed Mario and Luigi due to their thick, bushy mustaches and dramatically different heights, almost bullied us out of the shop when Mami had the nerve to ask for her salad dressing on the side. Thankfully I don't have to worry about either of them whispering about my little rendezvous with Julian to the remaining town gossips. They never cared about the vacationers before, and I can't imagine they're going to start now.

Mario is as crabby and his mustache as thick as I remember. At least some things are still the same. He taps his foot impatiently.

"I'll take a water."

Mario mutters something under his breath as he heads toward the fridge to grab a bottle.

"I promise I'll get something else too!" I tack on before darting to the bathroom. No way he'd let me stick around without ordering something worth at least $5. Maybe soup? I can't think of any death-by-contaminated-soup horror stories off the top of my head.

In the bathroom, I peel off my soaked hoodie, wringing out the dank stench of sweat as best I can before tucking it into my backpack. The hat and oversized sunglasses I pull out of my bag aren't exactly a foolproof disguise, but it'll do for now.

By the time I leave the bathroom, sweat-tacky and flushed down to my toes, Julian is sitting at a nearby table. He waves me down, pushing his bag off the seat across from him. He eyes the sweat stain lining the collar of my T-shirt but keeps any snarky comments to himself. His phone buzzes on the table as I sit down across from him, a photo of his mom lighting up the screen.

"Sorry," he says under his breath before sending the call to voice mail and shoving his phone into his pocket. "I didn't think you'd actually show."

"Should I not have?"

He shakes his head, toying with one of the takeout menus between us. "No, I'm glad you're here. I get why you wouldn't want to trust me."

"I'm still not sure that I do."

Julian nods, leaning back in his seat and crossing his arms. "That's fair."

Mario interrupts us, bustling over to our table to remind me that I'll have to leave if I don't order anything else. Julian orders a foot-long turkey sub before I can open my mouth, handing him a twenty and telling him to keep the change. Thank God Julian's a chronic over-tipper. Mario nods, tucking the money away with a pleased smile before shuffling back to the counter.

"To be clear, I haven't made up my mind yet," I clarify once he's out of earshot. "I just want to know more."

"About?"

"This." I wave my hand at the space between us. "How it will work. How *we* will work."

Julian props his chin up on his hand. "I don't know. Like any other couple?"

I hold back a scoff. "Except that we're not like any other couple."

"I'm not asking you to call me pookie and get my name tattooed on your chest. You just have to stand there and not look like you'd rather die."

I don't hold back my scoff this time. "Easier said than done."

We stay silent until Mario returns with a glass of water

for Julian and the three-dollar bottle I ordered when I walked in. I watch Julian fold, unfold, and refold his straw wrapper. "If we're going to do this, then I want something out of it."

Julian nods between sips of water. "Okay. How much?"

"I . . . uh . . . I don't want money."

Julian's lips tug into a frown. "You don't?"

I shake my head, willing my nerves to cool it for a second while I try to sound believable. "I want to come over to your house. Twice a week. Minimum." The request sounds as awkward as I feel.

And Julian looks as shocked as I was when Maya first suggested this plan. "Oh . . ." His cheeks flush as he leans back in his seat. "Uh . . . why?"

"I'm applying for this mentorship with a CalArts professor that's due after break." It's not a lie, so it rolls clean off my tongue. "I need to work on a piece for it, but my dad's making us do all of these DIY projects around the house, and Maya and Andy are already chaotic as it is, so I need a place where I can go to concentrate. Just for a few hours."

Once again, Maya's way better at coming up with believable lies than me.

Julian bites his lip, the cogs in his head clearly working at high speed.

"All right, fine," he answers after a pause. "That's it?"

I tuck my hands under my armpits to keep them from shaking. "That's it." This seems too easy, but I'm not going to question it. The hard part has barely begun. "So, what would I have to do?"

Julian reaches into his pocket, pulling out a folded piece of cardstock. He smooths it out on the table before pushing it toward me. It's an invitation. "Show up tonight at seven. Dress code is business casual. We say our hellos. Done."

The invitation alone is intimidating. It's printed on the good cardstock, the kind that costs more than any type of paper ever should. The date is written in elegant script, with a coat of arms at the bottom of the page. What kind of family has their own coat of arms?

The name written below the crest, in a less opulent, but more readable font, strikes me as familiar.

"Allegheny . . . like the water park?"

Julian nods, his eyes still avoiding mine. "The Alleghenys are loaded, super old money. My ex—*Liam*—his dad has always had a thing for amusement parks. Building their own was like the ultimate sandbox," he says with a shrug, as if having enough money to build a water park isn't absolutely wild.

My mouth hangs open, a bit of drool spilling out onto the table. Luckily Julian doesn't notice my graceful maneuver of wiping it up with my sleeve. Well, this confirms my theory that the rich only date within their tax bracket.

"How long were you two together?" I ask, feeling strangely drawn to Julian's history with this water park heir.

"Not long. Two months, maybe less. We tried the whole long-distance thing when I went home to Miami after the summer, but it wasn't really working." He sighs as he runs a hand through his hair. "And now he wants to pick things up where we left off."

"And you already tried telling him to buzz off?"

"Not in those words, but yes," he replies dryly. "But Liam's a . . . complicated person."

A gulp gets lodged in my throat. What could be more "complicated" than not knowing how to respect boundaries? Meeting Liam just skyrocketed to the top of my list of things I'm worried about—with "Mr. Cooke destroying our cabin," and "getting rabies from a possum" as very close seconds.

"You'll be fine, though," Julian assures me. He must've sensed my panic—guess that's something I'll have to work on if we want to pull this off.

I take one last look at the invitation, reminding myself that I can still get out of this if I want to. But the thought of Maya, of our cabin, of *winning* is stronger than the urge to run away.

"All right. I'm in."

Julian looks up at me with a raised brow. "Wait, seriously? You'll do it?"

"The fact that you're this shocked is making me think that I shouldn't."

He clams up, quickly shifting back to his side of the table. "I just didn't think you'd actually say yes."

I groan, burying my face in my hands. "Neither did I."

Luigi finally makes an appearance, bustling out of the kitchen and setting down the sandwich before Julian can reply. When I lift my head, there's a small green bottle sitting in front of me.

"It's tea tree oil," Julian explains. "My mom said it can help with infections."

I turn the bottle around in my hand. "You got this for me?"

"For your nose." He taps his plastic fork against his nose before slicing the sandwich down the middle, passing half to me.

"Oh, no, thank you." I quickly push the plate back toward Julian.

"C'mon, I can't eat an entire foot-long by myself," he pleads, pushing the plate back more intently.

Looking at the sandwich makes me woozy. "I'm fine, really." But my stomach betrays me, falling for the allure of carbs and mayo, growling loud enough that Julian chuckles.

"Consider this practice." He pushes the plate back again. "If we can survive eating together, we can make it through a cocktail party."

I frown at the sandwich. It does look better than I remembered . . .

"Thought so," Julian says under his breath when I let out a low moan around my first tentative bite.

"Shut up," I mutter, hanging my head in shame as I take another wolfish bite. It's not the best thing in the world, but I was stupid enough to think I could make it through a mile-long walk on half a granola bar. Maybe the food poisoning incident was partially our fault. We should've known something called a "Meat Mayhem" wasn't going to go down well.

"So, tell me about yourself," I say once I've eaten most of my sandwich half.

"Why?" he asks warily.

"If I'm going to pretend to be your boyfriend, I should actually know stuff about you, right?"

Julian purses his lips and scratches his head. "Like what?"

For someone who's trying to shake off an ex, he seems as inexperienced at romance as I am. "Anything, really. All I know is your family's loaded, your brother plays football, and your sister was in an Old Navy commercial."

"Fine. What do you want to know?"

Let's start off simple. "Favorite color?"

"Don't have one."

"Okay . . . Favorite movie?"

He hums before shaking his head. "I don't really watch movies."

I bite back a dramatic sigh. I figured Julian was dull, but I didn't think he was "I don't watch movies or have a favorite color'" dull. He dabs neatly at the mayo dripping from the sandwich before taking a bite. I don't think I've ever seen anyone eat a sub so neatly. It's unsettling.

"Favorite book?" I ask, tearing my eyes away from his plate.

This one stumps him. His face scrunches up and he snaps his fingers before replying, *"Titus Andronicus."*

"First of all, that's a play not a book. Second of all—seriously?"

"What?"

"Who picks *Titus Andronicus* as their favorite Shakespeare play?" I'm not a big Shakespeare fan to begin with, but the three weeks I spent reading *Titus* bored me to tears. I made it through the first fifty pages before SparkNote-ing my way through the rest of the class.

"Me," he retorts defensively. "What's your favorite book, then? Since you're apparently the pinnacle of good taste."

Easy. *"Catcher in the Rye."*

"Are you kidding me?" he scoffs. "That's the most pretentious book you could possibly pick."

"Is not!" Admittedly, I haven't read many books to begin with, but still. It's an American classic.

"Yes, it is! Holden even *says* he's pretentious."

"That doesn't mean the *book* is pretentious."

Julian wordlessly pulls out his phone. Seconds later he shoves it in my face, pulled up to an article listing the top twenty most pretentious books in American literature. *Catcher in the Rye* is number one.

It takes every bit of strength I have left in me not to shove my fork into Julian's thick skull. Mario and Luigi glare at us, gripping their mops like they're ready to step in if Julian and I come to blows. I sit up straighter, using Maya's breathing techniques to help compose myself.

"Favorite band?" I ask, calming down.

"New Nostalgia," he replies. All right, good, an actual answer—even if I have no idea who New Nostalgia is. "They're this indie rock band from Leeds," he adds.

I make a mental note to Google them and move on to the next topic. "Favorite TV show?"

Julian ducks his head sheepishly. I can tell by the color rising in his cheeks that he's going to give me another unhelpful answer. "I don't really have time to watch TV."

I let my head fall to the table with a clunk. I knew this wasn't going to be easy, but this is painful. "Do you have time to do anything fun in your life?" The question comes out without thinking. I swore I would play nice this time but bickering with Julian is second nature to me.

"Not really. Dad always told me TV rots your brain," he whispers, tearing his napkin into strips. "That's something I want to change, though."

"Rotting your brain?"

He shakes his head, lowering his eyes. "Listening to my dad."

He peeks up at me from beneath full lashes, turning away when I meet his gaze. I bite my lip, unsure of what to do. I could play the supportive soon-to-be-fake-boyfriend, tell him everything will be okay even though I have no idea if it will be.

Fortunately, he changes the topic before I can put my foot in my mouth. "Favorite flavor of ice cream?"

The question catches me off guard, but the shy smile budding on Julian's lips makes my chest feel less tight. I laugh, half out of relief and half because the absurdity of our situation is finally setting in. "Mint chocolate. You?"

"Vanilla."

I don't call him boring for picking the blandest possible flavor. Instead, I nod, take another bite, and move on.

See? Progress.

CHAPTER SEVEN

Julian's going to kill me.

In my defense, I didn't think it would take over thirty minutes for Lyft to find a driver in my area. After twenty minutes of waiting in the dark with nothing but owls and mosquitoes for company, I was ready to walk the two and a half miles myself. Finally Danny and his blue Honda SUV came to the rescue. He doesn't even mind when I start changing into a new outfit in the backseat. Five stars.

The Hillsdale Country Club is as intimidating as I thought it would be. The marble entryway looks like it's been plucked from a villa along the French Riviera. A man in a well-cut suit appears at my side after I drop off my backpack at the coat check, holding out a tray with a single champagne flute.

"Oh, I'm not twenty-one."

"My apologies." He sets the tray down on the entry table,

pulling a fresh flute practically out of thin air. "Sparkling cider?"

I warily accept the cider, letting the man usher me into the main dining room. Didn't Julian say this was supposed to be a low-key affair?

Dozens of waiters skate across the room with trays of hors d'oeuvres and flutes of champagne. A cellist is setting up in one corner while a man decked out in a full tux—cummerbund, tails, and all—takes a seat at a baby grand piano in the center of the room.

"Low-key, my ass," I mutter, leaning up on my tiptoes to scan the room for any sign of Julian.

None of the people here look familiar, but based on their designer handbags, suits, and dresses, I clearly missed the memo about the dress code. That's on me, though. I should've known that a dinosaur-print button-down wouldn't cut it at a country club. A passing waiter gives me a suspicious look, whispering behind a gloved hand to the man from the entry-way. The men exchange shrugs after looking me up and down, as confused by my presence as I am.

I need to find Julian before they smell the fraud on me.

Julian suddenly appears at my side, pulling me toward a more secluded area of the dining room. "You're late."

"My bad, I didn't realize how long it would take to get here."

"We're fifteen minutes from your house," he hisses, his grip on my arm getting a bit too tight.

"Yeah, but it took thirty minutes to find a rideshare willing to come get me." I pull my arm out of his hold, my mouth watering at the scent of something deep fried.

"It's fine." He smooths the lapel of his burgundy dinner jacket, a bold choice in the sea of gray and blue. "At least you're actually here."

"I considered standing you up." I snag a mini crab cake from a passing tray. "But I heard there would be free food."

He scowls before grabbing my arm again and dragging me toward the opposite end of the room. Only five minutes in and I'm already starting to feel less like a guest and more like prey.

"Wow, you're actually stupid enough to go through with this," says a voice from behind us.

Stella, like Julian, isn't much like the girl I remember throwing sand in my eyes. She arrives in a cloud of rose-scented perfume, wearing a silver sequined dress that would probably look hideous on anyone other than her. At sixteen, she's grown into the type of person who looks like they just walked out of a magazine—luminous skin, dark, thick hair braided down her back, high cheekbones, and full lips. A face worthy of eighty thousand Instagram followers and a brand ambassadorship with the latest flashy celebrity skin-care line. Something that has always infuriated Maya, who spent an entire paycheck on said celebrity's overpriced seven-step regimen.

The one thing that hasn't changed is Stella's voice, flat and disinterested, as if she's never experienced another emotion besides extreme boredom.

"Shut up, Stella," Julian mutters, glancing over her shoulder. "Have you seen Liam?"

"No." Stella crosses her arms, looking pointedly at the two of us. "You know he's never going to believe this, right?"

"Yeah, well, it's not like I have other options." Julian pushes past her, gesturing for me to follow.

"You could've just blocked him and moved on like a normal person," she replies.

Julian stops in his tracks, inhaling sharply as he turns back to his sister. "Can you please not be a pain in my ass for one night?"

She mulls the question over for a second before conceding and heading toward a table covered in champagne flutes.

Julian takes a deep breath, pinching the bridge of his nose. "Sorry, you can ignore her."

I peer over my shoulder at where Stella has helped herself to champagne and a bruschetta. "Should I be worried that your sister thinks this is a bad idea?"

Julian takes a concerning amount of time to answer. "No."

"Are you sure?"

Another pause. "No."

Great.

Julian stays rooted in place, staring at me with a frown that speaks volumes. It feels like he's thrown the ball into my court, like he wouldn't stop me if I walked away. I consider it. Walking away and saving myself from whatever disaster's waiting for me on the other end of the room. But I'll take chaos over losing our cabin, so I offer him my hand.

"Guess we'd better go find your ex."

Julian stares at my hand, lips parted but no sound coming out. His own hands tremble at his sides.

"Well, don't leave me hanging," I snap when my arm starts to ache.

"Right, right." He shakes himself off and takes my hand.

Our fingers slide together easily, Julian leaving them suspended in midair until I push them back down to our sides.

"Relax. You look like I'm holding you hostage." I send a friendly wave to the waiter who's eyeing us suspiciously.

"Sorry." Julian rolls his shoulders back, releasing some of the tension. "It's just weird."

"Yeah, I'm not exactly having the time of my life here either." I'm no expert in hand-holding, but Julian's hands are a special brand of weird. Ice cold, yet damp to the touch. I readjust my grip, grimacing at the slick glide of Julian's palm against mine.

We take a lap around the dining room, keeping our eyes peeled for any sign of Liam. I still don't have any idea what he looks like, but I have a hunch. Tall, stylish, and handsome enough to charm someone like Julian. He should be easy to spot based on age alone. This place is a sea of well-dressed middle-aged men.

"Why does your dad only hang out with people who look like him?" I ask after mistaking yet another random man for Mr. Cooke.

Julian's nervous expression quirks into an annoyed frown. "Does everything you say have to be sarcastic?"

I'm not being sarcastic. Everyone here resembles a sunburned Jon Hamm.

"Keep it moving," Julian snips when I release his hand to grab a passing shrimp cocktail.

"Excuse you," I reply around a mouthful of shrimp. "Aren't you the one who said free food was part of the deal?"

Julian groans. "Can you just—"

An unfamiliar voice cuts him off before he can finish that thought.

"Hey, stranger," a boy calls out as he slides up beside Julian, wrapping an arm low around his waist. "It's about time I tracked you down."

As expected, Liam is tall, handsome, and wearing a suit that's probably worth more than Dad's car. Clocking in at six-two with sandy hair and a tasteful artificial tan, he makes me feel impossibly small. He's the type who wears confidence like a second skin, exudes a certain type of charisma. Some might call it charm. I call it cockiness.

"Liam! Hi!" Julian exclaims. "We were just looking for you."

The "we" dawns on Liam slowly, his thick eyebrows knitting together in confusion until Julian grabs my waist and pulls me flush against his side. The arm Liam has around Julian jerks once I'm pressed up against it, his hand trapped between us in a weird throuple sandwich. Clearly, Liam asking to meet Julian's supposed new boyfriend was his way of calling Julian's bluff. But lo and behold, Julian delivered.

Despite his body's reaction, Liam's expression remains neutral. His eyes glaze over me, though not with the same interest he'd had for Julian. Less admiration, more "who the fuck is this?"

"I don't think we've met."

"This is Devin Báez," Julian replies on my behalf while wriggling himself out of Liam's grip. Once we're free, he drops the arm around my waist to take my hand again, holding it up like a badge of honor. "My boyfriend."

Watching Liam's eyes rake down between the two of us to

our linked fingers makes me go as clammy as Julian's hands. "Nice to meet you," I choke out.

"Likewise," he replies, snapping his eyes away from our hands and up to my face. He flashes me a megawatt smile as he holds out his hand for me to shake. Rows of perfectly straight white teeth glisten in the light of the crystal chandelier.

How could Julian want nothing to do with someone so aesthetically pleasing?

"Interesting interpretation of business casual." Liam waves his free hand at my ensemble. "Very 'secondhand' chic."

Ah, that's why.

My cheeks flush as I drop Liam's hand. Why didn't I think to bring a suit jacket with me?

Beside me, Julian's jaw clenches at the backhanded compliment. "Liam," he murmurs through gritted teeth, his grip on me going from uncomfortable to straight up painful.

"What?" Liam waves him off. "It's a compliment, I swear."

As much as I want to defend myself and my choice in dinosaur-print shirts, I bite my tongue. If Maya were here, Liam would've gotten his ass handed to him by now, but I'm not as quick-witted. She sucked up all of our potential confidence in the womb. Instead, I stand my ground and hope the heat of Liam's glare doesn't turn me to ash. Besides, I'm here to play nice. Not cause a scene.

Before Julian can open his mouth to defend my honor, a more familiar voice cuts him off.

"Julian!" Mr. Cooke shouts, earning the attention of half

the room. Julian pales while Liam's smirk grows tenfold as we watch Mr. Cooke shove through the crowd to get to us, his eyes fixed on me.

"Nice to see you again, Mr. Cooke," Liam greets when he finally reaches us. "I just finished listening to your interview on the Florida Entrepreneurship Society's podcast—really great stuff."

Mr. Cooke's frown drops long enough for him to beam at Liam. "You flatter me." He sidesteps me in favor of patting Liam on the shoulder. "Will we be seeing you out on the green next week? Your dad mentioned your wrist injury was healing nicely."

Liam holds up his right arm, not-at-all subtly flashing his Cartier watch. "Wouldn't miss it."

Seeing Liam and Mr. Cooke side by side is jarring. If the theory that you're more likely to date someone who looks like one of your parents is true, these two are a perfect example, with their matching coiffed hair and striking blue eyes. They're even wearing the same shade of forest-green silk tie. More importantly, they have the same smile. Cunning and vicious and as artificial as their hair color.

Mr. Cooke pats Liam on the back one last time. "Good man." Their bougie display of camaraderie comes to an end when Mr. Cooke's attention shifts back to me and Julian, his expression souring.

"Mind if I take a second to chat with Julian?" It's unclear if the question is aimed at me, Liam, or both of us.

"Of course." Liam holds up his champagne flute. "Don't forget to try the Brie before it's gone. It's imported from

France." Finally, mercifully, he starts to walk away. "Pleasure seeing you all again. And nice to meet you, David."

I don't bother correcting him, focusing instead on making my own grand escape in the opposite direction, but Julian yanks me to his side.

"Stay," he whispers to me out of the corner of his mouth.

"I'm not a dog."

"Hello, Devin," Mr. Cooke says, his face painfully stiff.

"Mr. Cooke." It's oddly thrilling watching cool, confident Paul Cooke squirm.

"It's very nice of you to stop by, but this event is really just for friends of the Alleghenys." He rests a hand on my shoulder. "You understand, don't you?"

"He's here as my plus-one," Julian says.

Mr. Cooke turns to him, annoyance morphing into horror as his eyes travel down to my and Julian's linked fingers.

"Your . . . plus-one?"

"The invitation said we could bring one if we wanted to." Julian pauses, straightening himself out. "Didn't it?"

I hold in a laugh. Mr. Cooke looks like he's going to either pee himself, explode, or both.

He checks us out, as if we're toxic waste. "Devin, can you excuse us for a moment?" He loops his arm around Julian's shoulders, tugging him toward a nearby hallway. Julian glances back at me as his dad pulls him away, mouthing *Be back soon* before disappearing from view.

Well . . . what now?

I rock on the balls of my feet, digging my hands into my pockets. I don't realize I've been relying on Julian as my shield until I'm left alone on the battlefield without armor. I'm not sure how long "soon" is, but I don't want to risk losing Julian in the crowd when he returns. Or getting cornered by Liam, who may try to stab me with an antique steak knife if he gets the chance.

After fifteen minutes of standing around, I start attracting the wrong kind of attention. A handful of people assume I'm a waiter, which feels like a microaggression on way too many levels. What waiter wears a dinosaur-print shirt?

Doing nothing isn't helping me seem any less out of place, so I might as well *try* to act like I belong. I confidently make my way toward the drinks table, grabbing a flute of champagne this time. What the Alleghenys don't know won't hurt them.

I sip my champagne and continue sampling the rest of the hors d'oeuvres. The Alleghenys clearly pulled out all the stops for their "modest" affair. There's a surprising amount of meat wrapped up inside other meats, and a burrata so light and wonderful I hear angels sing after I take my first bite. As for the Brie, if anything, it was imported from a Whole Foods.

While I take a lap with a plate of finger sandwiches, I make sure to keep tabs on the people who have it out for me. Liam is throwing eye daggers at me from across the room. Thankfully he's too preoccupied with schmoozing to attack. Henry skulks around the bar, clearly trying to sneak himself something stronger than champagne, but the bartenders don't look like they'll be caving anytime soon.

The only person I haven't spotted is Mrs. Seo, though I

wouldn't be surprised if she wasn't here tonight. She's a busy lady, busier than her husband's ever been. She's a name partner at a law firm that does . . . lawyer things. Doing actual work while Mr. Cooke "networks" with the upper crust until he can charm them into investing in his (probably stolen) business ventures. Spotting her name on the notable alumni roster when I visited UCLA was a jump scare straight out of a horror movie. Turns out she's a born and bred Angelino—and a beloved one at that. The Seo-Cookes still haunt me even when I'm across the country.

My suspicion radar pings as I watch Liam cross the room to grab a passing waiter. His red-hot gaze doesn't leave me as he whispers something in the waiter's ear, pointing right at me before stalking off. The waiter glances nervously between the two of us before hesitantly approaching me.

Liam can't get me kicked out of here . . . can he?

Either way, I'm not sticking around to find out. I carefully weave my way through the crowd, avoiding the waiter on my tail, until I finally spot a familiar face at a secluded table in a back corner.

Stella doesn't glance up from her phone when I throw myself down into the seat beside her. "You're still here?"

"I can't believe it either," I mutter, more to myself than her. The waiter hasn't caught up to me yet, so I make myself unassuming. An impossible task considering how out of place I am.

"Why is *he* here?" sneers a voice to my left.

Henry's slim-cut suit makes him look impossibly larger, like he's one flex away from bursting at the seams. I wonder if there's an ounce of fat left on him, or if he's grown into one giant mass of pure muscle with a neck as thick as his head.

Stella pops her gum before replying, sounding as disinterested as ever. "Julian invited him."

"He's actually going through with it?" Henry softens but keeps a wary eye on me. "After I told him they hid my stuff?!"

"Apparently."

"Technically, my sister hid your stuff," I add. "Not me." No shame in throwing Maya under the bus if it saves my ass tonight.

The three of us turn at the sound of an exaggerated groan, watching Julian flop into the chair beside me.

"Well, if it isn't the traitor," Henry greets.

Julian shrugs out of his suit jacket and loosens his tie the second he's seated. "What now?"

"You didn't tell us we'd have to babysit Dickwad Báez for you."

"Calm down, it was five minutes," Julian replies. It was a lot longer than five minutes, but I'm in no position to argue. At least I have him to defend me if that waiter tracks me down. "And it wouldn't kill you to play nice for once."

Henry scowls, crossing his arms like a toddler on the brink of a tantrum. "I'm not the one who's fake dating him, so why do I have to pretend to like him?"

"I'm right here, you know." No one pays attention to me.

"He's better than Liam," Stella mutters.

Henry scoffs. "No way. Liam's chill."

Stella and Julian exchange wary expressions. It makes

sense that Henry and Liam are friends. They're a match made in frat bro heaven.

But the mention of Liam brings an unsettling silence to the table. Stella doesn't turn back to her phone. She peers at Julian while Henry huffs like a gassy baby.

The only thing more painful than being surrounded by Seo-Cookes is being surrounded by silence. Foolishly, I take a stab at breaking the ice. "Is your mom here?"

One second everyone stiffens, the next they're staring me down. Stella's jaw drops while Henry's face reddens. And I can't even bear to meet Julian's eye. No one says anything, the air between us shifting from awkward to tense enough to suffocate me.

"I . . . I'm sorry," I sputter, even though I don't know what I'm apologizing for.

Slowly, Stella and Henry turn to their brother. They wait until the cellist finishes off their latest piece, using the light smattering of applause to cover up the sound of the tirade they launch into, talking over one another and taking turns smacking Julian on the shoulder or over the head.

"What is wrong with you?!"

"You didn't tell him?!"

"What kind of fake boyfriend are you?!"

"This is like New Boyfriend 101!"

"Can you both shut up?!" Julian shouts after Stella nearly pokes his eye out with her acrylic nails.

We've earned ourselves enough dirty looks that they give up without protest, settling back in their seats with furrowed brows and pink cheeks.

"C'mon." Julian grabs my hand and tugs me toward the entrance. "I'll drive you home."

"Really?" I look around in confusion but let him pull me along. "That's it?" Not that I don't want to get out of here ASAP, but it's barely been an hour.

"We saw Liam. You got your free food. No reason to stick around." Julian halts so suddenly I almost run into him. "Unless you want to stay?"

Instead of replying, I push right past him and head straight for the exit.

"Well, don't look *that* excited to get out of here," he whispers once he catches up to me.

Considering his ex may be trying to get me forcibly removed from this party, and his siblings are apparently pissed at me, it's in our best interest to haul ass.

We grab my stuff from the coat check, then navigate through the sea of sports cars and convertibles until we get to an Audi so white and pristine, I'd be terrified to ever take it out of the garage. I climb into the backseat, taking my extra clothes out of my backpack while Julian slides into the driver's seat.

"What're you doing?" He looks at me in the rearview mirror.

"Changing," I reply as I start unbuttoning my top. "Eyes that way—this show costs extra."

Julian's cheeks flush as he averts his gaze. "And why are you changing?"

"Because I haven't told my family that I sold my soul to the devil, and I'd like to keep it that way."

Julian taps his thumb against the steering wheel as he pulls out of the lot. "Are you going to tell them anything?"

I stay quiet and focus on changing. It's harder to take your pants off in the back of a sedan than it is in an SUV. It gives me time to mull over how to respond, whether I should tell him that Maya knows or keep that to myself. Barely twenty-four hours into this plan and I already can't keep up with my lies.

"Maybe." A diplomatic enough answer, but I change the topic before he can press further. "So, your dad really likes Liam. A lot more than he likes me at least."

Switching topics does the trick. Julian lets out a hollow sigh, sagging against the steering wheel. "Yeah . . ." He shakes his head, letting his eyes close while we idle at a red light. "Liam doesn't come around to our side of the lake much, but Dad's always excited when he does. I think he was hoping one of us would wind up with him. Especially with the water park stuff. The amount of money amusement parks can make in a single hour . . ." He shudders. "Dad's been trying to get in good with the Alleghenys since they moved here. So me and Liam just . . . made sense, I guess. For business."

It does. One obnoxious rich boy dates another obnoxious rich boy, and the King of the (Stolen) Idea Empire gets the chance to add another zero to his back account.

"Until it didn't?" I ask when the car starts moving again.

Julian takes his time replying, his brows furrowed and his jaw locked. If I wasn't so occupied with getting dressed, I might even apologize for prying.

"I don't think it ever really did," he says finally.

His reply makes me think back to that afternoon at Dixon's. The way he'd had that same look of frustration. *That's something I want to change,* he'd said—listening to his dad. Maybe ending things with Liam was the first step.

After a prolonged silence, Julian's eyes flicker to the rearview mirror again, catching me the exact moment I finish unbuttoning my shirt. "Hey, I said no peeking!"

"Sorry, sorry, sorry," he says in one quick breath, knuckles going white around the steering wheel.

Getting caught peeping shuts Julian up. He keeps his eyes on the road while I finish pulling on my T-shirt and paint-stained jeans. Changing out of my boyfriend costume doesn't settle the unease that's still clinging to me, though.

"I screwed up, didn't I?" I say once I've finished changing, unable to shake off my curiosity. "Asking about your mom?"

Julian sighs, running a hand over his face, massaging the sharp edge of his jaw. "No, you didn't. It's a recent thing; there's no way you could've known." His voice is gentle, kind. Soft in a way that actually makes me feel less guilty.

"Is your mom sick?" It's strange being on the opposite end of that familiar question. Asking feels almost as hard as answering had been.

But Julian doesn't answer the way I always did. His eyes don't go misty, and his body doesn't tense up over words he's said thousands of times but that still don't feel real. He just shakes his head and sighs.

"Our parents are getting divorced."

Oh.

"I'm sorry," I say, my voice as hollow as my answer.

Still, a small part of me can't help but feel vindicated on Mrs. Seo's behalf. We loathed the Seo-Cookes as a whole, but their mom never took cheap shots at us. She was sweet, even. One year, she dropped off those snack cakes we loved after she overheard Maya talking about how much we missed them. When the box showed up on our doorstep, we assumed she'd finally joined the rest of her family in the war against us. A trap we never would've expected. So they sat unopened on the kitchen table until we tossed them in the trash.

Maybe she was never a player in our game.

Julian doesn't reply, and I'm grateful for it. We may be fake boyfriends, but that doesn't mean we need to have therapeutic heart-to-hearts about our family traumas. We keep to ourselves for the remainder of the short drive back, Julian parking a few feet away from my driveaway, at my insistence. The headlights switch off, and we're swallowed by the darkness. The world beyond the windshield is almost pitch-black, the lights from my cabin barely visible through the trees. My breath hitches at the sound of Julian shifting in his seat. On instinct, I prepare myself for some kind of attack. He's got me exactly where he wants me: alone and defenseless in the dark.

"Thank you again. For everything," he says, his voice as soft and warm as the breeze coming through the window. "I know this was really weird and awkward, but . . . thank you."

I hesitate for another second, clutching my backpack so tightly my shoulders start to tremble. There's still no knife in my back, and as my eyes adjust to the dark, his shy smile comes into view.

"Y-yeah. Sure."

If I were a better person, I'd tell him I was sorry. Not because I did anything wrong, but because I can finally see what a shitty situation he's in. I'm sure Julian's dad had more sway in his decision to start seeing Liam than he's willing to tell me. Mr. Cooke is overbearing even with people who aren't related to him. Living under the same roof must feel like a prison. A well-decorated prison, but still.

But I'm not here to become friends with Julian Seo-Cooke.

We sit in silence for a few more seconds, the breeze coming through the open window cooling the sweat on the back of my neck. Julian looks over at my cabin, nudging his head toward it like he's granting me permission to run. I don't need it, but I take it, reaching for the door and bolting.

The car idles on that dark patch of road until I make it to my doorstep, driving away once I pull out my keys. Just to be safe, I pat myself down before I head in. No bugs (listening or living) slipped into my pockets, or notes taped to me. Tonight was weird, but I actually managed to make it through unscathed, and maybe even earned some of Julian's trust. A weapon worth its weight in gold.

Maybe we'll be able to pull this off after all.

CHAPTER EIGHT

Maya puts her megaphone to work the second it arrives.

The morning after the cocktail party from hell, a shrill siren jolts me awake. A quick look around confirms the apocalypse hasn't come early—it's just Maya. After the megaphone's blaring doesn't do the trick, she resorts to banging on every bedroom door, summoning us in a colorful mix of Spanglish expletives.

Everyone shuffles into the living room, where she's waiting for us in her usual training gear.

"Good morning, team!"

"Why?" is all I can manage to say.

She rolls her eyes before shepherding us into the kitchen. "We need to go sign up for the games ASAP."

Dear God. I know the games are high stakes this year, but not enough to make us be first in line for sign-ups. Registering early doesn't give us an advantage. Sure, we'll finally know what events we're up against, but that's a moot point considering we've already started training.

Dad and Isabel don't put up a fight, blearily walking to the coffee maker. Maya pulls me aside while they're distracted, elbowing me in the ribs once she has me alone. "You're supposed to agree with me, dingus. We need to get in and out before the Seo-Cookes show up." She flicks my forehead. "Unless you want to play Future Mr. Seo-Cooke in front of Dad."

The warning wakes me up faster than five cups of coffee. Nothing like the fear of pretending to date your archenemy in front of your dad to get you going. "Right."

Panic in place, I help Maya hustle everyone out of the kitchen as fast as we can. It's easy enough to convince Andy to face the morning after promising him homemade breakfast in exchange for the trek.

We're not sure what to expect from sign-ups, but none of us could've anticipated that a small crowd would be gathered around the bulletin board in front of the visitors center.

"Where did all these people come from?" Maya scans the crowd, shaking her head in disbelief.

I can't place any of the faces, though they do look more like the crowd I've come to expect at Lake Andreas. Swim trunks and halter dresses paired with oversized sunglasses and vicious sunburns. They don't take the time to chat and mingle either like the locals from my memories. They bustle in and out of the visitors center, grabbing flyers and downing coffees from Dixon's.

"I thought Old Bob said they were having trouble getting people to sign up for the games this year," I say, scanning the crowd for any sign of the Seo-Cookes.

Andy clears his throat to collect our attention, then holds up a flyer he grabbed off the ground. "Isn't this that new water park?"

Smack at the top of the Winter Games flyer is a very new addition. A massive Allegheny Park logo beneath the words PROUDLY SPONSORED BY.

Old Bob appears out of nowhere, leaning heavily on his eagle head cane after snatching the flyer out of Andy's hand. "The Alleghenys have *graciously* offered to host this year's Winter Games at the park. And donated a family pack of season memberships as the grand prize," he says through gritted teeth as he balls up the flyer and tosses it into the trash. "Thought they'd 'give back to the community' by helping us generate some buzz."

It's bad enough Allegheny Park has sucked up Old Bob's usual business. Now they're taking his magnum opus: the games.

"We'll actually get to go inside the park? For free?!" Andy asks, practically bouncing on his toes.

If looks could kill, Old Bob would've murdered Andy in cold blood. Thankfully, he huffs off to return to his place behind the sign-up table instead, leaving Andy to audibly gulp in relief.

"That explains the crowd," Maya whispers to me once Old Bob is out of earshot.

At least the admission fees go to a good cause. Lake Andreas could use a face-lift. Still, more contestants mean more competition. Though I can't imagine anyone here knows what they're getting into stepping onto a Seo-Cooke/Báez battlefield.

"Dev, go check out the schedule," Maya orders, pushing

me toward the bulletin board. "I'll fill out the form. Then we're out of here." She loops her arm through Andy's, bringing him with her to the table.

Another scan of the crowd confirms that the Seo-Cookes aren't around—yet. If we're quick, we can make it out of here in the next five minutes. I make my way to the front of the crowd, noting the list of events. There's nothing out of the ordinary. Pie eating, two memorization challenges, a tug-of-war, along with a handful of other events, all leading up to a game of capture the flag in the event of a tie. Not so off base from what Maya predicted, though she'd been hoping for a three-legged race instead of a 5K. That might be a problem, considering my inability to run more than five feet without feeling like my lungs are going to collapse. But it's too early in the game to be a pessimist. I snap a picture of the schedule to be safe.

The crowd has emptied out, making it easier to spot the rest of my group. Maya and Andy are almost to the front of the sign-up line, Dad and Isabel are making small talk with the Khans—who are in town after all—and Liam is handing out Allegheny Park coupons.

Wait. Liam?

Before I can grab my family and get the hell out of here, an arm wraps around my waist.

"Hey, Devin," Julian says with a Jokeresque grin.

"If you keep sneaking up on me, you're going to kill me," I snap at him, pressing my hand against my chest. "Or I'll kill you, whichever comes first."

Julian laughs loud enough to attract an uncomfortable amount of attention. "You're so funny."

"What're you doing?" I hiss.

"Liam's right there," he whispers back. As if on cue, Liam catches sight of Julian, waving to him with a devious smile. "We can't just stand around and act like we don't know each other."

Of course we can't, because that would be too easy. "Why couldn't they just send a disgruntled teenage employee like any other theme park?"

We watch Liam stall in his tracks to hand an elderly woman a bright red slip of paper. She seems more enamored with him than the discount, making sure to rest her hand on the breast pocket of his puffer vest before begrudgingly letting him leave. Old Bob glowers at Liam, abandoning his post at the table to trail behind him at a careful distance. Gotta give it to Liam—showing up here was a ballsy move. Old Bob is feisty. I wouldn't put it past him to take a swing at Liam with his cane if push comes to shove.

"Hello, lovebirds," Liam says once he finally reaches us. "Signing up for the games?"

"We are," Julian replies, holding me tight against his side. Sweat trickles down my temples as I attempt to discreetly survey the dissipating crowd for any sign of my family. Dad and Isabel are still caught up in conversation, but they won't be for long. We need to send Liam packing before Dad can find me in any compromising positions with the enemy.

"Fun. I'll see you there." Instead of walking away, Liam shifts his attention to me. His steel-blue eyes are piercing even when they're narrowed to slits. "I thought your name sounded familiar."

I rack my brain for a time when Liam and I would've met before the cocktail party. It'd be hard to forget meeting someone whose dad owns a water park. Besides the Seo-Cookes, the most interesting person I've met is the guy who broke the world record for eating the most peanut butter cups in one minute.

"You're from that neighbor family," Liam supplies before turning to Julian. "The one Henry said you guys can't stand."

"That's me," I reply with a nervous laugh.

"We started texting after we ran into each other at the Tallahassee airport." Julian lets go of my waist to turn and face me, smiling like I'm his sun and stars. "Turns out we had more in common than we thought." He punctuates the sentiment with a kiss to my knuckles.

He's laying it on a little too thick if you ask me. . . .

"Cute." There's a hint of a sneer on Liam's lips. "Your dad mentioned you're going on a hiking trip next week."

Julian nods warily. "We are . . . Why?"

"He said you have room for one more." His eyes flicker over to me for a moment, his confident façade cracking when I don't wither under his gaze. "Unless Devin's coming along."

"He is," Julian replies before I'm given the option. "We've been looking forward to it."

I'd rather eat glass than go hiking with the Seo-Cookes. Julian hasn't delivered on his end of our deal—he can't just pencil me in for extra fake boyfriend shifts when I haven't gotten within five feet of his house yet.

Julian lovingly runs his hand along my back. His palm against the small of my back makes me want to recoil, but I force myself to relax into his touch, leaning my head against his shoulder. The sooner we can get Liam to leave, the better.

Liam lets out a dark, humorless laugh. "Funny, your dad didn't seem to think Devin was coming."

"I guess you missed the memo," I reply with a smile as sharp as my tone.

Julian's calm expression falters for a second as he blinks over at me in surprise. What? Spite is a powerful motivator, something Julian and I know all too well.

If the shock of my response gets to Liam, he doesn't let it show. Instead, he holds out one of the coupons. Any desire I had to visit Allegheny Park went down the drain the day I met him, but I accept the coupon anyway. Liam stalks off after I've thanked him for the generous gift, giving Julian a cheeky wink before returning to soliciting the last of the crowd.

"Your ex is the worst," I whisper to Julian once Liam is out of earshot.

Julian sags, letting out the breath he seemed to be holding since Liam walked away, his hand going limp in mine. "I know."

My romantic exploits aren't wide or varied. Just an ill-advised hookup sophomore year with my lab partner, Briana, and a horrendous double date with Maya and another pair of twins—which was as weird as it sounds. Still, I know having an ex like Liam would drive me up a wall. Maybe even make me desperate enough to spend time with the enemy next door.

I'm not sure what to say—whether I should console him or smack him for forcing me into another round of Seo-Cooke Dinner Theater.

Unfortunately, I don't have to say anything, because Dad is walking straight toward us.

"Hiking, huh?" Dad says, completely perplexed.

If Julian wasn't holding me up, I'd definitely be on the ground.

Dad's eyes are laser focused on where Julian's arm rests around my waist. "I didn't know you two had gotten so close."

"We, uh . . ." I pause to wriggle my way out of Julian's hold. Why didn't Maya and I think of an emergency signal before we left the house? "We just—"

"Is there a problem here, Tony?" Mr. Cooke interrupts as he saunters over to our tense circle.

Sweet merciful Lord, this is a motherfucking nightmare.

Dad chuckles awkwardly. "No, no, just a little confused. I wasn't aware that Devin and Julian were um . . ." He trails off, looking uncomfortably bashful. "Seeing each other."

"Can't say I saw it coming either," Mr. Cooke replies with a chuckle of his own. "I guess this is what happens when we don't keep a closer eye on our kids."

Dad flips like a switch, his eyes darkening and fingers clenching into fists. Mr. Cooke starts to walk away before Dad can respond to the taunt.

"Julian, let's go," Mr. Cooke orders. Julian turns to me, lips parted as though he's going to say something, when his dad adds "Now!" with enough force to startle all of us.

We watch Julian trail behind his dad, leaving me to pick up the pieces.

Old Bob cackles so hard it sends him into a coughing fit. "Well ain't that the plot twist of the century!"

My throat feels painfully dry, and if someone doesn't say

something soon, my heart might beat out of my chest. I'd welcome it at this point; at least then I wouldn't have to explain myself.

Before I can think of something to say that isn't an incoherent plea for forgiveness, Andy and Isabel come along bearing Allegheny Park–branded popsicles.

"Hey!" Andy rushes up to me, pouting like a grounded toddler. "How come you get to date one of the neighbors? You said they were off-limits!"

Dad looks as though he's going to pass out at any second, a feeling I can very much relate to. "Let's discuss this at home."

Yes, please, anywhere but in front of half the town.

We're headed toward the path when a scream stops us in our tracks.

"Those assholes!" Maya storms toward us, her Dutch braids coming undone and dripping with what looks like muddy water.

Isabel goes into mother hen mode, cradling Maya's cheeks and checking for cuts or bruises. "Are you okay? Did you hit anything?"

"I'm fine," she mumbles bitterly, sliding out of Isabel's grip to undo her braids and wring out her curls. "Some guy came up to me and offered me a soda, but I should've freakin' known better." She turns around with narrowed eyes, glaring somewhere beyond the trees. Even dozens of feet away, I can still make out the shape of Henry Seo-Cooke. Maya was right—he is impossible to miss. Like a mountain troll.

"Did soda explode on you?" Andy asks, scratching his head.

"No, it shot glitter at me," she replies sarcastically.

Well, Henry was bound to retaliate for the bush incident at some point.

"Let's go," Dad insists, rubbing his temples as he leads the charge back toward home. "We've been here long enough."

Isabel rushes to his side, whispering something to him about being dramatic, while Andy hands Maya his second Allegheny popsicle in solidarity.

"Did I miss something?" Maya asks as she falls into step beside me, shaking herself off like a wet dog.

I heave a sigh, squeezing my eyes shut and preparing for the lashing she's about to give me. "Dad knows about me and Julian."

But the tirade doesn't come. Instead, Maya lets out a low whistle and unwraps her popsicle. "Less than forty-eight hours and you already beefed it."

"What was I supposed to do?" I hiss, turning down a bite of her Popsicle.

"Hide from Julian until it was time to leave."

If only it had been that easy. "His ex was right there. We couldn't just stand around ignoring each other."

Maya's brow furrows. "Who's his ex? The Martinezes son? Isn't he, like, thirty?"

"The one who was handing out the water park vouchers." I hold up my own crushed coupon as evidence. "His dad owns the place."

Maya's eyes go wide as saucers, her jaw hanging open to reveal a bright red, cherry-stained tongue. "Holy shit."

My thoughts exactly.

Her shock quickly shifts into excitement. "You think he can get us free day passes?" she asks while nudging me in the ribs.

"Not likely. I'm pretty sure he hates my guts." I don't know what kind of power Liam holds over Allegheny Park, but I wouldn't be surprised if he made sure to have me and the rest of my family permanently blacklisted.

Maya rolls her eyes. "You ruin everything." With that, she takes off ahead of me.

The walk back to our cabin is excruciatingly silent. Whatever Isabel tried to argue on my behalf doesn't get through to Dad. By the time we get back, he's still pale all the way down to his sockless ankles, as if he's seen a ghost. We gather around in the living room, spread out in a circle like we're the goddamn United Nations. Isabel, our moderator, takes center stage.

"So, Dev, it seems we have a *situation* your dad would like to discuss with you."

Great, a family mediation about my love life. "It's not a situation. It's—"

"It's a betrayal!" Maya easily slips into the role of the scorned sister, slamming her fist down on the arm of the love seat.

Isabel winces, holding her arms out to keep the opposing sides at bay. " 'Betrayal' might be a bit dramatic. Dev, why don't you tell us about what happened between you and Jude?"

"Julian," Maya and I say at the same time.

"Julian, right." She winces a second time, settling down beside Andy.

Burying my head in my hands doesn't shield me from the burn of the four pairs of eyes staring me down, waiting for me to come clean. I lift my head up and inhale sharply, trying to figure out what in the world could bring two people like me and Julian together.

"We started DM'ing each other a while back, and . . .

things . . . just happened." Not my best work, but you try rewriting *Romeo and Juliet*.

Maya deflates, covering her eyes so she doesn't have to witness the bloodbath that's about to unfold over my pathetic excuse of a love story. It's a terrible half-hearted, half-baked, half-assed lie, yet Dad reacts like it's the full truth. He throws his hands up into the air, startling Andy and Isabel as he slaps them back down onto his thighs.

"Dev, I know you're living on your own now, making your own decisions." He pauses to take off his cap and pinch the bridge of his nose. "But you couldn't have picked anybody else?"

"Maybe this is a good thing," Isabel proposes, ignoring the blank stares she gets for such a bold statement. "I'm serious!" She comes behind me, resting a supportive hand on my shoulder. "Clearly Devin and Julian found something in each other that made them want to put the past behind them. Maybe the rest of us can too." She gives my shoulder a squeeze that makes my stomach churn.

Maya snorts, shaking her head. "So we're just supposed to forgive the Seo-Cookes for years of pain and suffering because Devin and Julian want to make out?"

There's a collective grimace, myself included, at the thought of me and Julian making out. No one needed that mental image.

Isabel, though, maintains her composure. "You don't have to forgive them, especially not their dad. But we can learn to coexist peacefully."

Maya puts on an overdramatic pout and gives me a thumbs-up when no one's looking.

"I don't know," Dad mumbles, rubbing his bald spot as though the answers are buried in its wrinkles.

"Why don't we start off easy?" Isabel does a little dance and claps her hands to try to lift the mood. No one budges. "How about you invite Julian over for dinner tomorrow?" Dad goes pale while Maya looks hopeful.

This day is getting worse and worse by the minute.

Isabel doesn't let our hesitance bring her down. "Dev, ask him if he's free." She holds her hand up when Dad opens his mouth. "This is a good thing," she tells him.

"I don't think that's—" I start.

"Come on, Dev!" Isabel interrupts, nudging my arm. "We're talking about your boyfriend. You should feel comfortable inviting him over."

"He's just . . . really busy . . . with college prep stuff . . ." Killed it.

"Too busy to eat dinner?" she asks with a raised brow.

I chance a peek at Maya over Isabel's shoulder, silently begging her to find a way to get me out of this mess. All she offers me is a shrug.

"O-okay." I finally give in, and Isabel cheers.

My hand shakes as I open up my thread with Julian, scrambling to find a way to word the text without looking like I'm sending a Tolkien-length message.

> My stepmom wants you to come over for dinner tomorrow

I don't bother to phrase it as a question. Isabel's made it clear that she's not going to let this go. Still, I hold on to the hope that he can think of a way to turn down the invite. Julian's response comes a few seconds later.

Sure.

I'm sorry for the way things went down today.

So much for him putting up a fight. I don't have time to process Julian's apology. Isabel's still waiting for a response, so I give her the most eager thumbs-up I can muster.

"Perfect!" She beams, turning to the others. "And we'll all be on our best behavior, right?" She stomps her foot when no one responds. "Right?"

"Right," Dad, Andy, and Maya mutter.

I wish I could sink down beneath the floorboards and spend the rest of my life as a spirit haunting the crawl space with the possums instead of live this painfully awkward existence.

Maya shoots me a discreet wink while Isabel rattles off plans for tomorrow's dinner. Knowing her, she'll find a way to spin this as a good thing. Get the enemy on our turf, show him what they'll be taking from us if they win, try to get the weakest link on our side. The framed pictures of Mami on the mantel, the smell of her still lingering on her favorite couch throw pillow—the type of mementos that could tug even ice-cold heartstrings.

We can try to do the impossible: give a Seo-Cooke a conscience.

CHAPTER NINE

Somehow, I become an even more strung-out, nervous wreck than I already am. I can't so much as glance at Dad without feeling the truth crawl up my throat like bile, only stopping myself when I catch Maya glaring at me.

Strangely enough, our home renovations become a welcome distraction. I don't have to talk to Dad about my fake boyfriend when I'm busy wiping gunk out of the crevices in the living room windows. For now, anyway. Maya's half of the deal doesn't kick in until I've made it through an afternoon at the Seo-Cookes. Cosmetology may be her passion, but she'd make an excellent, and very ruthless, lawyer.

After morning training, I barely have enough energy to lift a pencil, let alone work on my mentorship piece. Not when all of my extra energy has to go toward renovations. The lack of time for productivity actually has me looking forward to my first day at the Seo-Cookes'. Desperate times.

Dad takes a certain pride in sprucing up the house before dinner. He pauses replacing the wood on our dock in favor of dusting the living room mantel so we can hang up the stockings Mami knit for us. They've seen better days, especially next to Andy's and Isabel's new ones, but the message is clear: this home is rich with memories. Our names, written in dull red yarn, have become too frayed by time to still be legible, the edges chewed on by moths. But we don't have the heart to put them back in the closet. With just a few small changes, our cabin begins to feel like a living museum. A memorial to the life we used to have.

It should feel comforting, watching our cabin revert to the holiday haven it used to be, having all these pieces of Mami, of her story, out proudly on display. Maybe it could even be better than the cabin we knew. With all the changes, it'll start to look like the place Mami always dreamt it could be. But running my fingers along the edges of my moth-eaten stocking just feels like a stark reminder of everything we stand to lose.

Once Julian texts me that he'll be over in ten, my hands start trembling so hard I can't button my shirt.

"That's what you're going to wear?" Maya asks when I storm into her room half-dressed.

"Does it really matter?" I cross the room to check myself out in her full-length mirror. "It's not like he's actually my boyfriend." I may not have any experience in the boyfriend department, but my paint-splattered jeans and gray flannel aren't going to offend anyone.

"That doesn't mean you can get away with looking like you got dressed in the dark," she replies, rolling off her bed with a sigh. "C'mon, let's find something we can work with." She sticks her fingers through my belt loops and drags me toward my and Andy's room.

I groan for the sake of appearances, but I'm secretly grateful for her help. Being forced to reevaluate my entire wardrobe for fifteen minutes will at least keep my mind off dinner.

Maya wrinkles her nose as she sorts through my shirts, pinching the sleeve of a yellow plaid shirt. "We seriously need to go shopping before you leave." She tosses the shirt straight into the hamper. "It's a miracle the Californians haven't eaten you alive yet."

That's the first time she's mentioned California without grimacing or rolling her eyes. Scheming against the Seo-Cookes, while stressful, has worked its wonders on closing the gap that's grown between us. Granted, I haven't had a moment's peace to work on my mentorship application this week. Having the Seo-Cookes' place to work will definitely help, but with three weeks left until my deadline and zero progress, I'll have to work on my art piece around her at some point. Until then, I can revel in the temporary. Us, the way we used to be.

"I'm not *that* bad." I'm definitely not as stylish as she is, but at least I don't dress like I walked off the set of *Riverdale* like Andy. I snatch the plaid shirt out of the hamper, ignoring her huff as I hang it back up.

"For a regular teenage boy, yeah. But you're my twin. Fraternal or not, you should know that this"—she holds up a shirt patterned with tiny rocket ships—"is unacceptable."

I pout, snatching that shirt too. "I thought it was nice," I mumble under my breath.

She ignores me, flipping more frantically through my options. "You're lucky Julian's bougie ex didn't kick you to the curb when you showed up in this," she says when she gets to the dinosaur-print shirt. Well, he *did* try. "How are you eighteen years old and don't own a single blazer?"

"Are you here to insult or help me?"

She hums in thought, replying, "Both," before handing me a shirt to try on.

We settle on an outfit Maya deems "acceptable, at best"—a royal-blue button-up and black jeans—before she drags me off to the bathroom. She lathers an obscene amount of mousse through my curls, artfully twirling the dark brown coils around her finger until they look effortlessly windswept instead of overgrown. Once she's happy with my hair, she dabs a tasteful amount of concealer under my eyes. Just enough to cover up the imperfections. I'm still nervous, but it's comforting to let Maya thrive in her element and work her magic—transforming me from an anxious wreck to a slightly more attractive wreck. It's so easy, teasing and cracking jokes like there's not still something tense and strange lingering between us. My world is so much brighter, so much less daunting, with her in it.

But once she leaves to finish getting herself ready, the panic settles back in. I turn to the mirror with a sigh. Considering how much I'm sweating already, an extra layer of deodorant wouldn't be a bad idea. A small green bottle catches my eye, buried in the back of the medicine cabinet—the tea tree oil Julian gave me. I'd shoved it in there without a second thought. I examine the bottle again, scanning the ingredients and giving it a tentative whiff. The seal is still intact, so it shouldn't pose a threat. I use the dropper to squeeze a bit out onto my nose, wincing at the burn. I blink up at my reflection once the pain passes, the skin around the piercing an angry shade of red.

I hope this works . . .

Once the doorbell rings, the flush has spread down to my collarbone. When I open the door, I see Julian looks as terrified as I do, which is oddly comforting.

"Hi." Julian shoves a plastic-wrapped bowl into my hands. "I thought I should bring something."

"Uh, thanks." I can't really tell what's beneath the plastic wrap, but there's a concerning amount of orange and blood-red. "What is it exactly?"

"Parsnip confit with pickled currants."

I have no idea what half of those words mean. "Currants?" I ask, at the risk of embarrassing myself.

"They're like raisins," he replies, loosening his tie before he's even inside.

I consider asking about the other words, but ultimately decide against it. Google is my friend. "That's really sweet of you, thanks."

"Well, at least one of you knows how to put together an outfit," Maya praises as she steps into the living room decked out in a velvet minidress and her finest wig—a honey-blond bob she made for our prom. "Nice loafers."

The compliment soothes Julian's nerves. He's certainly dressed up for the occasion, wearing an emerald suit jacket paired with a simple white button-down and matching green slacks. For someone who doesn't have a favorite color, he has a surprisingly vibrant wardrobe. He blushes as he stares at the leather loafers. "Thanks, my sister got them for me."

Maya sneers at the mention of Stella, looking as though she regrets giving the compliment. I clear my throat before she can say something cynical. On cue, she loops her arm through Julian's and guides him to the couch, forcing him to sit down beside her and Andy, where she can keep an eye on him. For all we know, he could be sneaking behind enemy lines with an agenda of his own. Julian glances at me for help, his eyes wary and his expression desperate, but I trust Maya not to kill him—not tonight at least—and excuse myself to the kitchen.

I set the wrapped bowl in front of Isabel. "Do you know what a currant is?"

She shakes her head. "Is it like an anchovy?"

"Julian said it's like a raisin."

She hums, pulling back the plastic wrap covering the bowl. "It looks pretty good," she says before spearing what I think is a parsnip. She moans around her first bite, eyes blown with wonder as she licks the glaze off her fork. "That is amazing." She helps herself to another forkful before pushing me out of the kitchen with a wave of her oven mitt and a promise that dinner will be ready in ten.

Maya and Andy are still on their best behavior, giggling with their heads together as they watch something on Maya's phone. Julian doesn't seem any less tense, though. He's perched on the edge of the couch, as if he's ready to make a run for it. His hands are clasped primly on his lap, a layer of sweat dotting his brow.

"Calm down, we're not going to roast you over a fire and

serve you for dinner," I tease, tossing him the TV remote as I settle into the armchair across from him. "Control over the remote is the highest honor we can bestow upon you in this house. Use it wisely."

He sets it back down on the coffee table. "Thanks, just nervous," he replies, wiping his brow on the hem of his sleeve.

Maya snorts. "Yeah, we can tell. You look like you're going to shit your pants any second now."

"Hey, I get it." Andy nudges his fist against Julian's shoulder in solidarity. "I sorta freaked out the first time I came over for dinner." He nods his head toward me and Maya. "These two are super intimidating."

Maya and I turn with matching indignant looks. "We are not!" we reply in almost perfect unison.

Andy ignores our protests, mouthing, *They totally are* to Julian. "I'm Andy, by the way. Nice to meet you."

"Julian. Nice to meet you too." The bro-y handshake and pleasantries do the trick. Julian loosens up, unclasping his hands and leaning back in his seat. Seeing him relax lets me breathe a little easier too. "So, how long have you and Maya been together?"

Oh, sweet Jesus.

Andy's jaw drops while Maya starts flapping her arms wildly at me, signaling for me to fix the mess Julian walked himself into. Julian pales once he sees the look on Andy's face, and soon enough he's looking to me for backup.

"I . . . uh . . . I'm their stepbrother." Andy shifts uncomfortably, putting some distance between him and Julian. "Did Devin not mention that?"

My brain is about ten seconds from short-circuiting, and

I have no idea what I can do besides shove a pillow over Julian's face, so I go with the next best thing I can think of. I slide into Julian's lap, wrapping an arm around his neck and laughing like I've absolutely lost my mind—which I might if the night continues on like this.

"I meant to tell him once we got here! But we've just been so busy this week," I say. I toy with Julian's tie in what I hope looks like a fun and flirtatious game but is actually a signal for him to shut up.

"Oooookay," Andy answers slowly, scratching his head.

"Yep, haven't had much time for talking," Julian tacks on as he reaches up to hug me like he isn't the biggest moron on the planet. He actually has the nerve to look proud of himself. The urge to murder him is strong, but I'd also take spontaneous combustion.

"Gross," Maya mutters, her nose wrinkled in disgust.

Julian looks around, slowly realizing what he implied. His lips form a silent O as he goes beet red. "That's not— I . . . I didn't mean—"

"It's cool," Andy reassures before Julian can finish. "You guys do you."

If we're lucky, Andy will forget this conversation ever happened and never bring it up again. But if there's one thing I've learned during this trip, it's that I'm an unlucky bastard.

I tighten my grip on Julian's silk tie, tugging just enough to make him cough.

"Y-you're choking me," he whispers, blanching when Andy appears concerned. "Sweetheart," he adds.

Dad winds up being Julian's saving grace. He clears his

throat to get our attention, clearly unamused. I let go of Julian's tie and jump off his lap as quickly as I can, brushing myself off and greeting Dad with a wave.

"Hi! Dinner's almost ready! Come sit at the table!" I'm shouting, and the room is starting to spin, and I think I might be sick, but I hold it together long enough to rest a hand on Julian's shoulder, slap on a smile, and pray that my nerves pass for love.

Dad raises a critical brow. "In the meantime, let's try to keep our hands to ourselves." He waves a finger at me and Julian before heading into the kitchen to help Isabel carry out the food.

"Jesus Christ." Without thinking, I run my fingers through my hair, only for them to get entangled in the sticky mousse.

Maya shrugs, nudging my shoulder with hers. "Could've been worse."

God, I really hope she's right.

• • •

Dinner is maddeningly awkward. Isabel, bless her, does her best to engage everyone in conversation, but even her best efforts fall flat. No matter how hard she tries, there's no way she can mend a decade-long divide over a single dinner. There's an unspoken agreement between us and Julian: We all want to get this night over with.

"Julian," Isabel says more loudly than necessary after an especially prolonged silence. "Doesn't your brother play football up at Florida State?"

"Your brother plays for FSU?" Andy asks around a mouthful of rice.

"Yeah, he's a sophomore," Julian answers weakly, his voice growing quieter with every moment of strained silence.

"That's sick!" Andy nearly chokes on his food in excitement. "What's it like? Does he have to train, like, a bajillion hours a day?"

Julian shrugs, shoulders sagging now that the air is less loaded with tension. "I'm not sure, but it's definitely intense. He has to drink these weird protein shakes that smell like death, and get up at six a.m., even in the summer, so he doesn't throw off his sleeping schedule for training season."

Andy's eyes are full of amazement. Our high school football team never inspired much spirit, but Andy is the team's bright spot. A beacon of hope after years of lackluster seasons. They even made it to the playoffs last year, a first for this millennium. In a way, it's what brought Dad and Isabel together. Maya, the head cheerleader, and Andy, the quarterback, falling in love would've been a cliché as classic as apple pie. Except in our version our parents fell head over heels at the snack stand instead.

"That's *so* cool." Andy nudges his mom's arm insistently.

"Very cool." Isabel pats Andy's hand before turning her attention back to Julian. "Are you planning on playing any sports at Princeton?"

Julian's smile falls, his brows knitting together. "Princeton?"

All the tension we'd chipped away comes rushing back as Dad turns to glare suspiciously at Julian. "Your dad said you're enrolled for the fall."

"He still has to interview at Yale, so it's all up in the air," I blurt. "Such an overachiever, isn't he?" I wrap my arm around his shoulders, giving them a reassuring squeeze.

Julian nods, patting my hand. "That's me." He lets out the world's saddest chuckle.

We're quite possibly the worst liars in the entire state of Florida. I've managed to sweat through any semblance of style Maya worked into my hair, and Julian has gone as pale as the tablecloth. Maybe I should call this whole thing off, tell everyone the truth now and beg for forgiveness.

Isabel swoops in to save the day before we can dig ourselves into an even deeper grave.

"Well, if the whole Ivy League thing doesn't work out, you should seriously consider culinary school. Because this"—she points her fork at the bowl—"is so good. I have no idea what a currant is, but if you can make it taste like that, I'll eat it every day."

The change of topic calms Julian down enough for some color to return to his cheeks. She takes the praise one step further, doling out servings onto everyone's plate.

"Try it," she says to the table. It's a command, not a suggestion.

I happily let go of Julian, smiling gratefully at Isabel before slicing one of my parsnips in half. My eyes widen around my first tentative bite, much like Isabel's had. I can't say it's like anything I've had before. Autumn flavors bloom on the tip of my tongue—crisp November air and the sweet smell of pumpkin and apple cider–flavored treats wafting from the kitchen. I've never had such a visceral, emotional experience with food before, and definitely not with something as mundane as parsnips. This must be what that critic from *Ratatouille* felt like.

"Whoa," Maya whispers after she takes her first bite.

"Julian, this is amazing," I say, and it's not even a part of the performance. A milestone: my first genuine compliment for a Seo-Cooke. The boy may be dull as a rock, but *damn*, can he cook.

Julian ducks his head with a shy smile, toying with his sterling-silver cuff links. "It's just a recipe I found online."

I tune out the rest of the conversation in favor of trying to snag seconds. Maya grabs the bowl first, grinning triumphantly as she claims the last of the parsnips. Right when I go to swipe some off her plate, she leans in and gives them a good lick, marking her territory.

"Bitch," I mutter, earning me a warning slap on the wrist from Dad. I turn my attention to Andy's plate, where his parsnips are still untouched. "Andy, give me yours." I reach my fork across the table to take them myself.

Andy bats me away. "No, they're mine."

Isabel sticks her arm between us when I go to poke Andy with my fork. "Andy, eat your parsnips or give them to Devin."

I reluctantly lower my weapon, watching Andy prod his parsnips limply before closing his eyes and taking a bite. "Dude, this is the best vegetable I've ever had," he says to Julian with delight. "Like, ever." He scarfs down the rest of his parsnips in two wolfish bites. I'm not as annoyed about the loss now that Julian doesn't look like he's going to throw up anymore.

"Andy doesn't just compliment any vegetable," says Maya.

"He's forty-five percent dinosaur chicken nugget." Andy nods, cheeks full as a chipmunk.

Julian straightens up, accepting the praise with pride and a nervous smile. For a few seconds, it's as if this isn't the weirdest thing in the world. We're just a group of people getting to know one another. But Dad, the only person who hasn't fallen under Julian's cooking spell, brings the tension back with full force.

He waves his fork at me and Julian. "So, when exactly did this happen?"

It takes me a second to process the question. Julian's new-found confidence quickly deflates. We exchange fleeting, harried expressions before we both turn to answer.

"Last week—" I begin the exact moment Julian says, "Two months ago—"

Dad's brow wrinkles as he narrows his eyes at us. "Was it a week or two months?"

"We made it official last week, after seeing each other in person," I answer quickly, shoving my elbow into Julian's ribs. "But we started texting two months ago."

Julian adds, "It's been such a whirlwind, it all blends to-gether."

Dad hums, a deep frown still set on his face. "It's odd, though. You two didn't even seem interested in being friends last week."

"I figured you might be upset, so we wanted to wait be-fore breaking the news to everyone." I laugh as I turn to Julian, using this as an opportunity to communicate "shut up and let me handle this" with my eyes. "Guess I've always had a soft spot for him."

"You called him a dipshit three days ago," Andy interrupts.

I give him a strained smile, taking Julian's hand. "But he's *my* dipshit."

Dad hums, taking a drawn-out sip of his beer. "Well, Dev, you know the rules. If he comes over, your door stays open and he leaves by eight. If you're meeting up, make sure you're back home by ten."

I nod so quickly it makes me light-headed, pinching Julian's arm until he does too. I can't imagine Dad's rules will be an issue, considering I don't plan on spending any more time with Julian than I have to. There'll be no climbing through windows, or sneaking through back doors, or covering the smell of alcohol on my breath and the shape of a boy's lips on my neck.

But just when I think we're out of the woods, Dad turns his attention to Julian, eyes narrowed. "And if you even *think* about trying to hurt my son, I'll kick your ass into next year." He points his butter knife at Julian as menacingly as a balding middle-aged man can.

Julian audibly gulps. Dad's never had to play the Big Bad Authority Figure card with me before. Maya, the cool twin, is the one he had to chase down with threats of grounding. While she spent her high school career staying out past curfew and exploring her pansexuality with actual people, I spent mine Googling "how do I know if I'm bi" and perpetually single.

"Y-yes, sir," Julian stammers out.

Julian's already clammy hand becomes even more unpleasantly damp, nearly slipping out of my grip when I give it a reassuring squeeze. God, his hands are gross. But I fight the urge to pull away, tightening my grip instead and slapping on yet another fake, plastic smile and gazing at Julian like he's the most perfect mistake I've ever made.

◆ ◆ ◆

Julian doesn't stay for the dessert, not that I give him a choice. I bustle him away from the table the second our plates are cleared, insisting that he needs to go home and get some rest. Julian follows my lead, waving to everyone and thanking Isabel for the meal. We linger in the doorway while he pulls his jacket on, unsure of how to say goodbye to one another.

"Are they looking?" I whisper.

He peeks over my shoulder. "Just your stepmom."

"I guess we should . . . hug or something?"

Before I can propose something, Julian leans forward and presses a kiss to my cheek that's close enough to my mouth to make my heart stutter. "Was that okay?"

My skin burns, white-hot and angry. Like an allergic reaction. "Y-yeah, that was okay."

"Cool." He nods. "Wanna come over tomorrow? To work on your art stuff."

"Yep, great, bye," I sputter before slamming the door right in Julian's face.

While Andy and Maya bicker over dessert, I excuse myself and head straight for my room. Between having to cover my ass and unraveling the mystery that is Julian Seo-Cooke, I've had enough excitement for one night.

In the safety of my room, I collapse against the door and

exhale slowly, trying to calm my racing heart. I can't tell if it's the belated surge of adrenaline or fear, but my skin is all tingles, my stomach is in knots, and I really, *really* don't like feeling this way. The worst part is knowing that it's nowhere near over yet. I still have to survive braving his fortress of a house.

When I open my eyes again, I catch sight of a new addition to the room. A picture of me and Mami in the backyard. Me in her arms, Maya running from the kitchen to join us. The memory wraps around me like her arms—the scent of lake water on my skin, the sound of Maya's giggles as she tackled me and Mami to the ground. Grass staining our clothes, the brightest joy in our smiles.

I exhale slowly, running a finger along the edge of the frame. Dust floats free, and the memory becomes replaced by the image of our cabin in pieces. Nothing left of it but dust in the air.

My heart doesn't slow, but it races with purpose this time. If this is what it takes to win, so be it.

We've lost enough.

CHAPTER TEN

Either I forgot what the inside of the Seo-Cookes' house looks like, or it tripled in size. I'm a whole lot taller than the last time they let us onto the premises, but the sprawling twenty-foot-high ceilings are as daunting at eighteen as they were when I was five. The dramatic oil painting of the family hanging in the foyer is definitely new, though.

"Watch it," Stella warns when I lean in to get a closer look at the portrait. "Henry knocked that over once and got grounded for a month."

I quickly step back. Lord knows what Mr. Cooke would think up to punish me. Stella returns to filing her nails once I'm a safe distance away. She'd called Julian down after she opened the door for me, but apparently she doesn't trust me enough to leave me in the foyer alone.

Since I can't stand still when I'm nervous, I make my way to a less prized possession. I wander over to the picture frames hanging beneath the winding staircase, a timeline of the Seo-Cookes' childhood. On closer inspection, it's clear that, with the exception of a shot of Henry and Julian as toddlers wearing matching bowl cuts, Mrs. Seo is missing from all of the photos. Shocker: Mr. Cooke handles breakups as well as Maya does.

"Hey," Julian greets as he comes down the stairs, dressed in a T-shirt and the type of low-hanging sweatpants that always look terrible on me but look runway-ready on him.

Stella relieves herself of her watch post to block his path when he makes it to the last step, holding her hand out for payment.

He groans, reaching into his pocket. "I didn't ask you to watch him."

"But I did," she insists, accepting the red package he slaps into her hand and brushing past him to head up the staircase.

Julian rolls his eyes as he crosses the staircase over to me. "Sorry about the guard dog. I'll call her off next time," he says before tossing me the same red foil package he'd paid Stella off with.

"What's a choco pie?" I ask, inspecting the package.

"Chocolate on the outside, cake and marshmallow on the inside. My mom always used to pack them in our lunches in middle school. Made us into sugar fiends." He pauses, pulling yet another one out of his pocket. "I didn't poison them, if that's what you're thinking." He unwraps his and takes a bite to demonstrate the point.

While I wouldn't put it past the Seo-Cookes to find a way to sneak sand or mud or crickets into a prepackaged snack cake, the reassurance does make me feel better. I unwrap it and take a tentative first bite. In the blink of an eye, our first year at the lake comes rushing back. The first time I ever came to visit this place, sitting pretzel-style on the carpet while Maya and I ate enough snack cakes—choco pies—that we stayed up all night. The box that showed up on our doorstep, with a handwritten note from Mrs. Seo. The box we threw into the trash.

He's right—it's not poisoned, and it tastes just as amazing as I remember.

"Do you carry these around all the time?" I ask, covering my mouth as I chew through the chocolate and marshmallow.

He nods, jutting his chin toward the staircase. "I have to because Stella's a monster. She always steals a stack for herself if I leave the box out in the open but refuses to buy her own."

That I can sympathize with. If I leave a bag of chips unattended for more than fifteen minutes, my roommate always finds a way to swipe it. Not everything about college is supposed to be communal, especially when it's the only thing keeping me going after ten hours of staring at my tablet.

"Your nose looks better," Julian says.

On instinct, my fingers reach up to trace the scabbed edges of my piercing. It's the first time I've been able to touch my nose without wincing in weeks. I'm finally giving off less of a Rudolph vibe, and more of the cool, aloof artist vibe I was going for. "I used the tea tree oil."

He smirks but doesn't linger on the subject. "You came

prepared." He points to the canvas bag slung over my shoulder that's so heavy I have to hoist it onto my knee to readjust the strap.

While my bag *is* full of every artistic medium I could find—you never know what type of inspiration is going to hit—it's more notably stuffed with plastic baggies full of salami. Courtesy of Maya, who tasked me with getting back at the Seo-Cookes now that the prank ball is back in our court. "Art stuff."

"Cool." Julian takes my sneakers, tucking them onto a gilded rack beside the door before guiding me down the hall. Our footsteps echo against the high ceilings, ringing back to us as we cross the dining room (very big) to get to the living room (even bigger). The space seems to be designed around aesthetic rather than comfort, plucked straight from a Pinterest board. There's not even a proper couch, only high-back wing chairs that make my lower back ache just from looking at them. Most of the Seo-Cookes' possessions make us bitter, but I'm not jealous of their choice in décor. Our cabin is far from perfect, but at least it feels like a home. Everything here feels like it should be roped off and guarded by someone with an earpiece and a Taser.

I settle down in the comfiest-looking chair, which is unusually low to the ground. And that's coming from me, someone who's already low to the ground. Julian leaves me to unpack, backing away slowly toward what I assume is the kitchen. "Want anything to drink? Water, coffee, soda?"

I shake my head. While the choco pies weren't poisoned, I should still be wary of any food or drink I don't see come from a spout. I double-check that there aren't any meddling siblings or dads lurking in the farther corners of this massive room before I let myself relax a bit. Not let my guard down, just relax.

A buzzing sound catches Julian's attention. Another call from his mom. He excuses himself before stepping into the hall.

"Hi, Umma . . . Yeah, everything's fine," I can hear him say before he switches to what I assume is Korean. His voice gets quieter and quieter, until a door closes, and it fades completely.

So much for eavesdropping.

Left to my own devices, I take in my temporary workspace. The room is as stiff as a library. It's a miracle a house with this many people living in it can be anything but pure chaos 24/7. Our house hasn't been this quiet since before we were born. Life in the Báez household means ignoring arguments that don't involve you, and the sound of the microwave beeping. Our family consumes an unholy amount of pizza rolls.

While I'd love to go find what I need and head home as soon as possible, I'm not just here for snooping. Coming here to be productive wasn't a lie, and I intend to follow through on that performance. A space where I don't have to concentrate through the sound of a buzz saw, or worry about upsetting Maya, is an asset I can't afford to lose.

While Maya's rule that I can't use the sketch of her ruined my initial plan, it did spark a new idea. This sketch of the cabin probably won't be my final submission piece, but it feels like a step in the right direction. The pieces I've created while at CalArts are about precision, but *my* work is about memories. Sentimentality. If I can't draw Maya, I can draw our cabin. The other piece of myself I'm worried I'll lose.

"Is that your house?" Julian asks, close enough that his breath tickles the back of my neck.

My sketchbook falls to the ground after I let out a yelp. "I'm begging you to stop sneaking up on me before you give me a heart attack."

Julian laughs, picking up the sketchbook before I can reach for it. "Stella once said I should wear a cowbell around the house."

"I hate to say it, but she's right." I reach for my sketchbook. It doesn't feel safe in anyone's hands but mine.

But Julian's too entranced to notice me. He stares down at my sketchbook in what I won't let myself think is awe. He lifts his hand to trace the page with his fingertips, as if he's searching for something.

"Is this your mom?" he asks, and I know instantly what page he's looking at.

It's the last portrait I did of Mami, a few pages behind the sketch of Maya. It's how I like to imagine her now— eternally twenty-seven, her favorite age, wearing the white cotton sundress she wore to her wedding because she refused to wear Abuela's powder-puff gown. Roses bloom from her fingertips, her curls full, dark, and free. Her skin glistens like copper embers as the sun sets over La Poza del Obispo in her hometown of Arecibo, the tide licking her bare toes. If I close my eyes, I can hear the distant sound of salsa music blasting from the radio while she took us by the hand and showed us how to swim in the sea.

My throat goes dry when Julian doesn't stop ogling. Allowing someone like him, someone who can use the things I love against me, see my most intimate works, my heart on the page, feels like pulling myself open at the seams.

"She's beautiful," Julian whispers, eyes fixed on the portrait even after he hands my sketchbook to me.

"She was," I reply, voice slightly hoarse.

"It's really beautiful too," he adds, pointing to the sketchbook. "Your artwork."

My cheeks grow warm, not that I'm letting a compliment from Julian Seo-Cooke get to me, thank you very much. I'm just not used to people who aren't my family or classmates admiring my work. Art school critique is brutal. My ego is in desperate need of stroking.

"You said you're applying for an internship?" he asks as he settles back into his seat with a mug of coffee.

"It's a mentorship." The correction isn't really necessary, but I'm still feeling jilted by Julian's invasion of my artistic privacy. "With a professor."

One of his eyebrows arches as he takes a sip. "Well, good luck with your *mentor*ship." His eyes travel back to my sketchbook, and even though he can't see the pages, it still feels invasive. "I've always wished I was better at art. I loved drawing as a kid but never got any better at it. Even my stick figures are terrible."

"Blame the universe," I reply. "You're good at pretty much everything but the one thing you wanted to do."

"I'm not good at everything," he protests sheepishly.

"Uh, yeah. You are. You can't be quadlingual, or whatever

it's called, an amazing cook, good at lacrosse, smart, *and* hot. It's not fair."

Julian's eyes widen. He lets out a quiet chuckle. "I never told you about lacrosse." Fuck. Shit. He didn't, and now I *definitely* look like a stalker. Before I can defend myself, he stares right at me with a cheeky smirk. "And you think I'm hot?"

Oh God, I didn't actually say that, did I?

Okay, apparently I did. But I won't let the sparkle in Julian's eyes intimidate me. Or the fact that he knows I snooped through his social media. Plus, it's not like *I* think he's hot. He just is. Objectively speaking. He's got the abs and the thick hair, and the thousand-kilowatt smile with the pretty, perfect teeth. It's an objective fact.

"I never said that."

Julian hums, his playfulness fading away as he turns his attention to a loose thread on his sleeve. "I'm really not," he insists. "Good at everything, I mean. The jury's still out on whether I'm hot." Then he has the audacity to wink. And not the kind of wink that's more like an eye twitch, but a good wink. The sexy, effortless kind of wink meant for slow-mo montages.

How dare he.

And no, I'm not flustered, not at all. Just caught off guard by the normalcy, by how *not* weird it feels to have a regular conversation with Julian. I should reply with something cool, too, something witty.

"So . . . you got more snacks?"

Not exactly what I was going for, but it does the trick. It takes Julian a second to process the question. "Uh, yeah, sure."

He beckons for me to follow him to the kitchen. I don't spend as much time ogling as I want to, can't let Julian know I'm impressed. The kitchen is as much a work of art as the rest of the house, pristine marble counters and glistening appliances so immaculate I can see my reflection in them. The type of kitchen Dad promised he'd give Mami one day. Looks like he could have, in another life where we play smarter. Meanwhile our kitchen hasn't looked this clean since Abuela gifted us the home deep clean she won at church bingo.

"We don't have much right now." Julian reemerges from the pantry with an armful of snack foods. "Henry laid his claim." He holds a bag of Doritos, Henry's name scrawled all over it in bright gold Sharpie.

"That seems obnoxious." How can someone at the big age of twenty, who grew up with two younger siblings, not have learned the importance of sharing?

"He's an obnoxious guy." Julian tosses the snacks back onto their shelf and walks over to the fridge. "Mind if I use you as a culinary guinea pig instead?"

My mouth waters at the memory of butter, rosemary, and whatever a currant is on my tongue. I'm not the most adventurous when it comes to trying new foods, but if Julian can make a parsnip taste like heaven, I'll gladly have anything he's willing to put together.

A shout makes both of us jump, my attention wandering to the kitchen window. Outside in the backyard, Stella shoves Henry's shoulder before stomping out of view, their voices too muffled for me to make out what they're saying.

"You can ignore them," Julian says, and I keep my eyes to myself but my ears pricked.

"Are you a 'leave me to my work in peace' kind of chef, or a 'doesn't mind help with the chopping' kind of chef?" I'm itching to get back to my sketchbook, but I can stall for ten minutes in the name of food.

Julian places some ingredients on the counter, followed by several mason jars. "Definitely the latter," he replies while grabbing some potatoes out of a basket hanging from the ceiling. "Mind slicing these?" I narrowly catch the potato he tosses me.

I nod and follow his directions to find the cutting board and knives. After washing the potatoes, I scan the mason jars Julian set down, each growing steadily larger in size. The contents all appear to be the same, some jars deeper red than others. "Why do you have four separate jars of kimchi?"

"Because kimchi goes with everything," he replies, stepping in front of them. He taps his fork against the largest of the four, labeled *Halmeoni* in bright purple. "My grandma's recipe." He taps the second and third jars, labeled *Umma* and *Umma w/extra garlic* in neon green. "My mom's recipe." And finally, he taps the smallest jar. No label, just a smiley face sticker. "And *this* is my recipe."

I lean in to inspect the largest jar, nearly four times bigger than the smallest. His grandma must be the expert. Julian's handwriting is tough to make out at first, a strange combination of Victorian-era script and chicken scratch. At least that's one thing he's bad at. When I look up, a forkful of kimchi from Julian's recipe jar is waiting for me.

"Try it." He holds the fork closer to my mouth.

The bite is deceptively spicy, the heat hidden beneath the

first sour notes of cabbage and ginger. Tears well in the corner of my eyes as the spice pricks my tongue and trickles slowly down my throat. Julian quickly passes me a glass of water, laughing while he slaps me on the back when I can't fight the urge to cough anymore.

"Too spicy?" he asks, rubbing circles between my shoulder blades until I finish my water.

I'm not the type to bow down to spice. I welcome all heat levels eagerly, but Julian's kimchi packed a punch I definitely wasn't ready for. "A little bit."

He takes a bite of his own. After a few seconds, he nods in agreement, wincing before putting the lid onto the jar. "Yeah, a little."

He pulls out a notebook from a nearby drawer, flipping to a heavily color-coded page. He scribbles something down and adds notes in the margins before returning his recipe jar to the fridge.

We slice and chop in comfortable silence, pausing long enough for me to sample Julian's grandma's and mom's recipes. Theirs are definitely much milder, more focused on highlighting individual ingredients than the heat behind each bite. Unsurprisingly, his grandma's is my favorite.

The rumblings of Stella and Henry's second argument are loud enough for me to almost make out what they're saying this time. I crane my neck to listen in, but their voices are drowned out by the sizzle of potatoes. "Are they okay?" I ask once Julian and I are safely out of range of the pops of oil.

He looks up from his phone at where the two of them

have gone red in the face, pointing at a stack of ten-pound bags of rice on the ground. "Yeah, they're fine. Probably arguing about the Winter Games."

My heart rockets into my throat. "O-oh . . ." Every part of me starts to sweat, my hands trembling at my sides. God, I'm so bad at lying—why did I agree to do so much of it?

"If that makes you uncomfortable, you can go sit in the living room." Julian nods toward the room we came from. "I can finish up here and bring it over to you."

"No!" I shout so loudly it startles him, my voice echoing off the pots and pans hanging above us. *Way to make it obvious that you're trying to eavesdrop, Devin.* Maybe I should try to create a diversion and escape before Julian catches on. Or I could try to hit him over the head with one of the pots. "I . . . uh. They're just so . . . intense. It caught me off guard."

Being generous, I have about a .0002 percent chance that he'll believe me. But, mercifully, he either does or he doesn't care. "Yeah, we can get pretty intense about it sometimes. No thanks to you guys." He knocks a fist against my shoulder, as if this is all some fun little game we play to pass the time. Like we don't have our entire home to lose.

Outside, Henry hoists three of the bags of rice onto his shoulder with ease, tossing them halfway across the yard like they weigh nothing. "Shouldn't you be out there too?" I ask while watching Stella lift and toss a bag of her own.

Julian brushes them off, pulling the curtain closed after he catches me staring. "They always leave me out of prep stuff."

Now that's good to know. Not useful information per se, but definitely worth noting. "Really?"

He yelps when a drop of oil splashes onto his hand. "Dad's pretty competitive." A massive understatement. "Usually he and Stella are in charge of coming up with stuff to help us get ready." He pauses, sucking the pad of his thumb into his mouth. "Dad says I don't have the right kind of attitude for winning a competition. Apparently I'm 'too nice.' So, better to leave me out of it."

Julian wasn't "too nice" when he helped his siblings lock me in a Porta Potty, or put a beetle down my shirt, or replace my shampoo with mayonnaise, but sure, whatever he needs to tell himself. Still, that doesn't help me figure out what the others are planning this year. He's got to know that they've been cheating. He may not know *what* they have in store, but he can't be that oblivious.

Behind the curtain, Stella and Henry get into yet another screaming match. It's hard to make out what they're saying through the window, but it's obvious that she's not happy. If it's games related, it's worth trying to listen in.

I pry my attention away from the window. "Do you have a bathroom?"

"Down the hall, make a left, up the stairs, make a right, third door on your left," he says in one breath.

"Sorry, can you repeat that again . . . but slower?"

Julian rips a page out of his recipe book and scribbles down a rough floor plan of the first and second floors. "In case you get lost," he explains when he hands me the map. "Which still happens to me."

"No promises I won't get lost anyway." I scramble out of my seat, slowing to a more normal pace when I realize how sketchy running away would seem. I cut through the sitting room to grab my bag and make a dash for the stairs.

I don't breathe until I've safely made it to the second floor. A quick glance out the window confirms that Stella and Henry are still outside, and Mr. Cooke evidently isn't home today, based on the eerie silence. My chest heaves as I brace myself against the top of the landing.

Day one in the beast's den and I'm already falling apart.

I duck into the first room at the end of the hall once I'm sure the coast is clear. It's an unassuming room, mostly storage from a quick scan. Cardboard and plastic boxes of toys and vinyl records are stacked in the corners. Another box on the folding table in the middle of the room is packed to the brim with all the framed photos Mrs. Seo is in. *Theresa* is scrawled on the side of the box in angry red Sharpie.

As much as I'd like to dig into Mr. Cooke's scandalous estrangement, I'm on a different kind of mission. Two, in fact. Carefully hiding myself from view, I look out the window at the far end of the room. Stella and Henry are in plain sight, still bickering over an abandoned sack of rice. I crack the window open, getting onto my knees to stay out of sight.

Opening my phone's camera, I start recording them in case my microphone can pick up something I can't hear. It's tough to make out what they're saying. Something about focus and needing to try harder. All the same things Maya shouts at me at our morning training sessions. I keep the camera rolling even when they get going again. It can't hurt to know what techniques they're using to train. Maya's training schedule is airtight, but we could take a leaf out of the enemy's handbook.

After two minutes, I stop recording. No use wasting my storage on Stella and Henry grunting over bags of rice. I send the video to Maya, waiting until the text is marked as delivered to close the window. Her response comes through exactly ten seconds later.

That's it?

Do better.

I'd respond telling her she should try putting her neck on the line next time, but I can't because she already did. There's a better chance of her getting mauled by a possum than the Seo-Cookes trapping me in the basement and turning me into a meat pie. Fair is fair.

That's enough sneaking around for one afternoon. I'm not sure what Maya's expecting, but I'm not going to crack this case in twenty minutes. The Seo-Cookes are cunning, and I don't have enough brain cells to Sherlock Holmes my way into an answer today.

My phone buzzes with one last message from Maya.

And don't forget about the salami!!!

How could I forget about the pound of deli meat in my bag?

Tucking my phone back into my pocket, I kneel down and pull out the carefully wrapped baggie. Unrolling a handful of salami, I lean up on the windowsill until I'm high enough to tuck the cold cuts into the curtain rod. It takes some finagling to get it out of view, and you can still spot it at some angles, but it'll do. It's not like anyone's going to walk in here expecting to find lunch meat. It'll be a nice surprise when the stench matures two weeks from now. A niggle of guilt tugs at my empathetic side, but I quickly squash it down.

We had to get back at them for the soda prank somehow.

With the meat in place, I pack up my bag and head for the door, stalling when another abandoned box catches my eye. A familiar, clunky contraption sitting on top of a stack of bedsheets. I lift it up carefully, a knot forming in my stomach as I run my hand along a weathered googly eye.

Suck-o. Abandoned and collecting dust in a storage room.

My gut tells me to tuck it under my shirt or find a way to sneak it into my bag downstairs. To smuggle it out of here so I can take it home, to where it rightfully belongs. They wouldn't notice anyway, not when it's clearly been sitting up here for years. Studying it, all of the dents and scrapes and dust, feels like they're twisting the knife they plunged into our backs years ago. First our cabin, and now this. Pieces of our lives that meant so much to us, treated like trash. Bruised or bulldozed so they can make it into something better.

"Devin?"

Immediately I throw Suck-o back into the box and race out of the room to the staircase. Julian's waiting for me at the bottom of the landing. He blushes at the sight of me. "Sorry, didn't mean to rush you."

I shrug, my heart hammering too fast and too hard for me to come up with a reply.

"Food's ready. And not to be a snob, but serving a dish lukewarm goes against my code of ethics."

Rich of someone from a family like his to talk about a code of ethics.

"Right, yeah. Be down in a second."

Julian nods and heads back toward the kitchen. I sag against the railing once he's out of view, sucking in a deep breath before following his lead. All I need to do is stay calm. They're not on to me. Not yet at least.

Julian gestures for me to take a seat once I step back into the kitchen. With a flourish, he puts the finishing touches—a healthy sprinkling of green onions—on his culinary masterpiece.

I sit down at one of the counter stools, instantly falling for the intoxicating scent of melted cheese and deep-fried potatoes. "Cheese fries?"

"*Kimchi* cheese fries," he corrects me. "The best kind of cheese fries."

He eagerly hands me a fork, waiting with his chin propped up on his fist for me to take my first bite. Having an audience while you eat is nerve-racking, especially when your first bite can only be described as euphoric. Sharp, sweet heat and spice meet the cool, savory crunch of the pickled cabbage and onions. "Oh my God."

I moan around my fork without an ounce of shame. Reservations be damned. Everything about it is so good that I can't help licking the cheese clinging to my fork to make sure I got it all. "Is there bacon in this too?" How did he manage to fry bacon in under ten minutes without setting off the smoke alarm? He really is a culinary wizard.

Julian nods, nudging a small bowl toward me. "Try dipping it in this."

Stars bloom behind my eyes as the creamy sriracha and mayo combo takes the already complexly perfect flavors to new heights. It's the most satisfying version of comfort food I've ever experienced, so rich in taste and design, yet still so purely indulgent.

"I hate you," I mumble between bites. "You're too nice to be a dick, and your cooking could resurrect the dead. It's not fair."

Julian holds back a quiet chuckle, shaking his head as he pulls a loaded fry from the center of the plate for himself. "I really wasn't kidding when I said I wasn't good at everything."

He's full of shit. Julian Seo-Cooke, a boy without a favorite color or movie, is the type of artist I've always wished I could be. Someone who can create things so wonderful they make you see stars. It makes me want to hunch over my sketchbook again, to draw until it's too dark to see, working until I find a way to create something that makes me feel half as intensely as that single cheesy French fry did.

"Name one thing you're bad at," I taunt, holding up a finger. "And don't say drawing."

He hums in thought before shrugging. "I'm allergic to poison ivy? Well, all three of us are. Makes us break out into major hives in, like, seconds."

I roll my eyes before helping myself to another fry. "An allergy isn't something you're bad at."

"It's something my body's bad at."

"Doesn't count." I gesture for him to come up with something else.

The amount of time it takes him to answer speaks volumes.

"I have a really hard time with math. And science. Anything with numbers, really," he says after what feels like an eternity. His eyes focus on a spilled drop of sriracha mayo, his shoulders locked. "They all kind of . . . blend together sometimes."

I can sense the hesitance in his voice, see it right in front of me. The fear of being vulnerable with the person who could hurt you the most. He wasn't searching for an answer; he was weighing whether it was worth telling the truth. "That makes your cooking skills even more impressive," I reply, worried I've let the silence sit for too long.

But instead, he beams. "My mom gets most of the credit for that. Dad's big on personal chefs, but it was different when we moved in with my mom after . . . everything," he says with a shrug. "Mom's schedule is all over the place, and I was always the first one home from school, so it just made sense that I'd handle getting dinner ready. I didn't think I'd like it as much as I did."

He pauses to reach into the drawer and pull his notebook out. He flips to a random page, a recipe for fried rice. Every margin is filled with notes scrawled down to the farthest edges of the page, every line color-coded.

"We started off without recipes, going by taste for the most part. When she was home, Mom helped me make up my own system, a way of doing things that made more sense to me. It makes recipes less intimidating, knowing I can figure things out my way." He brushes his thumb reverently against a note at the bottom of the page, not written in his handwriting.

Yours is my favorite—don't tell halmeoni xx love you

The intimacy feels jarring, like I'm intruding more than I already am. But I'm rooted in place, unable to tear my eyes from Julian. For a fleeting second, it doesn't feel so impossible to believe that he's changed. That he's now too nice to play dirty.

"Maybe you really should consider culinary school."

That makes him stiffen and chew on his bottom lip. "Yeah . . . maybe."

The longer the silence stretches, the more I want to ask the question sitting on the tip of my tongue. "Are you really going to Princeton?" I ask, telling myself it's because I want to know him. Not because I want to take him down.

Any trace of that old smile fades into a full-on frown as he puts the notebook away. I'm prepared to apologize for asking when he shakes his head slowly. "No." He meets my eyes, his lacking their casual confidence and charm. "Could you keep that to yourself, though. Please?"

Suddenly, I feel terrible for bringing it up at all. "Yeah, totally, I'm sorry. I shouldn't have asked."

I set my fork aside to shove my hands into my pockets, guilt ruining my appetite, but Julian grabs my hands before I can. "It's okay," he says, releasing me as quickly as he'd grabbed me. "You're fine. My dad doesn't know yet."

"Oh." With those few words, Julian becomes an even

more complex puzzle than I thought. "Do Stella and Henry know?"

He nods. "And my mom too. It's just Dad." He starts busying himself with throwing dirty dishes into the sink. "Sorry, I didn't mean to drop that on you."

I'm awful at consoling people. Maya once said I have the emotional intelligence of a broom, and honestly, she had a point. I like distance. Distance means I won't say the wrong thing or trip my way through saying the right thing.

"It's okay," I reply, an empty response to a loaded situation. "That's what fake boyfriends are for, right?" He turns with a quirked brow. "Saving you from your ex and accepting your baggage."

It's not sentimental or endearing or uplifting, but it calms him. Maybe, for once, I said the right thing after all.

"Guess I picked a good one, then." He returns to the counter with a certain glimmer in his warm brown eyes—maybe sadness, maybe hope.

"The very best," I reply, and let myself believe that it's the latter.

CHAPTER ELEVEN

For someone who's spent his entire winter break dreading having to return to student life, I'm really digging having a schedule again. Afternoons at the Seo-Cookes slot easily into this new routine, though I'd look forward to anything that doesn't involve jumping jacks at this point. After just a few days, the Seo-Cookes' home becomes an unexpected haven.

Without having to worry about upsetting Maya or the bats in the attic, my application piece finally starts to come together. The sketch of the cabin grows into something much bigger. A replica of the picture hanging in my room—me and Mami in the backyard, Maya running after us. I'm more productive at Julian's than I've ever been in my own home—so much so that he even lets me come over all week instead of just the two days he agreed to. It's a two-way street—Julian likes having a culinary guinea pig who isn't paleo, keto, or gluten free.

At the rate I'm working, I won't have to pull an all-nighter to finish my application after all. With a little over two weeks until the deadline and only a few finishing touches left, I might even be able to submit early. A first for my academic career.

While I spend most of my time at Julian's working, there's room for other activities when I'm not hunched over my sketchbook. Like coffee together in the kitchen, or banter about music or books or whether the corner piece of a brownie is better than the center piece (obviously not). We spend our afternoons on the couch, him binging the movies his dad warned him would rot his brain, and me sketching until my hand cramps. Evenings are spent on the back dock, sharing bites of whatever noodle, rice, or vegetable dish Julian's concocted.

Dad's been so consumed with the renovations that he hardly even notices that I'm gone half the time. He and Isabel tackle the more complicated tasks—anything that involves heavy machinery—while we're delegated the more mundane jobs, like luring the possums out and unclogging the sink.

Slowly but surely the cabin starts to come together, becoming the place Mami always knew it could be. Fresh, turquoise tiles for the kitchen backsplash. New curtains in the bedrooms. The living room now fully coated in Eggshell Breeze.

Everything *should* be calm.

Except Maya's pissed.

Infiltrating the Seo-Cookes' home isn't the gold mine she thought it would be. Either they aren't planning on cheating this year, or they're way better at covering up their tracks than we anticipated. Stella and Henry train every day, just like us, but there's nothing off about their routine. It's more cardio heavy than ours, but that's just because they're more athletically competent than we are.

Neither of them even seems to have time for scheming. Mr. Cooke's influence is strong even though he's never home. While he's off schmoozing, he keeps everyone else on strict regimented daily schedules, color-coded down to how long they're allowed to use their laptops and catered specifically to their "interests."

Henry spends most of his afternoons watching old football games or running drills in the backyard while Stella bounces between SAT, biology, and AP English prep sessions. Julian has it the easiest of his siblings; the only things on his schedule are seven a.m. yoga and tennis practice at noon. Mr. Cooke gave Julian a "Princeton-approved reading list" last summer before he'd even applied. The stack of books—including *The Catcher in the Rye*—sits untouched on his bedroom desk.

All my peeking into empty rooms and craning my neck to eavesdrop on whispered conversations hasn't yielded much valuable info. Surprise surprise, they're not keeping top-secret plans out in the open where anyone could see. The most useful things we've found are that they're all allergic to poison ivy and that they always leave their back door unlocked. The floor map Julian drew for me on my first day will come in handy if Maya and I follow through on our idea to lure a raccoon into their kitchen.

"You're sure that's it?" Maya asks during morning training. Her chin is balanced on my bent knees, her hands holding down my ankles while I struggle to do a crunch that she deems acceptable.

"Y-yes," I grunt as I pull my body up. My body collapses before I can lift myself high enough. She gives me a thumbs-down—that attempt didn't count. I still have twelve more to go.

The closer we get to the games, the more on edge she becomes. Fighting rodents and fixing leaky faucets has taken its toll on her. Her body is a map of cuts, bruises, and bite marks—thankfully the possums didn't have rabies. Though it did cost us a very pricey trip to the emergency room.

Despite our bargain, I pitch in and help with the renovations whenever I'm home. I'm productive enough at Julian's, and the responsible brother in me won't let her bear the brunt of two loads on her own. A helping hand isn't enough, though. Even without me working on my application at home, she still ices me out, pushing me further and further away every time I come home without a smoking gun. The cabin gets better every day, but no amount of paint or photos mounted on the walls will shake the looming, growing fear that soon enough, it might not be ours anymore.

And I can't help the twisted sense of guilt that washes over me whenever I come home from the Seo-Cookes, our cabin slightly different each time. The guilt of knowing that restoring the cabin to its former glory should be bringing us together.

But I'm spending my time with the enemy instead.

"Maybe they're gonna play fair this year," I offer, still sprawled out on the ground and struggling to catch my breath.

She scoffs, leaning back and letting go of my ankles. "You don't actually believe that, do you?"

I don't. My conversation with Julian the first day at their house basically confirmed that they're up to something. They know to keep their guard up when I'm around and to leave Julian in the dark. They don't trust each other as much as I don't trust them.

"We're running out of time," she says.

Now that she's not holding me down, I abandon the crunches, propping myself up on my elbows instead. "Ten days is plenty of time."

All it would take is a matter of hours to take them down if we found proof. Even if we didn't report them to Old Bob, it wouldn't take much to try to avoid whatever they've been plotting. Though the panic is setting in, letting it get the best of us just gives them the upper hand.

"We can't rely on this, Maya."

She doesn't respond. Her mouth crests into a stern, unreadable line as she pushes herself off the ground. "We're done for today," she says before heading toward the cabin.

Any other day I'd rejoice over cutting training short. Instead it feels like I've done something wrong. Like I'm being punished for a mistake I didn't even realize I'd made.

Struggling through crunches with no one to watch or spot me isn't worth the extra energy, so I follow her. She's in her room with the door locked and her music on full blast. An effective "stay away unless you want to get bit" sign. Andy, who finished his own set of crunches half an hour ago, is on his second bowl of cereal. I plop down into the chair opposite him, pulling my sketchbook out of my bag. Most days, I don't head to Julian's until a more humane hour of the day. Might as well try to keep my mind occupied by being productive in the meantime.

The cabin sketch feels like a beacon of hope in all this uncertainty. It's not a guarantee that I'll land the mentorship, but even if we lose our cabin, I'll still have this. Losing our past doesn't mean I'll lose my future too.

Or Andy can spill cereal milk all over my sketchbook and I can lose that too.

"What the hell?!" I shout, only narrowly pulling my sketchbook out of the way before the milk can soak more than just the top page.

"Shit, dude, I'm *so* sorry." Andy sets his half-empty glass down on the counter. "Here, I can—" He goes to wipe the page with the hem of his shirt.

I must've been a god-awful person in a past life. That's the only thing I can think of to explain this disaster of a winter break.

"It's fine," I tell him through gritted teeth, pushing his T-shirt away.

There's no saving the sketch now. Wiping away the milk turned it into a mess of smudged charcoal, Mami's and my smiles melting into blurred lines. My heart pounds up my temples, through my skull, until I feel the overwhelming urge to scream. For once, I felt like I was actually creating something special, something that felt like me. And I was *so* close to finishing. I know I can start over again, try something new, but I can't shake off the fear that the spark I'd felt with this piece was fleeting.

Without another word, I tuck my sketchbook safely back into my bag and head for a well-deserved shower. If I stay at the table, there's a chance I'll snap in front of Andy, and he doesn't deserve my rage. It was an innocent mistake.

Besides, I need some alone time to pray to the art gods for some divine inspiration.

After I've scrubbed the cereal milk off my arms and the sweat from my hair, I get dressed and make the trek across the backyard to Julian's. Alone time with my sketchbook is what I need to find my muse again, I tell myself. But even my internal monologue is a shit liar.

"Hey, we were just talking about you," Julian greets as I walk into the Seo-Cooke kitchen.

I eye him and Stella warily as I settle down at the table, pulling out my dry, but uncomfortably sticky, sketchbook. "That can't be good." While Stella and Henry have begrudgingly accepted my presence as a semi-regular thing, it hasn't kept them from making it clear how pissed they are about having to share their home with the enemy.

"We were talking about how you two should hang out at your house sometimes instead." Stella hops off the counter and narrows her eyes at me. "Maybe then we can shove deli meat into *your* curtain rods."

I gulp. Well, they figured that one out sooner than expected.

"No, we weren't," Julian interjects, kicking her shin when she sits down beside him. If it weren't for him, I'm sure Stella and Henry would be holding me down and shaving my head.

Or drawing on my face with Sharpie. Whatever their twisted minds came up with as payback. "We were talking about the hike tomorrow."

Right. The "I'd rather eat glass" hike. My stomach clenches at the thought of it. Hanging out with Julian and his family is intimidating enough without physical exertion thrown into the mix. And I *really* don't like the idea of being alone with them on a hike the day after they found out I hid salami in their house.

Julian pulls out a chair for me before crossing over to the coffee maker. "Do you have your own bike, or do you need to borrow one? Henry's old one should still be in the garage. Might be a little rusty, though." He sets a mug in front of me, pouring out the coffee, cream, and two sugars.

Before replying, I savor my first sip of coffee, giving Julian two enthusiastic thumbs-up. He may be a jack-of-all-trades, but his ability to make instant coffee drinkable is by far the most impressive thing about him. "Why would I need a bike?"

"The first part of the trail is on a bike path. Nothing too intense, just about a mile."

I swallow hard around my coffee, nearly choking as it burns my throat. "Y-you didn't mention biking would be involved."

Julian tosses an ice cube into my mug before pouring another cup for himself. "Don't worry, it's beginner friendly."

That's great, but I'm not even a beginner.

Stella looks up from her oatmeal. "Please tell me you know how to ride a bike."

"Of course he does," Julian replies for me, sneering at his

sister before turning to me with forced cheerfulness. "You do . . . right?" I shake my head, and Julian's jaw drops as if in slow motion. "You can't be serious."

Stella hides a snort behind her hand, ignoring Julian's glower.

"Why bother with a bike if you can drive?" I snap defensively. Learning how to ride a bike is just one of those things we never got around to. Sidewalks are basically nonexistent in our area of Tallahassee, and the paths in our local park are full of cracks. "Maya doesn't know how to either," I add, as if that makes the situation any better.

"Okay." Julian exhales slowly, rubbing his temples before continuing. "This is fine. We can try to teach you the basics."

"You can't teach someone how to ride a bike in a day," Stella replies, waving her spoon at the two of us. "You need a week, at least."

"Couldn't we just walk up the trail instead of biking?" I propose.

Julian and Stella shake their heads, finally looking away from one another. "It's way faster to bike than to walk," Stella explains. "Henry brought his ex last year. Huge mistake. Turns out she was afraid of heights and barfed the second she got off her bike. Dad almost gave himself a heart attack because she threw us fifteen minutes off schedule. She dumped Henry by the time we made it back to the car."

Cool, another reason for Mr. Cooke to hate me.

Julian starts to pace around the kitchen, biting his thumbnail. "If Dad finds out you're not coming, he'll probably try to invite Liam again."

"Well, you're screwed," Stella announces, patting Julian on the back on her way to the sink. "Have fun explaining to Dad."

"What do you suggest we do, then?" Julian snaps at her.

She shrugs as she throws her bowl into the dishwasher. "You try to teach him to ride a bike in a day."

My brows knit together. "Didn't you just say that was impossible?"

"Yep." She heads for the living room, turning around to give us a cynical smile. "Let's hope this is the one time I'm wrong."

Julian slumps back into his seat and rests his head on his arms. My hand goes to rest on his shoulder, but I catch myself in time, shoving my hands under my thighs.

A red mark cuts across Julian's cheek when he picks his head up, an imprint of where he was pressed against his watch. "You up for a bicycling lesson?" He lowers his voice to a whisper as he leans closer toward me. "Please, Dev?"

He's never called me Dev before. The gentle way he says it, the soft cadence of his voice, forces a kneejerk reaction in me.

It makes my stomach flutter.

Which makes me sick.

Focus, you moron. Your most promising sketch is down the drain, time is very much not *on your side, and this is probably just his way of playing mind games. I see you, Julian Seo-Cooke.*

Wasting a productive afternoon on something that feels like a guaranteed loss isn't in my best interest, but Julian can still play dirty. Bowing out of the hike gives him grounds to call off our agreement. No fake boyfriend duties, no reentry. As much as it hurts to admit, I can't lose him now. Not yet, anyway.

Putting on a brave face is easy enough; keeping my voice level is a different story. "How hard can it be?"

• • •

It's hard as hell.

Julian had reassured me that riding a bike would feel like second nature once I got the hang of it. We made our way over to a nearby park to start our lesson, and I'd naively thought I'd be Tour de France worthy by lunch. But "getting the hang of it" is the hardest part.

I roll over to clutch my searing forearm after I tumble to the pavement for the fourth time. Thankfully the pasta sauce wound is healed enough to be sore but scabbed over. If I wasn't wearing a helmet, my skull would've cracked open like an egg.

Julian hoists the bike off me, propping it up on its kickstand before helping me back up. "Maybe try that again, but I'll hold on to you this time."

"Do *not* let me fall. Helmet or no helmet, my brain can't handle that kind of jostling."

He bites back a grin, brushing dirt off my shoulder. "The ten-year-old in me really wants to call you a pea brain right now." He holds his hands up when I stick my tongue out at him. "But I won't, because I'm a *mature* adult."

"A mature adult who still uses a night-light," I say under my breath as I mount the bike again.

Julian pouts. "I told you that in confidence."

"And I kept it between us." And Maya.

Julian scoffs, but thankfully takes hold of the back of the bicycle seat. "Ready, champ?"

I swallow down the lump in my throat and tighten my grip on the handlebars. "My ears are ringing, but sure."

One hand grips the seat, the other rests on top of mine on the left handlebar. He leans in, cheek nearly pressed to mine, his chest flush against my arm. "I won't let you fall this time," he whispers, so close I can feel his breath.

It's too much and too close, and Julian smells like a pinewood-scented candle today, and my heart is going to beat out of my chest if he doesn't back off in the next ten seconds. I want space, but I don't want to fall, and maybe there's a tiny, tiny, *tiny* part of me that doesn't really mind him being so close. And that scares the absolute shit out of me.

Fortunately, or unfortunately, I have bigger things to worry about. Like keeping my balance. I clutch the handlebars for dear life after Julian pushes me, realizing too late that I should've asked him how to brake. The breeze stings my sweat-slick skin as my feet scramble to find the pedals. My left foot accidentally knocks into one of them, sending the pedal into a spinning frenzy.

"Shit shit shit," I mutter under my breath as I try to get it under control.

Julian kept his promise—he didn't let me fall.

I crash into a tree instead.

"Pedaling would help." Julian jogs over to me, holding his hand out to help me regain my balance.

"Gee thanks, I hadn't thought of that," I reply.

"You need to relax. It's all about centering yourself until you can get situated on the pedals, and then following through."

We pick the bike up, setting it against a tree while I clean blood off my skinned knee at a nearby water fountain. "Why can't your dad just be a regular embarrassing parent instead of a tyrant?" I ask, limping back toward Julian.

He stays silent, frowning at something on his phone. "I'll be right back," he says, so quiet I almost miss it.

"Oh. Okay. Should I keep—" He brushes past me, nearly knocking me over.

Yeesh. And I thought I was in a bad mood.

While Julian's gone, I do what I can to practice, but give up after I nearly decapitate myself trying to kick off. He's gone longer than I would've thought. There's no sign of him in the immediate vicinity, but I respect his privacy. That changes when ten minutes turns into twenty. I can only twiddle my thumbs on a bench for so long.

At first I don't even realize that Julian's returned. He's now beside me, pushing the bike into my hands without a word. Whatever kept him busy wasn't good news. The harsh, deeply etched frown, the locked shoulders, the clenched fists—it's written all over him.

"You okay?" I ask, following behind as he walks toward a patch of grass. "If this is because of what I said about your dad, then I'm sorry, I didn't—"

"Let's keep going." His voice is firm, sharp. Not at all what I've grown used to.

I nod slowly, swallowing hard around the apology he'd cut off. It's jarring, falling into an old, but not unfamiliar rhythm.

The stakes feel much higher when I mount the bike again. As if the only thing standing between us and catastrophe is my ability to stay on a bike for more than five minutes.

The added pressure doesn't do me any favors. I still don't understand how to "balance my weight" or "kick off with force." Unsurprisingly, I spend more time on the ground than I do on the bike.

"Brace yourself! Lean to the right!" Julian shouts into my ear.

"I am leaning!" I yell, throwing all my weight to the right, which sends me straight to the ground. "You said lean."

"You leaned too far." Julian lifts the bike off me and offers his hand.

The urge to sling petty insults like we used to is strong. I'm pissed off and I know Julian is, too, but for once it's not frustration with each other.

I take his hand.

"Again," I say once I've dusted off my shorts, reaching for the bike.

Biting my tongue quickly becomes a necessity. I've only marginally improved after another hour of practice. My body feels like it's one fall away from snapping like a twig. Kids and their families start to come along once the morning chill settles, and I go from shouting profanities to muffling them with my sleeve. I nearly slip after Julian accidentally runs the bike over my foot, shouting "FUDGE!" at the last second instead.

The light at the end of the tunnel starts fading after I mount the bike for the seventy-third time. At this rate, the only thing I'm going home with is a broken ankle. But

I try again, because Devin Armando Báez isn't scared of anything—except death, spiders, and mice—but certainly not a bike and a couple of bruises.

My body, on the other hand, doesn't have the same determination. I lose the last dregs of my strength seconds after I kick off and can feel myself falling over before my feet are even on the pedals. I know instantly that I've lost the battle and prepare for the wet smack of the unforgiving ground for the seventy-third time. And I do hit the ground, but not the way I thought I would.

I'm knocked over in the opposite direction by what feels like a battering ram. There's a weight on my chest, heavier than the bike, and hefty enough to push all the wind out of me. Tears stream down my cheeks as I cough and gasp for breath.

When I open my eyes, I half expect to find a bear straddling my chest. I *definitely* don't expect to see Julian, eyes wide and lips parted, the rapid *badum badum badum* of his heart burning against my chest like a countdown to disaster. We're both at a loss for words, breathing hard and fast, faces inches from one another. The kind of intimacy that sets my already frayed nerve endings on fire. The too-hot press of his body against mine should feel wrong, but it just feels terrifying.

"You were about to fall on top of a puppy," Julian chokes out, his breath warm against my dry, chapped lips.

I lift my head to look over his shoulder. A miniature golden retriever curls up on the grass beside our abandoned bike, tail wagging happily, completely oblivious to the chaos it caused.

"You're a lifesaver," I whisper as I turn to face Julian.

"That's what fake boyfriends are for," he replies with a hint of a smile where everything between us is okay.

I laugh quietly, afraid to part my lips any more than I have to.

"I can't breathe."

I can breathe fine. Julian may be all hard lines and taut muscle but he's surprisingly light, slotting easily into the curves of my body. It's just the first excuse I can think of to get him off me.

"Right, sorry," he mumbles before rolling off.

Julian's disgruntled attitude doesn't do much to help us with the task at hand. We're losing steam with each stumble, and as the sun starts to set and the shops begin to shutter for the afternoon, we realize we're fighting a losing battle.

"I can't believe I'm still alive," I mutter after I screech to a halt seconds before clipping a fire hydrant. My body has become a mess of blood, bruises, and mosquito bites. I sag over the handlebars, sucking in air while I can. I've developed a bad habit of holding my breath while riding. It softens the blow when I fall.

"You don't have to come tomorrow," Julian says so quietly I assume the dehydration has finally gotten to me and I must be seeing a mirage.

"Wait, what?" I prop myself up on the handlebars, arms trembling to hold myself and the bike upright.

"Don't come tomorrow. I'll figure something out to tell my dad." He brushes me off like a speck of dirt on his designer jeans, as if I haven't spent the entire day working myself to the brink of exhaustion hundreds of times over.

"Are you serious?! We put my sanity, and an innocent puppy's life, at risk, and now it's just 'eh, who cares, we'll make something up'? Where was this energy this morning?!" I'm exhausted, we wasted an entire day I could've spent working on a new application piece, and I'm tired of looking at a puzzle I can't solve.

"I'm sorry," Julian mumbles, and even when he's looking at the ground instead of me, his voice is so gentle that the sentiment still feels sincere.

"So, what? We brainstorm an excuse for bailing on the hike and that's it?" If we're officially giving up, I might as well stop wasting my energy on standing up. I toss the bike onto its side and flop onto a nearby bench, grateful to finally be off my feet.

"I can come up with something on my own."

As if. Julian's too much of a Mary Sue to jaywalk without feeling guilty.

But it turns out I'm at my wits' end too. "All right, fine." I slap my hands down on the bench with force I didn't know I had left in me. "Then why don't you tell me what's bothering you so much?"

Julian blinks up at me like a startled fawn, looking so much like the chubby-cheeked boy I remember that it feels like I've been pulled into a memory.

"M'not—"

"You are," I insist before he can finish. "You've been acting super weird."

"I'm sorry."

"Please stop saying you're sorry," I plead, pressing my palms together. "I know I'm not exactly your favorite person in the world, but just talk to me." The words *you can trust me* sit on the tip of my tongue, but I push them down.

Julian sucks his teeth, kicking at the ground in an uncharacteristically childish move. "We should both go home," he replies bitterly before turning on his heels and walking away.

Oh *hell* no. One doesn't just turn down a moment of compassion from Devin Báez, king of social ineptitude with an emotional IQ score of "broom." I push through the staggering pain in my joints to march right into Julian's path.

"We're walking home together, then."

"We don't have to." Julian tries to step around me, but I block him. A taste of his own medicine.

"Yes, we do. We're neighbors."

With a sigh, he realizes he literally can't escape me.

"I have errands to run first." He's as bad at lying as I am at riding bikes.

"Great, then I'm coming with you." I flash him a smile before heading over to the bike, picking it up, and wheeling it back to him. He stays rooted in place, so I ring the bike's bell to get him going.

"Go home, Devin."

"No." I punctuate the statement with another ring of the bell.

"Can you please not be pushy and annoying for five seconds?" Julian shouts, startling the elderly woman across the street.

It's another flash of the old Julian, the one who can't stand to be around me. It stings, as stupid as that may sound, to see Julian slip into his old role. The house of cards we've built wobbles, but I won't let it fall down. Not yet.

"Sure. I can be quiet instead." I ring the bell one last time.

Julian exhales slowly, his chin dropping to his chest. "I'm not going home," he confesses, words lost to the blare of a nearby car horn.

"What?"

"I don't want to go home," he repeats, louder this time.

My instinct is to ask why, but the question dies on my lips. "Then let's walk." I push the bike past Julian, looking back at him when he doesn't move. "Are you coming or not?"

"You don't have to do this." Julian's brown eyes glisten with flecks of gold, the sheen of tears threatening to burst.

I look away quickly. I've always hated crying in public, and I've done a hell of a lot of it over the past few years. I always wished everyone would look away and pretend they didn't see me. I try to extend the favor whenever I can.

"I know," I reply. "But I want to."

I wait on eggshells for Julian to reply or break down or lash out, but the only thing between us is the sound of crickets and the tension of things left unsaid.

"If you want to be alone, I'll go home," I say when I don't get a response. "Pinky swear this time." I hold out my pinky.

He breaks the tension with the sweetest laugh I've ever heard, pushing my hand back down to my side. "It's okay. Wouldn't kill me to have some company."

I nod.

"So, where do you wanna go?" I ask, gesturing to the sleepy glow of the lake.

Julian heads in the opposite direction of our street.

"Anywhere but here."

CHAPTER TWELVE

"Anywhere but here" doesn't wind up being far from where we started. I don't have enough strength left to make it any farther than half a mile, so we settle for the most secluded place I can think of.

The pier isn't exactly private. Anyone could stumble upon it if they made a wrong turn off the path toward Fulton Drive, but it's close enough. It's in surprisingly good condition considering no one's in charge of maintaining it. Weeds and overgrown bushes have sprouted since we were last here, but flowers have bloomed along the shoreline too. Dozens of dandelions and a small smattering of irises. The sagging branches of the willow tree hiding the pier from view is still holding strong, its leaves as warm, vibrant, and green as I remember. I hold my arm up before Julian can step onto the dock, cautiously leaning my weight on a worn plank of wood. It doesn't buckle under the pressure, unlike our front steps.

"How do you know about this place?" Julian asks as he props the bike up against a nearby tree.

I make myself comfortable, kicking off my shoes and lying flat along the edge of the pier, dipping my toes into the water. "My mom found it," I whisper. The words come out soft—a secret I don't have the right to tell.

This alcove has belonged to her since she and Dad discovered it our second year at the lake. It was her secret weapon, a place she could take me or Maya whenever we threw one of our tantrums. Nothing settled us down like one-on-one time with her. As if some part of us knew the time we did have was fleeting.

Julian sits beside me once he's kicked off his shoes, leaning on his elbows to look up at the first budding stars. There's a welcome silence as we adjust to the concept of being alone together. When I close my eyes, it's as if nothing has changed. Lake Andreas is alive again, buzzing with excitement as the day winds down. But the sound of Julian's voice is a stark reminder of how different things are now.

"How are you feeling?" he asks as he lies back.

"Like I was hit by a truck." I rub at one of the bites on my wrist. "A truck filled with mosquitoes."

He chuckles, stretching his arms behind his head. "I promise I'll never make you go anywhere near a bike again."

"It was for the best," I admit with a sigh. "Every year my mom would say, 'That's it, it's time you two learn how to ride bikes,' but she never got around to it."

Julian takes his time before replying, "I'm sorry."

"Eh, she was a busy lady."

"No." Julian sits up on his elbows. "I meant about . . . y'know. *Her.*"

"That she died?"

Julian nods, cheeks visibly pink even in the pale moonlight.

"You don't have to apologize; you didn't kill her. Unless you invented ovarian cancer. In which case, fuck you."

The joke is lost on him.

"Sorry, I'm just messing with you." I knock my bare ankle against his calf. "Though the Suck-o incident *did* take five years off all of our lives," I tease, but the way his brow furrows says it's gone over his head again.

He turns to look at me. "The what incident?"

The question catches me off guard. Like seeing Suck-o in that box, it feels like yet another backhanded strike. Did our loss mean so little to them that they don't even remember it? That we're the reason they have the second-floor expansion and the Jet Skis tied to their dock?

"That bet, from our first year here?" His expression remains unreadable. "The one where your dad stole my dad's invention and turned it into a million-dollar empire? The same bet your dad challenged us to again this year so he can turn our cabin into a boat garage?" My tone is harsher than I mean for it to be, but I can't help the rage that bubbles up as I dwell on the fact that they can't be bothered to remember screwing us over.

"That robot was yours?" Julian chokes out.

I prop myself up, eyes narrowed at him. "You didn't know?"

He shakes his head. "Dad told us it was something he'd been messing around with."

The weight of his reply makes my arms tremble. If they didn't know, then why did he throw eggs at our house? Why did I trip him and make his lip split open? Why have we been at each other's throats for a decade over something they had no part in?

"Then why did you hate us?" is all I can manage to say. It barely made sense before and even less sense now. We assumed they hated us because we had the power to threaten what they had. Because we knew the truth, even if we couldn't prove it. But if Julian and his siblings didn't see us as a threat, then why have we been feuding for twelve years?

Julian doesn't meet my eyes, shaking his head at the sky. "Because he told us to."

It's easy to hate someone when you're six. The neighbors had a pool and we didn't; that was enough. Dad told us that the Seo-Cookes hurt him. That just fueled us even more. But what if the person you trust most isn't trustworthy?

What if the person right in front of you was someone you could've trusted the entire time?

When Julian speaks up again, he still doesn't look at me.

"This is my dad's MO. He's always talking about how people like us need to be louder than everyone in the room, or no one'll listen. And maybe that's true, but now all he does is talk over everyone."

It's not a line of thought I can disagree with. Mr. Cooke knows as well as I do what it's like to be the only Latino in a room, how sometimes it feels like you'll never be heard. But that doesn't change what he did. That he didn't just shout over us—he silenced us entirely.

So much for solidarity.

"That was him. On the phone earlier." Julian's voice is thick.

My breath catches, and I fight back the urge to cough. I can hear how badly Julian wants to cry, so I give him space.

"He set up a lunch for me and some guy who knows the coach of the Princeton lacrosse team. Even though I told him I wasn't interested," Julian continues. "I did what I always do. Panic and say the worst possible thing." He stops for a moment, glancing over at me with a half-smirk. "Thankfully I didn't say I have another fake boyfriend."

I snort, all the breath I've been holding coming out at once. "Good. I can barely keep up with one fake relationship."

He nods, looking up at the stars again. "I should've told him then. About Princeton."

"What's your plan? If you're not going to Princeton, I mean."

I'm prepared for him to list off dozens of top-tier universities, not shrug and say, "I don't have one."

"You . . . don't?"

Julian Seo-Cooke, whose days are blocked out and color-coded to the minute, doesn't have a plan. That sounds as believable as our relationship.

"Not exactly." He sighs as he folds his arms behind his head. "I didn't get into Princeton. Didn't even make it onto the waitlist."

"But that doesn't mean you can't apply anywhere else. You still have a few days left." I should know. I didn't submit my CalArts application until the very last day, drenched in panic sweat when my laptop crashed twenty minutes before the application portal closed. Thankfully, Maya came to the rescue and let me borrow hers. Something I'm sure she regrets now.

Julian shakes his head. "I don't think I want to go anywhere else. It's not like I wanted to go to Princeton, either. But . . . I don't really know what I want." He inhales sharply, exhales slowly, and I resist the urge to lean in closer.

"It was easy for Henry to become the person Dad expected him to be. Sports have always been his thing, but I never had that. A *thing*. So I let Dad tell me what I wanted to be, even though I knew it was never going to work. I knew I wasn't going to get into Princeton. Or Wharton, or any of the other schools he made me apply to. Not after I flunked out of pre-calc last year." He stalls, turning to me with a small, sad smile. "See, there is something I'm bad at."

Something a lot like guilt burns my neck. "So, what're you going to do?"

"Take a break," he replies as he turns away again, his voice lighter this time. "Get a job. Figure out what I want to do—if I even want to go to college. Mom said a change of scenery might help, so we'll see."

"Are you going to be one of those kids who backpacks through Europe after graduation and never shuts up about it? Because that's about half the population at CalArts, and they are *insufferable*."

"Nothing that glamorous, no," he says with a snort.

"Mom's been thinking about moving for a while now. Most of her family is still out on the West Coast, and she hates the humidity here. I'm going to stay with my aunt for a bit. She knows practically every small business owner in the area, so she has a few leads lined up for potential jobs already. If everything works out, Mom'll come over after she takes the California bar exam."

I stiffen, hazarding a peek at him. "California?"

"Yeah . . ." He trails off.

"Oh . . ." I shift my attention to the tree hanging over us, grateful for the darkness cloaking my flushed cheeks.

California's one of the biggest states in the country. Julian being in California doesn't necessarily mean we're going to be in the same city. Sure, his mom is practically the pride and joy of Los Angeles, but maybe his aunt lives in Fresno. Or San Francisco. Or he could be off to become one with nature in Joshua Tree. No need to panic yet.

"Sorry, I should've mentioned it earlier," Julian says, an uneasy edge to his tone. "It never felt like the right time to blurt out, 'Hey, by the way, I'm sort of moving to LA after graduation.'"

Okay, never mind.

"It's okay. I don't own the city." I keep my voice calm. The polar opposite of how I'm feeling internally.

All semester I've held out hope that the universe would put someone new in my path. A classmate, a friend, a . . . something more. Someone who hasn't found their way yet either. Someone who's as afraid of the city and the prospect of failing as I am. Someone to conquer that fear with.

And the universe gave me Julian.

The universe has a terrible sense of humor.

"So, you haven't told your dad any of this?" I ask, trying to change the topic. I can wrestle with how I feel about everything I've just learned about Julian later, ideally not when he's lying right next to me in the dreamy moonlight.

He shakes his head, tapping his knuckles against the wood. "No. I got close, though. I told him I didn't want to play lacrosse anymore. I thought maybe if I started to come clean, it might help Stella feel like she could too. Dad wants her to focus on getting accepted into an Ivy next year, but she's had her heart set on UCLA since she was a freshman." He exhales, and the tapping stops abruptly. The pieces start to come together—the way he'd looked at his phone, the tension when he got back, the way he'd snapped at me.

"Dad always makes this stuff about my mom," he says, angrier than before. "That she's too easy on us, letting us skip practices or pull out of activities we don't want to do. That she doesn't care about our futures the way he does, which is *rich* coming from someone like him, when that's why Mom . . ." The anger in his voice that's been growing with each syllable reaches its peak, then dies altogether. He cuts himself off midbreath, and before I can process what he's said, he's sitting up and reaching for his shoes. "I'm sorry, you don't need to listen to all this. I can—"

"No." I sit upright so abruptly the world starts to spin. I grab Julian's arm, the way he always grabs mine. "You don't have to tell me anything you don't want to, but don't think that you're a burden."

I don't know where those words came from. But they make Julian stay in place for a few more seconds, and for that, I'm grateful.

He sags once I let go of him, his eyes falling to the water. "I don't want to make you feel weird, hearing about all of this."

"Everything about us is weird," I reply with a lopsided grin. "Why not make it weirder?"

Julian returns my smile with one of his own, setting his shoes aside and lying back down beside me. "This month's been hard," he whispers, so much closer this time. "Especially with the whole Liam thing." He nudges his shoulder against mine. "You've made it easier, though."

I ignore the goose bumps that blossom along my arm where it's pressed against his. "What can I say? I'm a lifesaver too."

The lack of distance between us is still unnerving, but I'm glad he's not able to feel my heart thrumming against my skin.

"Sorry for hijacking your winter break," he says. "When I came up with this plan, I didn't imagine you'd wind up with six hundred mosquito bites three days before Christmas."

I wave off the apology. "It's fine. Not like we had exciting plans anyway."

He lets out a sound that's between a snort and a scoff. "Us either. Dad insisted he gets us on Christmas, even though holidays have always been Mom's thing. He's probably just gonna ditch us after breakfast to go golfing with Liam's dad. *So* fun."

Nothing about that statement surprises me, but the way it makes my heart ache does. I know all too well how much the loss of a tradition can hurt.

"We almost didn't come, but Dad insisted." Julian's sigh cuts right through me. "It . . . feels weird not to have Mom around. She calls all the time to make sure we're doing okay, but . . . it's not the same."

Yeah. I get that.

He doesn't say anything else, so neither do I. It doesn't feel right to tell him that a part of me is glad he came after all. That, in a weird, twisted way, he's become the highlight of my winter break. Not when he still has the power to take so much from us. Instead, we just sit, listening to the breeze and the buzz of the lake.

"My mom loved tres leches cake," I say after what feels like hours go by. "Her sister, my titi Rosa, always made it the best. Dad used to make us drive out to her place thirty minutes early *every* Christmas Eve to make sure we got some before she ran out. But then she said some pretty nasty stuff after Maya said she wanted to marry a princess instead of a prince at our fifth birthday party. So she's dead to us, and we decided to spend Christmases here instead." Julian flips onto his side, brows knit in confusion, but he doesn't interrupt. "We would drive for hours to find the best tres leches cake, but nothing ever lived up to the original. So, one year, Mami said we'd figure out our own recipe. One that was ten times better than Titi Rosa's.

"Mami was really sick by then. She'd spent most of the year in the hospital, but she was able to come home in time for Christmas. Obviously, we couldn't come down here, but we were grateful to have her home, period. So Maya and I spent every day of our break trying to figure out that recipe. Since Mami couldn't really leave her bed, we brought everything to her to taste test. In the end, we didn't get super close to replicating the original. Honestly, ours was pretty gross. But Mami helped us decorate the one we had on Christmas Eve with a little smiley face made of cherries. That was my favorite part. Even though the rest of it sorta tasted like cottage cheese. We couldn't have any family over, so we sat in her room and talked. Played board games. It wasn't exciting, but it was still our favorite Christmas Eve." I let out a humorless laugh, willing myself not to cry over something I've already shed hundreds of tears for. "And then she left us. Three days later."

Julian lets out a muffled gasp, and for a second, I feel the warmth of his arm against mine, but it's gone as quickly as it appeared.

"Maya likes to wear one of Mami's old jackets when she misses her. Black leather with roses printed on the back. If you lean in close enough, it still smells like her." If I try hard enough, I can smell it now. Her favorite lilac perfume mixed with something we could never replicate. The one thing left behind that still feels like her.

The stars swim in and out of view as I fight back the tears that come every time I let my heart linger on her for too long.

"We don't really celebrate the holidays anymore, but I still make tres leches cake. On her birthday, on mine . . . on the days when I miss her. The kitchen smells like cherries and cream, and I'll blast her favorite salsa playlist, and it almost feels like she's there. Just for a few minutes, but it's something.

My something." I exhale slowly, bracing myself before facing Julian. Our faces are too close, but the discomfort doesn't feel scary anymore. "I know it's not the same, my mom and your mom. But maybe that could be something for you too. When you miss her, I mean. I saw that note she left on that recipe, the fried rice one. You could make it on the days when you miss her."

Julian doesn't respond. My chest seizes up, my body going warm down to my core. That's what I deserve for getting swept up in the moment, for trying to take a blow at the wall between us. For a foolish second, I'd let myself forget that wall was built for a reason. Even if that reason has a new meaning.

"It's stupid, sorry, I didn't mean to—"

"That's really sweet." This time it's Julian's turn to reach for me when I try to run. He waits until I've relaxed my shoulders to let me go. "Thank you. For telling me."

I nod, unsure of how else to respond, and even more unsure if I should still try to leave.

Julian points to a bright spot in the darkness on the opposite side of the lake. "Allegheny Park does a fireworks show every night before the park closes, if you want to stick around for that."

"Okay," I reply. Strangely enough, I *do* want to stick around.

My cheeks burn when I feel Julian's eyes on me. I wait for him to say something, to make the prickle beneath my skin go away. When he whispers something about stars and light pollution, I can't hear him over the thumping of my heart.

"You know how when you're a kid you don't like broccoli, and then you spend your whole adult life thinking that you hate it, even though you haven't had it in years?" he says after a moment of pause.

"I've always liked broccoli."

"It's a metaphor. Work with me here."

I gesture for him to continue.

"I think you're my broccoli."

Oh.

I can't say I disagree. Hating Julian has always felt like second nature, but finding reasons to keep hating him is getting harder every day. I told myself I had to because that's who we are, who our families expect us to be.

But who are we when no one's watching?

"Maybe you're my brussels sprouts," I say.

He smirks but doesn't say anything, and we turn back to the stars.

The sky erupts, painted neon green, gold, and red. Sparkles trickle down to earth, sprinkling the air with ash and a sense of wonder.

I'm so entranced by the display that I don't notice Julian's hand sliding into mine. I'd left my own palm upturned to the stars, my body inviting him before my mind could realize what I was doing. I don't pull away when his fingers close around mine. Instead, I squeeze back, gentle but firm, and seal a wordless promise that I'm not sure I understand.

CHAPTER THIRTEEN

The memory of my night with Julian nestles inside my chest, hidden as deep as I can bury it as I cross all my fingers that Maya won't ask me where I was.

"Where were you last night?"

Can just *one* thing go my way?

I was already running on borrowed time. If she'd stayed up, she would've pounced on me the second I came through the door. I slid into my room unseen, hiding my flushed cheeks in my pillow and trying not to dwell on what last night meant. Or didn't mean. Because it shouldn't have meant anything.

"Learning how to ride a bike," I reply staying focused on my sketchbook, brushing some toast crumbs off the page. My latest idea is as scrambled as I am. I'm not even sure what it's supposed to be. The page is a mess of scribbled lines that look like a Picasso-inspired Pikachu. Turns out my creative well is dry after all, and it's taking a whole lot of self-restraint not to go into crisis mode.

Maya's brow quirks, her mug of coffee stalling halfway to her lips. "Why?"

I run my hand along one of the mosquito bites on the back of my neck. "It's a long story."

Not a lie, I even have the battle scars to prove it. She shakes her head, finishing her coffee before pushing away from the table. "You two are weird."

Understatement of the century.

She grabs the back of my shirt, tugging me out of my seat. I open my mouth to protest, but brushing her off so I can work won't do me any favors.

Andy greedily eyes my abandoned slice of toast, his glass of orange juice way too close to my also abandoned sketch-book for comfort. I pull myself out of Maya's grip, making a dash to pull my sketchbook out of harm's way before trudging back to her room.

Once Maya locks the door, I take my usual seat at the foot of her bed. "I've been doing some thinking," she announces proudly.

"That never ends well."

She rolls her eyes, chucking a pillow at my head. "Shut up." Once I've ducked, she turns back around to examine the whiteboard above her vanity, our training schedule written in pink and blue marker. "I think we need to change our approach."

I pull my battered knees up to my chest. The aftermath of my bicycling lesson left me more sore this morning than I thought was humanly possible. It took fifteen minutes just to butter my toast. "What does that mean?"

She paces across the room, tugging one of her curls taut before wrapping it around her finger. "Has Julian told you anything?"

I shrug, ignoring the ache in my shoulders. "He's told me lots of things."

Thankfully she's out of nonlethal objects to throw at me. "I mean *personal* things. Things he wouldn't tell any of us."

Neither her tone nor her question sits right with me. "Why?"

My eyes follow her warily as she continues pacing. "If we can't find out what they're planning, then we should think of something on our own." She stops, letting her curl spring free. "Something that'll stop them."

The flicker in her eyes is familiar, as vicious as the day she proposed her original idea. But there's something harsher to it this time, angrier. "You want to cheat?"

For a flash of a second, the fire fades away. She shakes her head, but I know her well enough to see right through the façade. "I want to get creative." She grabs one of the markers off the whiteboard, scribbling some ideas in a corner. "Weigh their bags down with rocks or stick something in their shoes."

"We were already being creative, Maya."

Spying on them wasn't easily justifiable, but we talked ourselves into it. Things were different, the stakes higher, and they never played by the rules, so why should we? Except we hadn't broken the rules; we just found a way around them.

There's no justifying this, though. No telling ourselves that we're better because we're honest and fair. Not if we stoop down to their level.

I march over to the whiteboard, taking the marker out of her hand and circling the ideas she's already written down. "*This* is cheating."

"It doesn't have to be," she replies too quickly, as if she knew this was coming. "You're the one spending all day at Casa del Cabrón. It's not just one asshole—it's a house full of them. You've seen what they're like. We could turn them against each other, make them fall apart before we even get to the games."

The worst part is that she's right. Sabotage would be so easy. It would only take the truth—telling Julian's dad about Princeton, that he and Stella want to move with Mrs. Seo across the country—and they'd crumble. An argument that would leave them so fractured there's no way they'd be able to stand against us, a united front. We could even go the blackmail route—force Julian to sabotage his own family in exchange for our silence. Stella and Henry are still guilty of making our lives hell, but they're way more innocent than I thought they were two weeks ago. Their dad is our real enemy, but I can't tell Maya that. Not when it means sharing the very same things she needs to tear them apart.

"Jesus, Maya." I run a hand through my hair, willing my voice to stay even, but I can't help losing control. "This is about a fucking game; we're not destroying a family."

"It's not *just* a game!" she shouts, flushed down to her collarbone. The silence is consuming as she glares at me with what's either disgust, disappointment, or both. "Or did you already give up on this place?"

Now, *that* shuts me up.

A knock at the front door is my saving grace. The idea of visitors is so foreign the sound makes both of us jump. We crack Maya's door open enough to peek out into the living room. Dad and Isabel exchange puzzled looks, nearly leaping out of their seats when there's a second, much louder knock. Dad grabs a baseball bat from the coat closet and approaches the front door with caution.

What's waiting behind the door is ten times more terrifying than anything we could've imagined.

"Happy holidays, neighbors!" Mr. Cooke exclaims.

Dad discreetly hands off the bat to Isabel before pulling the door open the rest of the way. "Happy holidays, Paul," he replies with a stiff smile. "Going for a hike?" Dad gestures to the hiking backpack at Mr. Cooke's feet.

"Just got home. Shame Devin couldn't join us, though."

I gag. My name sounds so off-putting when he says it, like it's a profanity.

The age-old stomach bug excuse worked to get Julian, and therefore me, out of the hike. Thank god. Figuring out how to create fake vomit for him to plant in his bathroom was a pain, but well worth the payoff. And in the end, Liam got to take my spot. Granted, he didn't have Julian to flirt with, but I'm sure Mr. Cooke was still pleased.

"We're hosting a little holiday party tonight. Just us and a couple of friends from Hillsdale. The kids were nagging me up and down this morning asking if I'd invite you all over."

That's odd. Julian never mentioned a post-hike get-together, and if he wanted us to come, why wouldn't he just text me? Maya pokes me in the ribs, brows quirked as she waits for an answer, but I have nothing to offer her. This makes as little sense to me as it does to her.

"Oh, well, that's nice of you to offer, but we wouldn't want to intrude," Dad replies, already starting to close the door.

"Nonsense!" Mr. Cooke insists, inserting himself more firmly into our doorway, one foot inside the cabin. "The kids are always complaining that our holiday parties are so stuffy, too many country club types. So I thought, what's the harm in switching it up a bit this year? And no one livens up a party like the Báezes." He slaps Dad on the shoulder with a hearty chuckle.

"Did he just call us poor?" Maya whispers to me.

Dad pats Mr. Cooke's hand with enough force for us to hear the slap from the hallway. "We'll uh . . . see what we can do."

"Great. See you then!" Mr. Cooke says before taking off, completely missing the part where we didn't agree to anything.

Maya pulls me into her room, leaning against the door with a mischievous smirk. "This is perfect."

"You actually *want* to go?" I go there every day and I don't want to go.

"Duh, of course I do." She slaps her hand against my chest for questioning her. "You keep them distracted, and I'll dig up the *real* dirt," she explains while rummaging through the carefully curated selection of crop tops in her dresser.

My body creaks with a new kind of ache as I sink to the

floor. Arguing is pointless when she has her mind set on something. It doesn't matter how many times I've told her they don't keep their secrets out in the open. Yet, a part of me hopes I did miss something. A clue or a hint that'll keep her occupied enough to abandon her latest idea. There's still a chance that we can make it out of this without hurting anyone but Mr. Cooke.

Still, I can't shake the undeniable bad feeling surrounding this invitation. And something tells me Maya's only going to make it worse.

CHAPTER FOURTEEN

"Stop fidgeting; you're making me nervous." Maya yanks me down onto the settee beside her. "Have a bacon-wrapped date."

She holds her overflowing plate of appetizers under my nose, but I wave off the offer. "You don't think this is weird?"

Everything about this overly formal holiday barbecue is weird. There's an ice sculpture of a swan in the kitchen, a Bruce Springsteen cover band in the backyard, and no one stationed at the grill. Mr. Cooke's friends got the memo based on their crisp polos and slightly less-business-casual slacks. Meanwhile, Dad sticks out like a sore thumb in his Tito Puente T-shirt and ol' reliable grilling shoes. I'd made fun of Maya for breaking out *that* jacket, the one that used to belong to Mami, but she's the only one who's somewhat up to code, though the violet wig she's paired with her ensemble makes us stand out more than we already do. It's kind of nice, actually. The smell of Mami's perfume comes in lilac waves every time there's a slight breeze. A calming anchor in a sea of uncertainty.

"It's super weird, but I'm not here to have a good time." Maya pushes a mini slider to the edge of her plate so she can sample the potato salad. "I'm here to mooch, dig through their dirty laundry, and bounce."

"But we haven't seen Julian, Stella, *or* Henry yet," I reply, peeking over the crowd gathered by the bar for any sight of the people who supposedly "begged" for us to be here. Liam's here, of course, decked out in his Vineyard Vines best. He's just too busy sticking to Mr. Cooke like a leech to antagonize me.

"Don't worry." Maya waves me off, keeping her attention focused on the gaggle of gossiping women opposite us. She's been eavesdropping on their conversation about their pack leader Evelyn's affair for the past ten minutes. "They're probably off doing rich kid things like grooming their horses or ironing their Burberry socks."

Andy returns to us with a plate so loaded he can barely keep his French fries from spilling over. "Dev, this place is amazing. How come you never let us join you?" He squeezes himself between me and Maya, double-fisting a barbecue slider and a buffalo chicken wrap.

"It's not usually this exciting," I mumble, propping my chin up on my fist.

My text to Julian from earlier is still unread:

Hey, what's the deal with this party?

If he wanted me here so badly, why is he avoiding me like the plague?

Or maybe he doesn't want you here, I remind myself. There are still two other siblings in this family who could've invited us. Though Stella and Henry can't stand seeing me during the week. Why invite all of us on their day off from my presence?

Maya gasps, clutching her heart when Evelyn reveals that her lover is none other than her sister's husband. "Rich people really live like they're in a telenovela," Maya whispers.

Across the room, Dad and Isabel wrap up their latest conversation, their smiles falling the second they turn around. Unlike the rest of us, they've been doing a remarkable job of acting like they wouldn't rather be anywhere else. They trudge over to us, downing the last of their champagne.

"This is exhausting," Isabel mutters. "¿El siempre es así?" She juts her chin toward where Mr. Cooke and a gaggle of balding white men are comparing their Rolexes.

"Yep," Dad, Maya, and I answer at the same time. Confirming that, yes, he is always this obnoxious.

She shudders, grabbing two fresh champagne flutes from a nearby table, handing one of them to Dad. "You'll need this."

My phone buzzes and I nearly knock over Andy's plate in my rush to pull it out of my pocket. But alas, it's just a spam text about hot singles in my area. "I'm going to take a lap," I announce to the others, nudging Maya's foot with my own. "You coming?"

She shakes her head, keeping her attention focused on Evelyn. "I'll meet up with you in a sec. Keep an eye out for the others."

Like that night at the country club, I peek through crowds

and into mostly empty rooms in search of Julian. The sooner I find him and shake off this nagging feeling, the sooner we can head home.

While this is clearly a catered affair, I still make the kitchen my first stop. A handful of waiters dart carefully around one another, loading up trays of appetizers and sliced fruit to bring out to the tables in the backyard. I nearly walk right into a harried woman carrying a vat of what smells like New England clam chowder.

"Hey."

I turn at the sound of Julian's voice cutting through the chatter in the kitchen. He appears at the top of the stairs, dressed more casually than me. "What're you doing here?" he asks, pulling out one of his headphones.

"You invited us?" I reply, the excitement I'd felt about finding him fizzling. "Or I guess one of your siblings did."

Julian's lips part, and his brow furrows as he lets out a confused "Uuuuuh . . . that's weird."

I fold my arms across my chest, unsure what to do with myself now that I know I'm not wanted. "Should I be concerned?"

Our answer comes bounding down the stairs. Stella looks like she just ran a marathon, cheeks flushed and hair up in a messy bun. It's the least put together I've ever seen her, and the happiest she's ever been to see me.

"You made it!" she exclaims, pushing past her brother to loop her arm through mine.

The shock of seeing her smile instead of scowl at me leaves me at a loss for words. Did we make a wrong turn somewhere and wind up in a different dimension? Because this is *not* the timeline I know.

She starts tugging me toward a nearby hallway, but Julian steps in her way. "Did you invite them?"

"Duh. Aren't you the one who's always saying we should be nicer to him?"

The thought of Julian trying to bridge the gap between me and his siblings is sweet, but the reality is unsettling. I'd rather Stella hate my guts than whatever this is.

"And Maya too!" Stella shouts. Maya freezes in the entrance to the kitchen, halfway into a bite of a cannoli.

"Uh, hi." She covers her mouth as she finishes chewing. "Did I miss something?"

Stella shakes her head, abandoning me to pull Maya along instead. "These things are so boring. Usually we skip them, and Dad never notices. You can hang with us, though."

Maya and I exchange wary glances but let her lead the way. Julian follows at a distance, looking more confused than we do. Stella pulls open a door that I'd always thought led to another pantry but reveals a flight of stairs plunging into darkness. I've seen enough horror movies to know not to go anywhere near a dark, creepy basement.

"Nuh-uh." Maya finagles her way out of Stella's grip, coming to stand beside me. "That screams serial killer."

Stella rolls her eyes, heading halfway down the stairs and pulling on a chain dangling from the ceiling. The overhead light flickers, and the most outlandish den I've ever seen comes to life. Maya and I hold on to each other with one hand and clutch the banister for dear life with the other. I bite back the urge to gasp, the room somehow growing more unbelievable with every step.

Plush couches and armchairs surround the room's center-piece, a television so massive I can't figure out how the wall is supporting its weight. A row of pinball machines and arcade games light up like Christmas trees. Bowls of candies litter every surface; jars of popcorn and homemade cookies rest atop the bar in the corner of the room. The bar is a gleam-ing beacon of liquid courage, dozens of untouched, clearly top-shelf bottles in a locked cabinet behind the counter.

"Holy shit," Maya says under her breath.

I follow her eyes to a row of framed movie posters, all of them signed by at least one member of the cast. Holy shit indeed. The posters, like most things about the Seo-Cookes, make me feel painfully out of my element. We knew they were loaded, but I'd underestimated them by a tax bracket or two. Up until now, I've rolled my eyes at the overly posh non-sense they spend their unearned wealth on, but I wouldn't mind having a basement like this.

Stella loses interest in us as soon as she sits down, pulling out her phone. The grind never stops, as influencers love to remind the plebian public.

Julian gestures for us to make ourselves comfortable. "Can I get you guys anything to eat?"

Maya shakes her head, dusting her powdered sugar–coated fingers off on the hem of her skirt. "We're good." She nudges her elbow into my ribs, leaning in to whisper, "Don't trust any food you didn't serve yourself."

While I appreciate her concern, I'm well past worrying that Julian is poisoning my food by now. He's had me in the palm of his hand for over a week, and the worst thing he's done is accidentally over-salt his pasta water.

Julian takes a seat across from the two of us, glaring daggers at his sister. She's tapping at top speed like she has something to prove.

"So." Julian gives up on his sister and refocuses on us. "Want to watch a movie? Dev and I were talking about working our way through the *Lord of the Rings* since I've never seen them, but that might be a lot for one sitting."

"Since when does he call you Dev?" Maya whispers to me.

That's a story for another day, maybe never. "Sure," I tell Julian, ignoring my sister. "But maybe something with less orcs."

"Nerds," Maya says, loud enough this time for both of us to hear. I go to shove her with my shoulder, but she stands up before I can. "If we're going full-on dork, let me get Andy. He lives for this kind of stuff." She shoots me a wink as she heads toward the stairs. An obvious lie to anyone who's had more than two conversations with Andy. He couldn't tell an orc from an elf. My guess is she's off to do her digging, leaving me to distract the wolves. I get one last subtle whiff of her jacket before she leaves, but even Mami's scent doesn't do anything to calm my nerves.

"Wait!" Stella shouts, nearly throwing her phone across the room as she races over to Maya. I'm ready to pounce if she tries to hurt her, but what comes next is even more upsetting.

Stella hugs her.

Maya goes rigid in the embrace, her face screwed up in a

mix of confusion and discomfort. Even Julian sits up stiff as a board, the two of us on the edge of our seats.

"I'm so happy you decided to come," Stella says, still not letting go, her face tucked deep into Maya's curls.

"Uh . . . you're welcome?" Maya gives me a panicked look, but there's nothing I can do short of pulling them apart. Maybe this is just Stella's weird way of playing nice? One thing I've learned this year is that kindness comes with a steep learning curve.

Stella pulls away, flashing Maya a too-sweet smile before grabbing her phone and heading back to her seat without another word. She plops back onto the armchair, kicks her feet up on the coffee table, and starts texting again like nothing happened. Maya stays in place, mouthing, *What do I do?* to me and Julian. The two of us shrug. There's little relief in knowing that Julian is concerned too.

Maya backs away slowly, waiting until she's made it to the staircase to bolt. She's out of sight for a fraction of a second.

And then she starts screaming.

Pure adrenaline jerks me out of my seat and sends me flying up the stairs. I'm not a violent person, but I'm prepared to claw apart whatever, *whoever*, made my sister scream like that.

The top of the staircase looks like a culinary crime scene. Clam chowder instead of blood, a half-empty bucket instead of a weapon. My sister instead of a body.

She's curled up in the mess, her violet wig knocked askew and stained with chunks of clam and potato, the embroidered roses on her jacket barely visible beneath the gunk. I kneel down beside her, pushing through the unfortunate smell of soup to help her into a sitting position. The screams die down as soon as I'm with her, melting down to quiet, whimpered sobs. She holds on to my arm so tight it burns, her fingernails digging crescent moons into my already bruised skin, but I push the pain down and let her hold on as hard as she has to.

A cold, hollow cackle draws my attention away from Maya. Henry and Liam stand side by side a few feet away; Liam laughing until his cheeks turn pink while Henry records the spectacle on his phone. Henry blinks up at me with those stupid dopey eyes, shaking his head as he starts to lower his phone. Without thinking, I let go of Maya and lunge at him, grabbing the phone and throwing it to the ground with all the force I have left in me. It cracks on impact, but that's not enough. I want to crush it until it's nothing, until it's as broken as they've left my sister.

"What the hell!" Liam shouts on Henry's behalf, shoving me back from the two of them.

"Fuck you!" I snap back, taking the opportunity to grab the phone and throw it to the ground a second time. The force shatters it the rest of the way. Finally, Apple's shitty hardware design comes in handy.

Julian stumbles up the stairs, nearly slipping on the chowder. "What is wrong with you?!" The question is aimed at Henry.

"C'mon, we had to. They did the salami thing, so now it's our turn," Stella replies in between hiccupped laughs as she trails behind him. The laughter dies once she gets a look at the scene at the top of the stairs. Her smile morphs into a frown, her gaze suddenly shifting to Liam. "It was his idea."

That doesn't surprise me. That damn hike managed to wreak havoc on me even when I didn't go. "You think this shit is funny?" I wave the last remaining pieces of Henry's phone in front of Liam's face. "Hurting someone like that?"

"Oh please," Liam scoffs, shoving my hand out of his face. "First off, that little stunt was meant for *you*. You're lucky she came up first. And you've both been doing the same thing since you got here. You can't get mad because we decided to punch back."

We? The war our families waged has never been just or fair, but it's only ever been between us. Liam doesn't get to rewrite history, insert himself somewhere he doesn't belong. Whatever problem he has with me stays with me.

"This doesn't involve you," I spit back, knowing that I should stop there. Instead, my anger boils over, too fast and too scalding for me to hold in. "But you've never cared about boundaries, huh? If you did, you'd know to fuck off and stop trying to make passes at the guy who dumped you."

Liam goes beet red down to his frosted roots, and while he still towers over me, I've never felt taller.

"For the record"—his voice is low, strained as if the lightest touch would make him snap—"*I* broke up with *him*."

While that doesn't change what I think of him, his reply does spark Julian back into action.

"That's enough." Julian grabs Stella by the arm and carefully sidesteps around Maya to drag her toward Henry. "You two could've just shut up and been respectful like I asked, but no! You're assholes." He pauses, rounding on Liam this time. "All of you."

With the others occupied, I rush back over to Maya. I

wipe the chowder out of her eyes, pushing synthetic hair and clam bits off her face. "You okay?" I whisper.

She shakes her head. "Can we go home?"

My arm is around her before she's finished asking, delicately helping her stand back up. I guide her toward the back door at the end of the kitchen. Once we're home, we can text the others to get the hell out. The commotion behind us is a dull din, ringing in my ears as we rush out of the house. We're halfway across the backyard, shielding ourselves from dirty stares, when a hand closes around my arm.

"Devin, I'm so sorry," Julian pants out, struggling to catch his breath. "I swear, I had no idea, and if I did, I would've—"

"Let me go, Julian." I'm not mad at him. If anything, I'm grateful that we have him as a buffer between us and the real enemies. But I can't look at him, not right now.

He lets me go without question, backing away to give us space. He might've said something else, something about texting him if we need anything, but I only care about Maya.

We fall apart once we've made it back to the cabin. Maya's whimpers shift into sobs as we rush to the kitchen to turn on the tap. She peels herself out of the jacket, pushing away the damp towel I hold to her face to wipe at the sleeves instead. The chowder gunk is gone after some careful scrubbing, the leather marred with scratches and the first signs of peeled edges. We lean in too close, holding the jacket like a lifeline, bracing ourselves for the scent of lilac to keep us grounded.

But it's gone now. Just like that, they've taken a piece of Mami away from us. The first of many, if they get their way.

We sink to the floor, soaked in chowder and freshly shed tears, holding the jacket reverently between our laps. It's only a matter of time before the others come home. Even without the warning, the news must've spread.

My hand finds Maya's, our fingers linked on top of the jacket. There's nothing worth saying that'll make either of us feel any better, not plans for revenge or insults or schemes. So we say nothing and split the pain. The way we always have.

CHAPTER FIFTEEN

"So when you get 'the eagle has landed' text, what're you going to do?" Maya quizzes me for the fourth time that afternoon.

"Run away into the woods to live the rest of my life as a hermit."

She stops long enough to smack me over the head.

"I'm going to get them to come outside!" I concede, shielding myself from her wrath.

"Good." She backs off and settles down beside the chimney. "I'm still working on my aim, so I'd suggest ducking. Or taking cover, whatever's easier."

While I'm very on board with the idea of making the Seo-Cookes pay for what they did at the barbecue, I can't say the same about Maya's plan for revenge. To be clear, it's not that I'm opposed to slinging water balloons filled with pig's blood at Stella and Henry. I'd just rather not have to be the Trojan horse.

"Why can't we lure them out with a fake pizza delivery or something?"

Maya rolls her eyes, scoffing at my insolence. "Because that would only get one Seo-Cooke outside, and what good is using our secret weapon if we can't get a three-for-one?"

She has a point. We don't know how to track down Liam to get back at him, and we can't just stand around the water park hoping he might show up, so Stella and Henry will have to do.

Considering our cabin's less-than-stellar stability, I don't trust the idea of both of us being on the roof at the same time, but it seems to hold our weight pretty well. We set up camp behind the chimney, the one spot that's hidden enough to work. Finding pig's blood on Christmas Eve was no easy feat, but Dad pulled it off, disappearing in the middle of the afternoon and returning two hours later with enough pig's blood for two dozen balloons, no questions asked.

Despite Isabel's best efforts, Christmas was a somber affair. We threw on smiles for morning waffles and opening our few, modest presents while Mariah Carey belted out of Maya's new Bluetooth speaker. But in this cabin that feels trapped in time, we can't find it in us to embrace new traditions. Not when the old ones are rooted in something we don't have the heart to let go of.

Though, spending Christmas pouring pig's blood into water balloons does feel very on brand for this family.

Maya carefully arranges the box of blood balloons she

forced me to carry up here so that they're out of view. "Think we're hidden enough?"

There's a clear shot if I can get them to the right spot and Maya keeps her aim sharp. "We should be. Unless they're on the lookout for snipers."

She ignores my joke to admire her handiwork, picking up one of the balloons and lightly tossing it between her hands. "You ready?"

"No."

"Great." She pushes me toward the ladder back down to the living room. "Good luck in there."

Yeah, I'll need it.

I swallow hard, bracing myself as we both climb down the ladder. Maya heads back to her room to grab some last-minute materials while I make my way over to the Seo-Cookes' front door. I haven't had to ring the bell since my first visit, but today feels unusually formal. The few times Julian and I have texted since the incident have been stilted, mainly him apologizing profusely. We chatted briefly about our respective Christmases, both of which sounded equally depressing. As predicted, Mr. Cooke stuck around long enough to watch them open their presents before bailing to go play a round of golf.

If I wasn't being sent into the enemy's lair on yet another high-stakes mission, I might even look forward to it. The few days without Julian's culinary experiments or him sneaking up behind me have been weird. And full of animal blood and plans for revenge. Lonely, too. Christmas has been a loaded day ever since Mami died, and I could use a break right about now.

"Hey," Julian greets, his expression flipping between relief and panic.

"Hey."

"I'm sor—"

"Please don't say you're sorry again," I interrupt, holding my hand up before he can continue. "Not that I don't believe you," I clarify. "I'd rather move on from the whole thing. If that's okay?"

"Yeah." He nods, peeking up at me with those light brown eyes I've come to look forward to seeing. "You don't have your sketchbook today?"

My hand twitches at my side, reaching for where my canvas bag would usually be slung over my shoulder. So much for acting convincing. "Artistic block. Figured a change of scenery might break me out of the rut." Not true, but I've gotten better at lying without sweating bullets. With two weeks left until my application is due, I didn't have a choice but to kick myself into gear. My latest attempt, which came to me in a flash of inspiration last night, feels like the best one yet. Who would've thought practice would make perfect?

"Oh. Cool."

We idle in the doorway, Julian still blocking my path into the house. "Should I come in?"

Julian shakes himself off, jumping out of the entryway. "Right, yeah, you should. Sor—" He catches himself. "Not sorry."

"Ha ha." I flick his wrist with my forefinger.

The mood is lighter, but not any less awkward. I sway on the balls of my feet, tapping my hands against my thighs as I wait for Julian to lead the way like he always does. "Are Stella and Henry around?" I peer around him into the empty din-ing room. The house is unusually quiet.

He shakes his head. "I asked them to give us the house for the afternoon. I figured you might not be comfortable around them right now."

He digs his hands into his pockets and heads toward the kitchen. My rapid heart finally slows, not threatening to beat out of my chest anymore, as I breathe a sigh of relief and text Maya.

> Stella and Henry aren't here, just Julian.

No Stella and Henry, no blood balloon showdown.

The text is marked as read, three dots appearing on the screen for a fraction of a second before disappearing. She's pissed, I'm sure. And dumping blood down the drain as we speak.

"I wanted to show you something, actually," Julian says as he picks up the mug sitting on the counter, his voice uneven, nervous.

I'm too distracted by my phone to realize we've made it to the kitchen, and I walk right into Julian. The mug he'd been holding out toward me spills over, latte splashing across the blinding white tile.

Julian whips around, worried. "I'm sorry, I can make you a new one."

He sets down the half-full mug in his hands before rush-ing to the espresso maker on the opposite end of the room. The wail of the grinder doesn't leave room for conversation, so I settle down at the counter and watch the master work.

He places a fresh mug in front of me, taking his time to garnish the new latte with a cinnamon stick and dash of nutmeg. How he manages to remember so many minute details—how I like my coffee, my ranked lunch meat preferences, my mild almond and pineapple allergies—I'll never understand. There's so much care and precision in everything he makes, from morning coffee to ham sandwiches, that I can't help but marvel every chance I get.

"You said you wanted to show me something?" I ask after my first sip. Like with each of Julian's creations, the latte is perfectly balanced.

He wrings his fingers as he sits down across from me, biting his lip and ignoring his own untouched drink. All it took was one day to ruin weeks of work, to build our walls back up.

"It's a song, actually." He pulls his phone out of his pocket, setting it down on the counter. "But, um . . . maybe now's not a good day. We can watch TV or something."

My hand twitches, wanting to rest on top of Julian's, to keep his from trembling. But I hold myself back, shaking my head instead.

"Today's a good day."

He nods, smiling sheepishly as he opens a playlist on his phone, scrolling past Ariana Grande's entire discography before finding the songs he's looking for.

New Nostalgia, it turns out, is a total carbon copy of the dozens of British rock bands I've favorited on Spotify. Julian taps on one of their songs and sets his phone down between us. The lead singer, a guy with skater bangs and the cool kind of nose piercing I *should* have, sings about a love lost to the sea.

"I never would've pegged you as the rock band type," I say as the vocals bow down to a dramatic guitar solo.

"There's plenty you still don't know about me," Julian says with a wink.

"Like what?"

"I can do this." He stretches his tongue as long as he can, nearly down to his chin, before flicking it up to lick the tip of his nose.

It's simultaneously gross and very impressive. "You're a man of many talents."

He takes a bow, and for a second, it feels like things might be all right. That whatever it is we have together won't go to waste.

The song plays on, and I listen more closely now, as if it'll help me figure out the puzzle that is the boy sitting across from me. "This isn't exactly a 'fun vacation up at the lake' song," I tease. The melancholy ballad has more of a "sobbing in your room" vibe.

"I know. But it reminds me of you." I don't have enough time to read into why a song about a giant squid makes Julian think of me.

A new text comes in during the last round of the chorus. I break away from the hold Julian and New Nostalgia have on me to scan the message from Maya.

The eagle has landed.

Shit.

Hell hath no fury like Maya Nicole Báez scorned, but even she should be able to see that Julian doesn't deserve to pay for other people's mistakes. Empathy and forgiveness aren't our strong suits, but we're not so hell-bent on revenge that we'd punish an innocent bystander. She's probably just messing with me; she wouldn't do this. She wouldn't stoop to their level.

Or maybe she already has.

"If that's cool with you, though," Julian says, having gone pink in the few seconds I stopped listening to him.

"One second."

I push past Julian, racing to the front door as quickly as my legs will carry me. The world seems too bright when I step outside, the trees shrouded in glare. I hold my hand up to my eyes, squinting at our roof for any sign of Maya, but I don't spot her. We're safe.

Julian appears behind me, nearly out of breath. "Hey, you okay?"

"M'fine," I mumble, scrutinizing our cabin one last time before turning to face him. "Sorry, I . . . thought I heard something."

Julian scans the front yard, brow furrowed. "You could've just said no."

"What?"

"To the concert. You didn't have to run away."

That's the last time I storm out of a room in the middle of a conversation. "What concert?"

"New Nostalgia? In April?" His cheeks flush as he shifts his gaze down to his shoes. "I have an extra ticket since Stella decided to spend her spring break back home instead, but if you're busy, or you don't want to go, it's fine. I get it."

He launches into a new line of thought before I can process what he's said. "I knew this would be a bad day to do this. But we're going to be heading home soon and I thought, hey, maybe now's the time to finally ask him, and clearly that was a stupid idea, so—"

Over his shoulder, I spot her. Maya steps out from behind the chimney, closing one eye as she prepares to take aim, Andy right beside her. Their target is clear, and my stomach twists so painfully I almost double over.

"I need to go," I say, interrupting Julian midsentence.

All the color drains from him. It tears at me, but I can feel guilty later. I can think about what all of this, the invitation, the song, the everything about us, means then too.

"O-okay," he croaks out, sounding so close to tears that it makes *me* want to cry.

If Maya doesn't kill me, the look on Julian's face will. Everything that makes him so uniquely wonderful—the light in his eyes, the pink in his cheeks, the warmth in his smile— fades at once. We're those ten-year-olds again, standing on opposite sides of the battlefield, waiting to get hurt.

"I'm sorry," he adds.

I've never wanted to apologize more than I do in that moment. But I bite my tongue when I spot Maya gearing up to throw the first set of balloons. If I'm lucky, he'll go back inside. If I'm even luckier, he'll speak to me again.

For once, luck is on my side. He turns on his heels without another word, slamming the door behind him seconds after Maya launches her first attack.

The onslaught isn't as painful as I would've thought. Besides the smell, the blood feels oddly soothing on my still-sore body. The snap of the balloons bursting against my cheek, waist, and arms, stings more than the impact itself. The smell *is* horrendous, though. It's so far up my nose I don't think I'll ever be able to smell clearly again.

Either minutes or hours go by when a hand closes around my wrists, yanking me forward. I can hardly see through the gunk clinging to my eyelashes, tripping over myself as Maya drags me into the woods. Breaking my neck on an overgrown tree stump wouldn't be a bad solution at this point, though.

"What's wrong with you?!" she shouts once she's dragged me out of sight. "We had him!"

"I told you Stella and Henry weren't home." I wipe my face with my sleeve, blinking blood out of my eyes. "Why didn't you call it off?"

"Are you being serious right now?" She storms up to me, chest to chest, nose to nose. "You're *defending* him?"

Seeing her like this used to scare me, because I can't stand when she's mad at me. Today, I hold my ground. "He had nothing to do with what happened, Maya."

He had nothing to do with everything. The chowder incident. The cheating. Suck-o. But telling her about Suck-o means unraveling their entire history. How they've let themselves be bulldozed by their father into following plans they never wanted, and harboring hate for someone they barely knew. And I still don't trust that she won't use it against them.

"That doesn't change who he is," she sneers. "At the end of the day, he's still one of them."

But he's not. The Julian that I know is so unlike the person I expected him to be. He's kind, and respectful, and thoughtful. He's a bit of a dork, tripping over himself and getting flustered so easily and endearingly it makes my cheeks ache.

He has this way of listening that makes everything you say feel like it's exactly what he needed to hear. And he has those eyes. Those goddamn eyes that make me feel the most comfortable type of uneasy.

"That isn't fair, Maya," I reply.

"None of this is fair, Devin."

She's right. None of it is fair—to us or to them. We're both being forced to play a game we never should've been a part of. But isn't that what this plan is all about? Blurring the lines between what is and isn't fair?

Maya brushes past me with enough force to smack me against a tree, storming back toward the cabin without another word. She's fast when she's determined, and even faster when she's angry. She ignores me calling her name, slamming the door. I catch it before it can close and follow her inside. If I'd been a few seconds slower, it would've smacked me right in the face.

"Are we going to talk about this, or are you just going to be dramatic and ignore me until I go back to California?" Probably not the best way to open a civil discussion with your short-tempered sister, but I'm *really* tired of having to play this stupid, pointless game.

It does get her to stop, though. "I'm not being dramatic." She whips around, pointing a finger into my chest. "You may have forgotten everything they did to us, but I haven't. And if you don't want to be on our side anymore, that's fine. But stop trying to play on two teams. That's not how this works."

"So, what? Not being an asshole makes me a bad person now? Being *friends* with someone makes me your enemy?"

I know, I *know* I shouldn't argue with her. But I'm not

perfect, and I'm not going to let her stand there and accuse me of being anything but loyal to our family. Not wanting to hurt someone I care about doesn't make me a traitor.

"You're either on our side or you're not." Her finger turns into a palm, shoving me toward the door. "And you've clearly already made your choice."

"Maybe I don't want to be on your team," I shout, digging an even deeper grave. "A team that has to cheat to win isn't a team I want to be on."

I've spent so long mourning the family we used to be that I forgot who we are now. One last vacation won't bring me and Maya back together. Not when we're as warped and broken as the wood beneath our feet.

My reply makes her laugh, cruel and cold. "That's rich considering what side you're choosing." She nods her head to the Seo-Cookes' house.

"I'm not picking a side. I'm choosing to be mature for once." I push her hand away from me, standing my ground. "And weren't you the one who wanted me to spend time over there in the first place? This was all *your* idea; you don't get to be upset with me for seeing it through."

"I didn't tell you to fall in love with Julian, you idiot!"

My brain short-circuits.

Every argument I had locked and ready to fire falls apart, leaving me with fragments of the things I meant to say. My mouth hangs open. And that's enough of an answer for her.

"I . . . I didn't . . . I don't even *like* Julian," I finally reply with as much conviction as I can muster.

She blows me off with a roll of her eyes, shaking her head

as she turns toward her room. "Fine, Dev. Tell yourself whatever you need to hear."

"But—"

"But what, Devin?" She stops in her bedroom doorway. "Say I'm wrong. Tell me that you haven't been hiding things from me."

I can't.

So she slams the door in my face.

CHAPTER SIXTEEN

Andy must've filled Dad in—he knows to go to Maya's room first when he and Isabel get home. I left my door open on the off chance Maya decides she wants to speak to me again sometime this century. Dad stilled in the hallway, nodding when he caught my eye.

"Quédate aquí," he whispered, like I have somewhere else to go.

Their voices are muffled through the thin wood of her door, but I can still hear him pleading and her shouting. With her therapist, she's (mostly) learned to work through her anger in ways that don't build up to outbursts. This is the kind of meltdown she reserves for especially enraging occasions—breakups and bad grades. Failed love and failed tests. This isn't a breakup, I tell myself, chewing on my lower lip until it hurts. Siblings always make up. *We* always make up. Even after she ruined my favorite T-shirt in the fourth grade. Even after I accidentally read her diary. After every fight and bruise, we found our way back to one another.

Then why does this time feel so different?

The sun has set by the time Dad comes to me. I shove my sketchbook under my pillow when his shadow stretches across the floor. He's worn down, as if he's aged ten years in the span of one conversation. He closes the door, locking it before sitting down on the edge of my bed. This is a practiced routine, the post-sibling-fight talk. Sometimes he and Mami would flip a coin to see who would take who because the two of us were too much for one person. My instinct is to explain my side of the story as soon as he walks in the door, but I bite my tongue. He's shouldering two burdens tonight. I owe it to him to make it easy.

"Your sister's pretty upset."

I want to say, "Yeah, we're not sitting alone in the dark for our health," but instead I just say, "I know."

Dad sighs, long, drawn out, and tired. "It's a good thing you did, standing up for him."

I peek up from my hoodie cocoon. "Really?" Dad's the last person I'd expect to be on my side.

He nods, rubbing at the circles beneath his eyes before facing me. "What they did to Maya was horrible, but you knew better than to fight fire with fire. And I should've taught you that a long time ago, but I let my ego get the best of me." He rests a hand on my knee. "I'm glad you were mature enough to see that, though."

The tears start welling faster than I can control them. I

didn't need to hear that I was right, or that Dad was proud of me. Knowing that I don't need to feel guilty for feeling something other than contempt for Julian is enough.

"I should've been honest with you from the start of this whole trip." Dad pulls his hand away. My nerves come rushing back, settling in my stomach at the somber expression on his face.

"About what?"

He shakes his head, pinching the bridge of his nose and closing his eyes. "Your sister . . . She's been having a hard time lately. With you in California now."

My throat locks, so dry it burns. Dad stops me when I open my mouth, holding his hand up to let him finish.

"She's happy for you, we all are, and you know that. It's just . . . she misses you. After your mom, and the move, you two held on to each other so hard. It felt good, knowing you would always have each other. But she's worried, Dev. She said you can take days, weeks sometimes, to reply to her texts. You don't FaceTime like you used to. If this mentorship goes your way, she thinks maybe you'll stop coming home as often."

"I wouldn't—"

"I know you wouldn't, mijo," he interrupts, taking my hand. "But *she* doesn't know that. You two have been together since the day you were born. It's been hard for her, learning how to adjust."

The cold shoulders, the scoffs whenever I brought up California, the eye rolls every time I focused on my application instead of listening to her. At CalArts, I was so worried about catching up, so obsessed with trying to be like everybody else, that I shut out the one person who could've talked me through it. And even now I was too stupid and hung up on my own selfish goals that I hadn't stopped to ask myself *why* my sister was pulling away. I pulled away first.

"Isabel and I thought this trip would help," Dad continues. "Coming here, to this place you both loved so much. And at first, we thought it was working. Everything with the games . . . It felt just like old times. Maya looks so much like your mom sometimes, it . . ." He trails off, shaking off a buried memory. "We thought it was bringing you two together again, but . . . I guess we only saw what we wanted to see."

That makes two of us.

"I'm not saying you have to break up with Julian, or anything like that," he reassures. "I know I've been hard on the guy, but he really doesn't seem as bad as I thought. You should've seen him after you and Maya left. Got all up in his siblings' faces, shouting to the high heavens before laying into that boy in the overpriced polo shirt. Dios mío, he sounded like my mother." He chuckles softly, and I do too.

The thought of Julian is comforting. More comforting than it should be.

"Try to talk to her. Not today—you know she always needs time to cool down—but later. And have fun. I know the games mean a lot to you both and how complicated that must feel this year. Everything will be okay, win or lose. It would be tough, but losing this place doesn't mean we're losing her too." He fingers the gold chain around his neck, Mami's wedding band dangling at the end of it. "Took a while for me to accept that too." He nudges my shoulder with his own. "Don't let a game ruin what you have here." He points to his heart, then to Maya's room. "¿Entiendes?"

I nod because I don't trust my voice not to crack, and wipe my nose with my sleeve.

"We're proud of you. Never forget that," he adds more sternly. "Seeing you work so hard on this stuff for your mentorship . . . kinda makes me want to pull out some of those projects we left in the shed."

"You should," I say. "Give Mr. Cooke a run for his money."

Dad laughs, slapping me on the back. "Not this time. These'll just be for me."

We fist-bump before he ruffles my hair and heads into the hall, looking a bit less weary than when he came in.

He pauses. "Maybe take another shower. You smell like a slaughterhouse."

I've already taken two, but I give him a thumbs-up. My scalp is as raw as my chewed up lower lip, but hey, third time's the charm, right?

Dad closes the door with a promise to bring dinner once it's ready, and I'm left alone with my thoughts again.

I pull out my sketchbook. The latest sketch is still bare bones, but it makes my heart flutter the way none of the other pieces I've worked on have. For the first time, it feels like I'm creating something that might *really* define who I am, and what I can do as an artist. It may not be as flashy or high concept as the pieces I'll be up against to win over Professor Cardarelli, but like everything that lives in my sketchbook, it doesn't have to be. Because that's not what this piece is about.

A boy with untamable hair, a jaw carved by angels, and the most kind and wonderful smile I've ever known, gazing up at the starlit sky. A portrait that bottles every complex emotion I've felt about its subject, of a moment I'll always want to remember.

Okay . . . Maya may have had a point.

CHAPTER SEVENTEEN

I don't know if it's the guilt, regret, or longing, but I can't sleep.

My mind isn't allowed to wander unsupervised anymore. Every time it does, it goes somewhere it shouldn't. A slew of ASMR videos make me drowsy, but something always wakes me up, prickling down my spine until all the exhaustion melts from my body.

One can only go down so many YouTube rabbit holes. After seven true-crime videos in a row, I'm a new kind of nervous, because hello, we're in a remote cabin in the middle of the woods. How have we not revisited the possibility of an ax murderer in our midst? I shift over to music once I've figured out the perfect escape route in case the potential murderer decides to attack tonight.

I find my way to New Nostalgia without thinking, hovering over the title of the song Julian had played earlier. I hit play and settle into my blanket cocoon, cranking up the volume to drown out Andy's snoring.

It's easier to connect with the lyrics this time. On a closer listen, it's not really about a giant squid. Well, it is, but it's also about regret. About hurting someone you barely knew and falling slowly for them in the aftermath.

I'm only halfway through the song when I smash the Next button, unable to make it through to the end. It's too on the nose, as if it transcribed the static that rings in my ears whenever I think about Julian into lyrics and melodies. The next song isn't as loaded, a more upbeat track about new love in the spring. It takes three more songs until my heart slows down and I'm able to think coherently again. New Nostalgia's songs all sound a bit similar, but they're the type of catchy I won't be able to get out of my head for weeks.

After streaming the album twice over, skipping *that* song both times, I text Julian.

> Hey

> I'm really sorry about today.
> I was distracted by family stuff

Leaving it there doesn't feel like enough. Less is more when it comes to texting, but I don't know how to keep from word vomiting.

> are all of New Nostalgia's albums this heavy on
> the ocean creature imagery? or was this album a
> one-off?

219

> that said the amount of
> ways they managed to make octopus
> rhyme is very impressive

It's not an ideal way to bridge the gap between us following this afternoon. I could've led with the truth, but this sounds way better than "Hey, sorry I shut you down today; I had to protect you from a literal bloodbath." He doesn't owe me kindness, though, especially not after blowing him off. So I set my phone on my nightstand, not expecting a reply.

But his response comes almost immediately.

> Just this one. But their last album had
> a bunch of metaphors involving goats?
> Maybe they're very into animal imagery
> in general

I snort, double-checking that I haven't woken Andy up before hiding my phone beneath my comforter. While his reply is clearly casual, he didn't acknowledge the apology either. Maybe he's still pissed?

I'm halfway through typing out a response when I remember the time. With the exception of the night we'd spent at Mami's secret pier, I've never seen or heard from Julian past sundown. I assumed he's one of those gremlin people who can't be seen or fed after dark, which is fair considering his dad makes him get up at the ass crack of dawn every day.

> what're you still doing up? aren't you supposed to be waking up in three hours for a jog or hot yoga or something?

Ha ha. I'm taking the morning off. Watched a horror movie with Stella and now I can't sleep. The clothes on my desk chair are too suspicious.

The thought of him cowering under his own comforter makes me laugh so hard I have to cover my mouth, sure that I've woken up Andy this time. But thankfully he's as knocked out as ever.

> be careful, I heard deaths by clothing are on the rise

Well, guess I'm a goner. It's been nice knowing you. Mourn me for 30 days before you find a new fake lover.

I bite back a grin, holding my fist up to my mouth. Why can't everything be this easy? No drawn-out apologies, no explanations, just moving on as if nothing happened.

He sends another message before I can reply.

Why are you up so late?

I sigh, setting the phone down on my chest while I consider how to respond. Writing novel-length messages isn't my forte, and I don't know how to convey tone over text yet. Ultimately, I settle on something that isn't entirely off base.

> bad dream, can't fall back asleep

As nice as it is to have Julian to distract me from myself, he's bound to fall asleep any second...

> Wanna go for a drive?

I blink the sleep out of my eyes, double-checking the time. Why does Julian want to go for a drive at 2 a.m.?

> seriously???

> Yeah! Not like we've got anything better to do.

Fair enough. While I don't want to leave the comfort of my bed, the thought of seeing Julian again after the day I've had feels simultaneously terrifying and soothing.

> sure, why not

> 😃😃😃😃😃😃😃😃😃

> Pick you up in ten

My stomach flutters as I rush to the bathroom to make myself look presentable. There's not much I can do when my eyes are red rimmed, the skin beneath them purpled and heavy with exhaustion. I'm the perfect picture of a night gone wrong. All I can do is hope Julian won't look too closely.

The rest of the house is fast asleep, snores echoing through the halls as I tiptoe out the front door. One wrong move and I can add a grounding to the heap of disasters I've been through today.

Julian's parked out front with more energy than anyone should have at this hour. He's playing out a passionate finger drum solo on the steering wheel, mouthing along to a rock song I don't recognize.

"How are you still so awake?" I ask around a yawn.

"Pure adrenaline from the fear of someone hiding under my bed and murdering me," he explains casually, turning down the radio once I'm buckled in. "Also coffee. Lots of coffee."

"You drank coffee in the middle of the night?"

He scoffs as he starts up the car and pulls out of the driveway. "You would've too if you'd seen that movie."

True. The last time Maya and I watched a horror movie together, we spent the next two weeks sleeping on each other's floors because every shadow scared the life out of us.

"So, what's the plan?" I ask, stretching myself out. "Drive off into the sunset? Cross state lines?"

The road is as dark as the night he drove me home from the country club. Thinking back on that night feels odd, especially when I remember how afraid I was of someone who's actually harmless. Something in me is still afraid of Julian, but it's not the same. It's the kind of fear I'm willing to face.

Julian flashes a radiant smile, taking his eyes off the road long enough to meet mine. That's another thing I'm not afraid of anymore. Looking at him. And the things I feel when I do.

"I'm taking you to the greatest place in the known universe."

• • •

The greatest place in the known universe, it turns out, is a twenty-four-hour diner.

Julian takes us thirty minutes outside of Lake Andreas, driving down sleepy suburban roads until we're on the highway. A blinding neon sign welcomes us to AL'S DINER: SERVING ALL THE BEST PANCAKES AT ALL THE BEST TIMES. Julian hops out of the car, racing to the passenger side to whip my door open with a flourish.

"This is the greatest place in the known universe?" I ask skeptically.

"Shut up and prepare to have your mind blown."

The counters are sticky with long-dried maple syrup and the booths are torn at the seams, leaking cotton stuffing onto the checkerboard floors. The air is thick with the scent of fresh coffee and the crackle of bacon. Frank Sinatra croons from a radio beside the cash register. Julian greets the elderly waitress behind the counter like an old friend, stopping to chat with her about her grandson's first year at basketball camp before guiding me to a nearby booth. There's only one other patron, a trucker huddled over a mug of coffee and a platter of eggs, but Julian still picks a secluded table tucked away in a corner.

"The pancakes are their thing, but you *have* to try the milkshakes—they're wild. Or if you're not into breakfast foods—although if you aren't, I'm going to have to seriously reconsider this relationship—then the burgers are great. Or the disco fries. Apparently, that's a New Jersey thing—the owner grew up there. You haven't lived until you've had French fries smothered in mozzarella and gravy."

The menu is overwhelming, which is saying a lot considering how often our family goes to The Cheesecake Factory. The thick booklet spans from omelets to surf and turf to an assortment of holiday specials, ranging from Christmas ham to something called the Reindeer Special. The items start to blur together as I scan the pancake selection. What's the difference between a Reese's Pieces Extravaganza and a Peanut Butter Explosion?

"Why don't you order for us?" I suggest, setting my menu aside. Julian's clearly the expert.

He beams, happily accepting the challenge before waving over the waitress, Judy. He keeps it simple, ordering a cup of coffee for himself (which I don't protest, even though I'm sure he's had more than enough caffeine for one night), disco fries to share, and two shakes. Vanilla for him, mint chocolate for me.

It probably says something about my standards that a boy remembering my favorite flavor of ice cream makes my heart race.

Julian clinks his coffee mug against my shake after Judy returns with our drinks. "To not sleeping."

"To not sleeping," I echo, watching Julian savor his first sip. "Do you make a habit out of going to diners in the middle of the night?"

"I guess you could say that," he replies, cradling the mug close to his chest. "We used to come up here every weekend for breakfast. Mom can't cook eggs to save her life. But it's usually just me now," he says with a half-hearted shrug, letting go of his mug to start rearranging the sugar packets.

"Food's that good, huh?"

He nods weakly. "It is. But it's comforting too. Reminds me of when things weren't complicated . . . well, when they were less complicated. Plus, it's the only place that's still open past midnight, and sometimes I *really* need to get out of the house."

I groan, slouching against the table. "Tell me about it."

Julian bites his lip, tapping his fingers against his place mat and peeking at me from beneath his lashes. He looks away the moment I catch him eyeing me, shifting his gaze to the TV in the corner.

"You look like you're getting ready to tell me that my dog died," I say after Julian cautiously peeks at me again.

He curls in on himself, flushed down to his collar at having been caught. "You *look* like you just found out your dog died."

"Harsh." But fair. I probably look worse than that, to be honest. Fighting with your sister *and* processing your complicated emotions for someone you're supposed to hate is a lot to handle in one day. Also, I'm more of a cat person. "It's been a weird day."

Julian runs a finger along the rim of his mug, tendrils of steam bending around his fingertip. "Because I asked you to go to a concert with me, or because you got assaulted by water balloons filled with what I'm guessing was either real animal blood or puréed beets?"

I choke on my shake, narrowly covering my mouth before it sprays out all over the table.

"Y-you saw?" I ask between coughs into my sleeve, the corners of my eyes watering.

His grin is coy as he leans across the table to pat me on the back. "I did." He waits until I've made it through the coughing fit to slump back into his seat. "Would've been hard not to. It's not every day that someone stages a sneak attack in your driveway."

"Sorry," I mumble, pushing through the ache in my chest. Guess that's why he was willing to talk to me again. "I tried to stop her, but . . ." I trail off, shrugging in defeat.

"I get it," he replies, eyes falling to my place mat. "It's what we deserve."

"Not you, though." I shift forward, stomach pressed against the edge of the table, our hands a hairsbreadth apart. Every part of me itches to get closer. "You weren't involved."

"But I could've stopped them. If I'd paid more attention, I probably would've seen that something was up." He curls in on himself, pulling his hands back and pushing them deep into the pockets of his cardigan. "Stella and Henry really are sorry, though. I know that doesn't mean much coming from me, but . . . I told them about the jacket, the one Maya was wearing. It was your mom's, right?"

I nod slowly, stomach clenching at the memory. The confirmation makes Julian stall, like we're giving a moment of silence out of respect.

"They want to apologize to her," he says, "but I can understand if she doesn't want anything to do with us."

The idea of not just one, but *two* Seo-Cookes apologizing

to us should be laughable. If this were any other year, I'd claim to see right through them and laugh in Julian's face. I'd brush it off as a decoy for yet another prank, a trick to get us to lower our guard. But because this is the weirdest month of my life, I smile.

"Thanks for taking a bullet for me," Julian adds. "Or balloon."

A little more physical contact won't kill me, so I knock my ankle against his. "That's what fake boyfriends are for."

The lamp flickers to full brightness, bathing our corner of the diner in harsh fluorescent lighting. Everything grows smaller, more intimate, like there's no one else in the world but us.

"Can I ask you something personal?"

"Sure." He goes to take a sip of coffee but pauses with the mug halfway to his lips. "Unless it's my social security number. Only my fake husbands get access to that."

"There goes that plan," I tease, taking a second to calm my racing heart before asking the question that's nagged me since the night of the chowder incident. "Liam said he broke up with you?"

It shouldn't matter, and it doesn't. Not really. The semantics of Liam and Julian's relationship aren't any of my business, and I don't have any interest in knowing more about Liam than I need to. And yet . . . I haven't been able to shake off what Liam said since he hissed it at me. Julian—frustrating, confusing, and strangely wonderful—has trusted me with a lot worse than the details of a breakup. It's what sets him apart from his siblings, and the boy I knew all those years ago. This Julian's never acted like he has something to hide from me.

He runs one hand along his arm as he lets out a long, slow sigh.

"I'm sorry, you don't have to answer that. Too personal," I say in one swift breath before downing enough milkshake to give me brain freeze.

"No, it's fine," he replies, eyes on his place mat. "He did. Break up with me."

There's a bitterness in him that I've never seen before. Beyond sadness or anger. Disappointment, maybe?

The thought of a selfish blowhard like Liam dumping someone like Julian seems impossible. People like Liam are meant to be dumped once the glitter of their bank account wears off. They're not supposed to dump kind, gentle, sweet boys who make your heart flutter with a single latte.

"Apparently, he doesn't 'do' relationships. Or, not with guys like me, I guess," he mutters. "He was always complaining that I held his hand too tight, or I picked the wrong movie to watch, or I wouldn't remember to keep his favorite snacks in the house. . . . I told Dad it was my idea, though. I thought if he knew . . . he'd find some way to blame me for screwing up things for him with Liam's dad." His frown ticks into a bitter smirk. "Like he didn't ruin that all on his own."

I nod slowly. "So, why's Liam still lurking around if he dumped you? Why not go be a bachelor on a yacht in Ibiza, or something?"

Julian laughs, but it's not enough to keep the tension from washing over him again. "He wanted someone to have 'fun' with while he was in town, no strings attached." He stares at the dark, desolate highway beyond the window. "People like him aren't used to not getting what they want."

And here I thought it wasn't possible to dislike Liam more than I already do. I'm not a violent person, but I hope he stubs his toe every night for the next year. No, next decade.

"Liam's an idiot," I say, because I can't let the silence linger. Not when there are so many things I want to say sitting on the tip of my tongue. "I mention something once and you always remember it." I gesture to my milkshake. "And you're not even my real boyfriend."

The corners of his lips tug upward as he starts to fold the edges of his place mat. I can just make out the pink dusting the apples of his cheeks. His hand is so close to mine it aches not to reach out and close the distance.

"Some things are worth remembering."

Okay, that was pretty swoon-worthy.

We're not touching, but we still recoil when Judy returns with our fries, tucking our hands under our thighs and keeping our legs to our respective sides of the table. This far away from the lake we don't have to pretend to be something we aren't. Judy winks at Julian as she sets the plate down, pinching his cheek before returning to work. The red mark stands out on his already flushed cheeks.

When I tear my eyes away from my milkshake, Julian's already done the honor of spearing a fry from the center of the plate, dripping with gravy and coated in cheese, holding it up to my mouth. "Get ready, your life's never going to be the same after this bite."

"You have a thing for French fries, don't you?" I tease with a raised brow.

"Why wouldn't I? They're the best food."

Now's not the time to get into why I'm a mozzarella stick

man myself. But if anyone has the power to convert me to the fry side, it's him. I open my mouth wide and accept the forkful. The heavens don't open up, and my life is still as confusing as ever, but it's a damn good first bite. Gooey cheesy goodness and the salty tang of gravy.

"Pretty good," I reply.

"Pretty good? That's it?" Julian shakes his head in outrage, pulling the plate closer to his side of the table and spearing an extra cheesy fry for himself.

Right before he can bite down, I snatch the fry off his fork for myself. "I've had better."

Julian reaches forward, wiping gravy off my lower lip. "Oh really?"

The touch makes me freeze, my mind going into overdrive as I struggle to decide whether I want to lick the pad of his thumb, kiss him, or stab him with my fork. "Mmm-hmm," I manage to croak out, the sound a garbled mess.

Before I can retaliate, Julian leans back in his seat with a satisfied smirk. I snatch up my milkshake, taking a long sip and letting the brain freeze dull my frazzled nerves.

"I happen to know a very talented chef," I say once I've composed myself again. "He makes these kimchi fries . . ." I let out a low whistle. "Once you have them, no other cheesy potato compares."

Julian smiles around his fork, trying and failing to hide his rosy cheeks behind his hands. "He sounds like a prick."

"Oh, he definitely is." The light flickers again, a momentary darkness. We lean in, knees touching under the table, hanging on to the edge of our seats. "But he's all right sometimes."

I've never pulled an all-nighter before. I'd rather not make a habit out of doing something that involves this much caffeine, but if all-nighters mean nights like this one, I can make some unhealthy exceptions.

Julian talks me into my first cup of coffee. The second one is all me. The third one is a mistake, but my eyes are starting to droop, and I don't want to fall asleep. Reenergized by greasy carbs and to-go iced lattes, Julian and I finally leave Al's at a quarter to four with full bellies and jittery hands. We drive aimlessly and sing along to an embarrassingly sappy playlist Julian made for an ex until our throats are hoarse, moving onto air guitar solos and slapping our hands against the dashboard when our voices refuse to keep up.

Winding roads and dimly lit streets lead us to the north side of the lake, only a few miles away from Allegheny Park. A behemoth of a waterslide towers over the tops of the trees, lit up by a spotlight even though the park is closed for the night. If I'd spotted it weeks ago, it would've made me drool, and Maya and I would've found a way to sneak in without tickets. Getting to know Liam may have soured all things Allegheny Park, but the thought of going doesn't interest me much anymore. I loved Lake Andreas when I was five, when it was bursting with new faces and the possibility of adventure. And I think I might love it even more now with its frayed, yellowed edges.

We settle down on the grass, leaning against mighty oak trees. The adrenaline that had been thrumming through our veins has run its course, so we sip our iced lattes slowly, stretching the caffeine as far as it'll take us. Julian is opposite me, closing his eyes and playing music off his phone because we're too exhausted to make conversation.

Bringing my sketchbook had seemed like a silly decision at the time, but I'd brought it just in case. You never know when you might need something to occupy your hands. I balance it on my lap, straining my eyes until the page comes into view. Having Julian in front of me as a reference is helpful. Even better with his eyes closed. There are lots of things I'd missed while working off memory—the scar on his upper lip, the one strand of hair above his left ear that never seems to behave.

"Wow. What a handsome young man," Julian says, voice weighed down by sleepiness and warm against my cheek.

The pencil flies out of my hand when I realize how close he is. I'd been so focused on the sketch that I hadn't noticed him waking up or coming over to sit beside me. The ache in my eyes eases as the glow of the rising sun slowly stretches toward us.

"It's the latest installment in my 'obnoxious hot guys with huge egos' series."

I don't need the sun to tell that he's smirking; I can hear it in his voice. "So you *do* think I'm hot."

I press myself farther back against the tree with a sigh. "I think you have a serious case of selective hearing. You should get that checked out."

He laughs, quiet and adorable, crawling back to the tree opposite me.

I could tell him to stay, but I don't. I could say something else, but I don't do that either.

"You should use the portrait of your mom," he says once he's settled back down against his tree. "For the mentorship."

It takes a second for me to ground myself and shake off the jitters that bubble up whenever Julian gets too close. "You think?"

"Yeah." There's a hint of a smile playing at the corners of his lips, his eyes focused over my shoulder, his mind somewhere else. "When I saw that portrait, I just . . . *got* it. All these intense feelings . . . like I was there and knew her—like, *really* knew her." He holds up his index finger. "And I never 'get' art."

The undignified snort I let out makes him laugh again and me blush down to my toes. It's a welcome distraction as I sit with what he's said, smiling to myself as I consider the drawing of him, wondering if it had the same effect on him.

"Did it scare you?" he asks when I don't respond, knees pulled up to his chest. "Art school? Moving to California?"

"Shitless," I reply, one of the few times I don't have to overthink a reply to him. "*Beyond* shitless. And it still does, every day." A moment of pause as I set down my pencil. "Does it scare you?"

He nods, picking at blades of grass until they pull free. "Sometimes it doesn't feel worth it. I could probably work in business management or consulting, if I studied hard enough. Not at Princeton." He yanks the blade between his fingers, earth coming up with it. "But somewhere else. Play it safe, be miserable, probably. But safe. Stable."

"Yeah, I get that."

It's an argument I've had with myself dozens, if not hundreds, of times over this past semester. Late at night and during class and every time I found myself panicking over the stack of unfinished assignments on my desk.

Dad and Mami didn't give themselves the luxury of options because they knew it meant they could pass them down to us instead. Medicine. Engineering. Stable work, stable money. The kind of money that could help get you out of the pit you dug to get the job in the first place. It didn't matter that Mami liked literature more than biology or that Dad wanted to design comics instead of buildings. They gave up passion for practicality so that I wouldn't have to.

And I'm barely staying above water.

There'll never be enough words in either of our languages for me to thank them for putting our lives ahead of theirs before they even knew us. But even luxuries come with fine print. Nightmares in the form of Dad's voice. A question I'm terrified he'll ask me someday.

Are you sure you made the right choice?

What if I'm not good enough? What if I fail at the one thing I thought was meant for me? What if we sank all this money into a dream I can't deliver on? Maya gave up on her dream when she saw the price tag—why did I think I could still have mine? I can't even come up with a subject for a piece that's supposed to be about me. How can I expect to compete with people who've known they were going to be artists since they could hold a pencil?

What if my parents gave up their possibilities for me to pick the wrong one?

"It's weird," Julian says, pulling me back to the present. "I thought I'd feel better about giving up on the whole Princeton thing. But I think I'm just as scared of not knowing what I want to do as I was of doing something I'd regret."

"Whatever you decide to do, you're going to be amazing at it," I say, because at least that's something I'm sure of. "Since you're good at everything."

He chuckles, slow and soft like he's half asleep. "And you're going to be a great artist." He leans down onto the grass, stretching himself out until his head is resting beside my knee. His eyes twinkle in the darkness. "You already are."

I set my sketchbook beside him, Portrait Julian looking over his shoulder at his living, breathing counterpart. There's a sadness in Portrait Julian's eyes, as if he knows he'll never live up to the real thing.

Without thinking, I grip the corner of the page and rip it free. The sound cuts through my heart, makes me wince, but not as much as I thought it would. It was a good idea, but something like this, a piece that was closer to my heart than I ever intended for it to be, isn't right for the mentorship either. I'd rather let it live with him than let a stranger—albeit an impressive stranger—analyze it. Wonder who he was and what he meant to me when I'm not even sure myself.

He marvels at the drawing now that I've given it to him, blinking up at me with wide eyes.

Looking down at Julian, the real one, as the sun finally reaches us, his skin dewy and golden, I find the courage to say one of the hundreds of things I wanted to but couldn't.

"I made this list last year." I dig my phone out of my pocket, pulling open my Notes app. "Things I wanted to do in LA." Julian rolls over to watch me scroll up through all the restaurants Andy added, back up to the title of the list: DEVIN'S GREAT CALIFORNIA ADVENTURE.

"I haven't had a chance to cross anything off yet," I say as I scroll through the most touristy section: see the Hollywood sign, find Shrek's star on the Walk of Fame, look at the stores on Rodeo Drive (but don't go in, they'll know you're a broke college student). "Turns out art school is way harder and time-consuming than people think."

He gives me *that* smile. The one that makes every thought that isn't about him feel enormously insignificant.

If I were a stronger person, I'd lean down and kiss him until the sun finishes rising. Then kiss him again and again until we're back to where we began: alone in the middle of the night with the only person who matters.

But I'm not that person, so instead I say, "I thought maybe we could check some of them out. Before the concert. Or after. If you want."

I'm worried I'll break when he doesn't reply, reminding myself that he still doesn't owe me kindness after this afternoon. He takes my phone, sitting up and typing something before handing it back. He updated the title of the list.

DEVIN & JULIAN'S GREAT CALIFORNIA ADVENTURE

He smiles, knocking his knee against mine when my lips part. "I'd like that."

And, somehow, those three words make me feel more than any kiss ever has.

CHAPTER EIGHTEEN

Grudges are Maya's thing. She excels in many areas—hairstyling, dancing, knowing everything about everyone—but this is her specialty. One of the girls from her middle school clique accidentally forgot to text her an invitation to a sleepover; they haven't spoken since. After the "girls can't marry girls" incident with Titi Rosa, Maya refuses to acknowledge her existence.

Being on the receiving end of one of her grudges is daunting. She ices me out from training before the final crunch and avoids me in common areas as best she can. Usually I wouldn't question getting out of physical activity, but it feels like the final nail in my coffin. I'm not on our team anymore.

Instead, I spend my morning researching how long I can survive without food or water. Maya practically bites my head off every time we so much as breathe the same air for too long, so my best bet is staying in my room for as long as possible. According to Google, I have four days to either suck it up and learn to coexist with her in communal spaces or find a way to harvest rainwater so I don't die of dehydration.

My cavalry comes in the form of a text message from Julian.

> Want to come over?

We don't usually hang out on Wednesdays, but anything is better than sitting in my room contemplating starvation. While heading to Julian's doesn't exactly help my case with Maya, I can't bring myself to care. The past few days have been shitty, and I'm not walking away from the one thing that could make it worthwhile.

Julian's waiting for me on the deck, leaning against the back door. While he's not wearing his usual name-brand athleisure, his more standard jeans-and-a-button-down outfit is still more upscale than most of my wardrobe. His shirt does have tiny penguins on it, though. It's really cute, and I feel very catered to.

He perks up the moment he spots me, pushing off the door to meet me halfway. "Hi!"

"Hi," I reply, taking a second longer than I should to admire his bone structure.

He runs a self-conscious hand along his jaw. "Is there something on my face?"

"No," I answer quickly, my neck growing uncomfortably warm. "You, um . . . you look really nice." He always looks nice, and based on how hell-bent he is on proving that I think he's hot, he knows that. But when you're as perpetually nervous as I am, paying compliments always feels like pulling teeth.

Yet he smiles like he doesn't know it, his cheeks the loveliest shade of pink. "Thank you. You do too."

"Is there a reason you're out here waiting for me?" I ask. "Didn't think I could make it across the yard on my own?"

His left brow arches and the corners of his lips curl impishly. "There were some coyote sightings last week, and I've heard through the grapevine that you're the slowest runner in your family."

That should *not* be common knowledge. Leave it to Maya to spread the news that I'm terrible at exercise.

"I have a surprise for you, actually," Julian clarifies before I can reply.

It's my turn to raise a brow. "You have my attention."

"It's nothing super exciting, just something I thought might be fun—I mean, not fun—cool. Wait, not cool—"

I rest my hand on his shoulder, and he cuts short like a record scratch. "The last time you surprised me, you asked me to pretend to be your boyfriend." When he doesn't recoil from the touch, I press my luck, running my thumb along the collar of his shirt. "Anything will be cooler than that."

He runs his hand along my arm, letting it rest on top of my hand, holding it down to his heart. His is beating faster than mine. My hands tremble as he takes them in his, losing the confidence that kept me afloat two seconds ago.

"Close your eyes?"

"O-okay." Tentatively, I close them, leaving my lips slightly parted.

My heart echoes in my ears, pounding so loud I'm sure

he can hear it, but all he does is take my hands and tug me forward. I close my mouth, pressing my lips into a tight, thin line, and let him guide me. We haven't gone very far, probably not even past the kitchen, when Julian lets go.

"Don't peek," he warns, and I can hear his padded footsteps against the tile.

"If the surprise is that you're going to murder me, I should warn you that my Fitbit has a GPS tracker. The police will know exactly where to go."

His voice sounds farther away, likely from across the room. "If I wanted to murder you, don't you think I would've done it by now?"

I rock on my toes, palms beginning to sweat. "You could be playing the long game."

We must be in the kitchen, based on the sound of drawers opening and utensils clattering. His voice returns, whispering in my ear. "You're too entertaining to kill off yet."

I wipe my hands on my jeans. It's the only thing I can think of to keep them from shaking. My eyes fly open the second he tells me I can look, scanning the room to confirm that we're in the kitchen. Julian's on my left, nothing on my right. He nudges his head forward, telling me to look down.

"Is this . . ." I can't manage the last few words.

"It's probably not as good as your aunt's, and I know it's a few days late, but I thought I'd take a stab at it."

There's probably something cool or eloquent that I could say, but I'm at a loss.

Julian, someone I hated with every fiber of my being three weeks ago, has made me a tres leches cake.

"W-why?" The cake looks so much like the one Mami

used to make, down to the cherry smiley face, it makes me want to cry.

"You said Christmases are always hard, and . . . I thought it might make you smile." His own falters when I look up at him. Tears cloud my vision, blurring him at the edges. "Oh God, I'm sorry. I thought—"

I don't let him finish. Fuck caution, fuck sides, and fuck who we are and who we're supposed to be to each other. I've spent long enough afraid of pursuing what I want, so I do the one thing that scares me the most. The one real thing *I've* wanted to do since I first saw him at the grocery store.

I kiss him.

And it is so much better than the aimless daydreams and 3:00 a.m. musings, because Julian tastes like espresso, whipped cream, and endless possibilities.

Before I can doubt myself, Julian loops his arms around my waist and kisses me back with everything he has. The force of it knocks me back, so I wrap my arms around his neck, and trust that he won't let me fall.

"Hi," he whispers when we pull apart, as giddy and playful and smitten as I am.

"Hi." I would kiss him again, but I want to keep looking at those eyes.

This time, he kisses me. His fingers curl at the base of my neck and his thumb tilts my chin up until my lips meet his. "I've wanted to do that for a while now," he says against my lips.

The hesitation is gone when I take the lead, kissing him again, and again, and again, spelling the words I didn't get to say with lips and fingertips. *Me too.*

We kiss until the bitter tang of espresso on Julian's lips fades into the sharp sting of my peppermint lip balm. From slow to fast to too much to too little until all that's left is the thrum of our hearts and the hitch of our breath. When breathing becomes too necessary to put off, we stop and hold still. We're the type of people with the worst kind of luck, so I brace myself for the sound of footsteps or a jingling doorknob.

When we're left with nothing but silence, Julian pulls me back in. He presses soft, chaste kisses to my shoulder, up to my neck, and settling in the curve of my jaw. Lips on bare skin is *very* different from what I imagined it would be like, and six hundred times better. My lips part in a silent gasp when his teeth graze my skin, sharp but gentle. Like the start of our story.

There are so many games we still have to play, but it's enough for me to win this one. Our game was the longest, and our reward the sweetest.

"Do you want to—"

"Yes." I don't need to know what it is. I want everything Julian has to offer.

He rolls his eyes, but there's no malice behind it. "I was going to ask if you wanted to go to my room."

"Fuck yes," I amend, pulling him in for one last bruising kiss. "And bring the cake."

• • •

Julian's room isn't all that more private than the kitchen had been. We can hear the rumblings of a baseball game coming from Henry's room and the bass of a pop song from Stella's.

The bedrooms are all big enough to do backflips in, but no one thought to soundproof the walls. Where's the logic in that? But the door locks, and the air is thick with the scent of cinnamon and Earl Grey tea and something distinctly Julian, and that's all I can ask for.

Julian sets the cake on the edge of his desk, pushing aside a stack of books and laminated recipe cards. "We . . . uh . . . we don't have to do anything just because we're in here, but I figured it might be a little quieter." He's as red as the cherries. "We could eat cake, if you want."

Of course I want cake—if I didn't, I'd be concerned—but there's something I want more.

I close the distance between us, cradling that immaculate jaw before leaning in for a kiss as sweet as the smell of the room. My body speaks its own language—shy smiles, trembling hands, and longing glances that say what I can't. But Julian meets every push with a pull and every tug with a touch like this language was made for him too.

When I lean back, it's not because I want to stop—I'd gladly give up breathing if it meant kissing Julian longer—but because I really do want to try the cake.

I make myself at home on the edge of his bed, holding my greedy little hands out. "Cake, please."

Julian's too kiss-stunned to respond, blinking rapidly and shaking himself off before grinning. "As you wish."

He cuts two pieces, handing the bigger one to me. A man after my own heart. I can hear him suck in a breath while he watches me take my first bite. Having an audience while you eat hasn't gotten any less intimidating, but my confidence in Julian's abilities makes it easier.

It's amazing, obviously. Better than amazing. And while I may be evolving and all that, I still can't turn down an opportunity to tease Julian, so I scrunch up my nose and shake my head.

"Oh God, it's terrible. I'm sorry, I knew I added too much condensed milk. I can—"

"Julian." He stops apologizing, but I wait until his eyes meet mine.

I've had hundreds of tres leches cakes in my life, and even if Julian's still has the classic flavors that taste like childhood nostalgia, there's something special about knowing that this one is just for me. It makes the whipped cream lighter, the coconut smoother, the cherries sweeter, knowing that this only exists because Julian wanted to see me happy.

The familiar taste still brings back memories of Nochebuenas at Titi Rosa's, barbecues with my cousins, and the sound of Mami's laugh, but there's something new now too. Lying on the edge of the hidden pier, secrets whispered against cool night air, the glow of Julian's eyes as he watched the fireworks.

"Titi Rosa is going to be so pissed, because *this* is the best tres leches cake I've ever had."

Watching Julian's smile blossom puts every sunrise to shame.

"You're just saying that," he replies bashfully, staring at his own untouched plate.

I shake my head, taking our plates and setting them down on the nightstand. Kissing is great and all, but I'm not about to ruin a perfectly good cake because of it. "I don't just say anything," I whisper, then kiss him until he believes me.

"You've made a very compelling point," he chokes out when we come apart for air.

I know I have, but I can still drive this point all the way home. I lean across him to grab my plate, holding up a spoonful to his kiss-swollen lips. "See for yourself."

He doesn't seem to like being fed, wrinkling his nose in protest, but I don't give in. This is what he gets for how many times he's fed me. "Not bad," he says before he's done chewing.

I poke him with the spoon. "It's better than not bad and you know it."

He shrugs but accepts the second bite I offer him. "Should've used less condensed milk."

"Shut up and accept the compliment."

He drags the spoon out of his mouth with a pop that shouldn't be allowed to sound so sinful. "Make me."

Finally, a challenge that I will *gladly* accept.

CHAPTER NINETEEN

I never thought I'd say this, and I hope I never have to say it again, but . . . thank God for the Seo-Cookes.

Well, mostly Julian. Actually, just Julian. Thank God for Julian.

Having somewhere to go during the day makes the last few days of our trip bearable. Existing under the same roof as someone who hates your guts is emotionally taxing. Granted, Stella and Henry don't like me much either, but they hate me slightly less than Maya does right now. The day after what I've now affectionately dubbed Tres Leches Day, Henry even gave me a 'sup nod. That might've come from the lingering guilt over the chowder incident, but still. Undeniable progress.

Meanwhile, I can't get my own sister to so much as look at me. Breakfasts are torturous. Maya will stare at her cereal until I excuse myself and take my toast to my room. Dinners aren't as bad—at least I'm allowed to stay at the table—but watching Dad try and fail to get Maya to engage with me is painful for us both. She doesn't even lurk on the front steps when I come back from the Seo-Cookes' anymore, ready to pounce on me for information.

I'd feel guilty about not exerting any extra effort into reconciling with her if she hadn't made it clear she's not going to talk to me anytime soon. I don't see why I should have to subject myself to feeling unwelcome in my own home.

Now that Maya has dropped me as her spy, I'm free to come and go from the Seo-Cookes without needing to snoop through their dirty laundry. The afternoons post–Tres Leches Day pass by in a haze of cups of coffee, sketches on napkins, and dozens, maybe even hundreds of kisses. Kisses behind trees and in the back of parked cars. Kisses in the moonlight and kisses at sunrise. Fleeting kisses that leave me trembling and all-consuming kisses that make my skin ignite.

In between kisses, Julian and I let ourselves dream about California, about going to galleries and picnics on the beach and hikes through the hills—a testament to how much I like spending time with him. When I sit with those dreams for too long, they melt down slowly, achingly bittersweet as I wonder if they'll actually become realities. Lake Andreas is our bubble. A shabby but sweet utopia where we've convinced everyone that we're two lovestruck, star-crossed saps who can't get enough of each other.

But tomorrow we'll be back on opposite ends of the battlefield.

With Maya icing me out of all forms of communication, I'm not even sure if I'm competing with our family at the games. With her as our self-appointed leader, she could easily remove me from the roster the day of. Losing their slowest runner wouldn't be a major loss, but I *am* their best puzzle solver. And a team of five is always stronger than a team of four. I would never forgive myself if they lost because of me. I'm not their saving grace, but if we're going to let go of our cabin, then we should do it together. But maybe I've hurt Maya too deep for her to let me join them.

It's been easy to skirt around the games while I'm with Julian, but that doesn't stop it from nagging me every time we're together. That my home might belong to him by the end of tomorrow. That his dad wants to destroy it for a boat garage.

Our near future may scare the shit out of me, but I've spent enough time this year hung up on worrying about things I can't control. So I stop thinking about the future for once and start focusing on the present, savoring every bit of my newest routine. Mornings and afternoons without classes or mentorships or work study, drinking coffee with Julian in his kitchen, napping together on the couch in their den, listening to music I'm not sure if I like because it sounds good or because it makes him happy. The days don't have to be exciting. They just have to be with him. That's enough to make this trip feel worthwhile.

Like today's wild afternoon: eating leftover takeout and watching a low-budget horror movie about Santa's most murderous elf. For someone who's so easily scared, Julian has developed an unusual penchant for the terrifying during his quest to rot his brain. At this rate his favorite movie is going to be *The Exorcist*.

"Come on, that wasn't even scary!" I shout at the screen after Glitter the Elf takes a swing at his next victim with a candy cane sharpened into a knife. The most horrifying thing about this movie is the acting.

It's easy to feel brave with Julian squirming beside me, jumping at every sound. He spends more time buried in the dip where my neck meets my collarbone than he does actually watching the screen.

"Felt scary to me," Julian mumbles indignantly, nuzzling closer to me. Either he knows exactly what he's doing, or he needs to change up his taste in movies.

"That's because you're a wimp."

He pinches my side, which I definitely deserve, but he doesn't pull away. I shift my hand from the top of his knee to rest around his shoulders, pulling him in even closer. I had my reservations about watching *Glitter's Gut-tastic Christmas,* but with Julian tucked into me and my fingers tracing lazy circles along his arm, it's the best movie I've seen this year.

Light floods the den, ruining the following jump scare, but startling us enough to fly to opposite ends of the couch. Stella is standing at the top of the stairs, hands over her eyes.

"This is your warning to stop making out," she shouts. Neither she nor Henry have caught us in any PG-13 situations so far, and we'd all prefer to keep it that way.

Julian lets out an exaggerated sigh. "Is anyone dying?"

"No, but—"

"Then go away." He unpauses the movie and tugs me into his arms.

The minor display of affection isn't enough to get Stella to leave. She marches in front of the TV, thoroughly killing the mood, and waits until Julian begrudgingly pauses the movie to speak. "I'm hungry."

"And? There's food in the fridge."

Stella pouts. "Dad didn't go grocery shopping this week and all that's left are Henry's weird protein shakes."

Julian parts his lips as if to protest, but ultimately decides against it. "Order a pizza."

"Stop being a dick and give me one of your choco pies." She holds out her hand inches from Julian's face.

This is one of the few times he isn't carrying a stash around with him. He lets go of me to pull the pockets of his sweatpants inside out, holding his hands up in the air. "Sorry, fresh out."

She rolls her eyes, dropping her hand down to her side. "Then tell me where you keep them, and I'll get one myself."

"Nope. Absolutely not." He starts the movie, turning up the murderous screams to drown out her protest.

"Come on!" She lunges for the remote, and Julian only narrowly manages to push me out of the line of fire. The two of them wrestle over the remote until they tumble off the couch, Stella claiming victory after biting Julian's hand. "Hand them over."

Julian scowls, readjusting his shirt once he's back on the couch. "Devin, please go get her one."

I really don't want to get involved. I was already a split second away from having Stella's elbow shoved in my face. But I think I'm the saving grace here.

"Just tell me where they are," she snaps, the two of them staring each other down.

"No." Without breaking eye contact with her, Julian reaches for my hand. "If you know where they are, you'll start stealing them again."

There's a gentle pressure on my hand, his thumb against my palm. Along with making me a tres leches cake, Julian had entrusted me with the hiding spot for his beloved snack collection that same day. Turns out they're just under his bed.

They continue glaring at one another as I head toward the door. "I liked you two better when you were pretending to date," Stella says once I'm at the top of the stairs.

I'm sure Julian can handle arguing on our behalf, so I close the door behind me. The top-secret location isn't very top secret at all, but I still check over my shoulder to make sure I'm not being followed. I don't think our fledgling relationship could survive me accidentally giving up his choco pie hiding spot.

Wrenching out the plastic bin from beneath Julian's bed is easy enough. I push aside the old tennis trophies to grab two green tea and three plain (four for me and Julian, one for Stella), stuffing them into my pockets. Shoving the bin back into place is another story. It's hardly a fourth of the way in when it snags on something. A closer look confirms my suspicions that Julian isn't one of those rare teenagers who actually keeps their room neat. He just shoves everything under his bed. The culprit is a box that's slightly bigger than the hidden stash bin. It takes two good pulls to yank the black box free, sending me tumbling onto my butt.

When I sit up, I'm surrounded by small slips of paper, the box knocked onto its side. They're not like the note cards Julian sometimes writes his recipes on. They're smaller, edges jagged and creased. Notebook paper and Post-its, phrases scrawled hastily. I pluck one out from beneath my foot, a bright blue Post-it.

Mint chocolate

Is this like some kind of culinary mad lib? Curiosity piqued, I grab another one, a crumpled piece of paper with the spindly bits of the notebook still attached.

Allergic to pineapple and almonds (nonlethal, gives him a rash)

My throat tightens while I read, as if I've swallowed either of those things. What're the odds that someone else has those two specific allergies? I pick up another slip of paper.

Wakes up at 7 for training. Done by 10, sometimes 10:30 if he has extra laps. Usually nobody leaves the house past 9.

Okay, what the fuck is going on?

I collect every scrap and note I can find, gathering them into a pile. At first I try to keep count, but I lose track after thirty-three. They remind me of the flash cards I would always make before midterms. Thinking of myself as a subject worth studying makes my stomach churn. Despite my unease, I don't jump to conclusions yet. It doesn't look like his siblings wrote any of these—it's that same familiar chicken scratch. As much as he's grown on me, Julian *is* kind of a weird dude. This could be romantic, maybe. He cared enough about what I had to say to write it all down, so he wouldn't forget.

But then I find a new slip of paper, a list instead of a fact, and realize this is anything but romantic.

Winter Games Brainstorm

1. Find fishing wire to trip them during the 5K
2. Devin's afraid of spiders. Sneak them into his backpack before the 5K?
3. Tie their shoelaces together before the three-legged race (how would I distract them?)
4. Replace their marshmallows with cotton balls? (they'd probably notice)
5. Give Devin almond oil lotion, tell him it's sunscreen
6. Convince Stella to flirt with their stepbrother/ bring him to our side (she tried already, didn't work)
7. Try bicycling lessons again. Maybe he'll break his leg?

This one isn't just loopy scrawl. New handwriting litters the page, notes in the margins and between each line (*way too complicated, not bad, could you even pull this off?*). Bubbly, elegant handwriting and scratch that seems almost illegible.

Stella and Henry.

I'm going to be sick. The list crumples in my closed hand as I keel over, clutching my stomach while the room starts to spin. How did I miss this? How could I not see it coming? Were there signs at all, or did I only see what I wanted to? A boy who was different from the rest of his family. A boy who would set the past aside for me. To think, I'd let him lure me in with his honesty, and this whole time it was just an act.

I was right; he has changed. He became a better liar.

The uneasiness digs itself so deep beneath me I don't think anything can hurt more than this does. But then I spot a new note, still tucked inside the black box.

Makes tres leches cake whenever he misses his mom

And a message in his sister's handwriting.

this is good, look up recipe

Beneath it, the sketch I'd given him. I hold my art against my chest, willing it to become a part of me again. But it's too late, this piece of my heart doesn't belong to me anymore.

I'm not sure how much time passes. Seconds, maybe minutes. I can't bring myself to look at the rest of the notes, not when I know what they all must say. Every little thing I've told him, all the things I'd been so impressed that he'd remembered. My mind flashes back to that night at the diner, when I'd let myself fall because he told me that I was worth remembering.

I want to throw up.

"Hey, are you . . ." Julian's voice trails off the moment he steps into the doorway. He freezes in place, but I can't bear to look up at him. My eyes stay on the tres leches note, his shadow enveloping me. "Devin . . ."

The way he says my name used to make me feel weightless. Tonight it makes my blood boil.

"What is this?" I ask, even though I'm sure I've figured it out. But I want to hear him say it himself.

"I can explain." He kneels down beside me, covering the notes with his hands as if he can take it all back, as if

I haven't already seen everything. "These were just stupid ideas and—"

"What? What was the plan here?" My fist clenches around the crinkled paper.

"I . . . I thought I could come up with something for the games . . . through getting to know you," he confesses, reaching out to take my hand. I snatch it away before he can touch me. "I just . . . with Princeton, and Liam, and everything else with Dad, I thought maybe winning the games could be the one thing I didn't screw up. Something Dad could be proud of . . . for once."

That's what this was all about: winning. It has been since day one. I was the only one who was too stupid to see the truth.

"Was this always your strategy? Bait me with the Liam thing, then keep me around by being nice?"

He shakes his head, looking as though he's going to reach for me again, but keeps his distance when I retreat. "Just after you started coming over here." His head lowers in shame. "I figured two birds, one stone."

Everything hurts, but that stings the worst. I'd let myself think I was an endgame when I was just a means to an end.

"How much of this was lies?" I spit out through gritted teeth.

"None," he replies quickly.

"Lies of omission are still lies." If my righteous Catholic abuela taught me anything, it's that keeping secrets and telling lies hold the same weight.

He doesn't have a response for that, and I've heard enough anyway. He stays on the floor, kneeling beside the mess as I pick myself up. When I cross to the door, he leaps back into action, standing so quickly he nearly loses his balance.

"You and Maya were doing the same thing. That's why you were here. To look through our stuff."

I don't want to stop moving until I'm back in my room and under my covers, but I freeze, still unwilling to face him. "How do you know that?"

"Every time you came over, she'd blow up your phone asking if you found any dirt yet." A bitter edge to his voice. "You weren't exactly discreet."

I know how it must come across, but my heart knows there's a difference. That he chose to hurt me, and I pushed away my own sister just so I wouldn't have to do the same to him. "It wasn't my idea, and I didn't want to do it."

"But you still did."

Finally, I turn to him.

The pain dulls as rage takes over. "And I ended it!" I shout, the picture frames on the wall beside us rattling. "You *saw* me protect you instead of taking her side, and you still thought I was going to turn against you?"

My chest heaves as I pause for breath, launching into a new tirade before he can respond.

"And is that really so unfair? Trying to catch you doing something you shouldn't have been doing in the first place? All we wanted was to keep it fair this year, that's it. We bet our fucking cabin on this. Can you blame us for trying to save the last place where we have happy memories with our mom from being turned into your dad's goddamn boat garage?"

I lean down to grab a handful of paper from the pile

between us, waving it in Julian's face. "*This* is different." My eyes sting, tears clouding my vision, but I will myself not to cry. Not yet, not in front of him. "You wanted to hurt us. Hurt *me*. And you didn't care."

"Of course I cared." His voice cracks on the last syllable. "We didn't know. About the bet, at first, I swear. When you mentioned it that night at the pier, I called off the plan. That's . . ." He trails off, composes himself, then starts again. "That's where the chowder plan came from. Stella and Henry were pissed at me, at *you,* for the salami thing, and because the games meant something to us too. Working together as a family, with Dad. I know we never played fair, but at least we were playing together. And . . . I guess we missed that. But if we couldn't do anything at the games, then they wanted to make sure they got the last laugh. Even though that's fucked up and wrong and I'm *sorry.*"

"Why should I believe you?" I hold up the tres leches note. "I told you this less than two weeks ago."

This catches him off guard. "That wasn't . . . that was different."

There's no telling how far he's willing to go. Even if he really didn't know about the bet, about what we would lose just so he could get some brownie points with his dad, it doesn't matter. It doesn't change that I've been nothing but a pawn in his game since the beginning. We could stand here for hours, pulling apart the fact from the fiction, but what's the point? Our relationship has always been a lie.

I toss the note onto the ground with the rest of the slips of paper. All the small pieces that make up our story. "Doesn't look different to me."

I don't have enough energy to keep arguing. He doesn't chase after me or call out my name when I storm out of the room. If Stella or Henry spot me, they stay out of my way. I slam the door behind me with as much force as I can, willing the glass to shatter. It doesn't. I'm the only thing that's broken.

Of course, Maya's sitting in the kitchen when I finally make it back to our cabin. It'd be too easy for me to head straight to my room without running into the one person who saw this coming.

She peeks up from her sandwich, the first time she's actually acknowledged my existence this week. Her hard-set frown softens, but she doesn't say anything. My legs are unwilling to carry me the rest of the way to my room, keeping me in the doorway, locked under her gaze.

"You were right," I say, willing my body to move now. "He hasn't changed. Happy now?"

She stands up from the table, taking a tentative step toward me. "Devin . . ."

As badly as I want to tell her everything, I can't. My body finally unlocks, carrying me past her and out the front door to the one place I know I can be alone. When the door closes behind me, I fall apart.

CHAPTER TWENTY

Mami's pier is quiet. So quiet I'm not sure how long I've spent lying here, skimming my toes along the water. It's long enough that the sky grows dark, and my stomach starts to grumble, but I can't bring myself to head home yet. When there's a rustle in the bushes, I assume it's Dad coming to collect me, but I'm still not up for conversation. With how raw my throat feels I don't think I'd have much of a voice anyway.

"Devin?" Maya whispers.

"If you're here to say I told you so, then you can leave," I mutter, the words muffled by the cool evening breeze.

The wood creaks as she approaches me. "I'm not."

Then why is she here? After almost a full week of the silent treatment, *this* is the day she decides to stop pretending I don't exist?

"What did he do?" she asks quietly.

I let my eyes slip closed. "I don't want to talk about it."

She drops the prim, polite act. "If he hurt you, I'll go over there and kick his ass."

The determination on her face would make me laugh any other day. She scrunches up her nose just like Mami used to whenever she was on a mission. "It's fine. It . . . was something I should've seen coming."

Her eyes lose their spark. "I'm sorry," she mumbles, lying down beside me. It reminds me of our last trip four years ago, when we tried to come to the pier without Mami. We didn't know she was sick yet, but the signs had started to show. She was too tired to bring us here, so we set out on our own. Within minutes, we both knew something felt off. Uneasy. Maya whispered something about feeling creeped out and we both ran back to the cabin as if we'd seen a ghost in the water.

"Don't be," I reply. "Like I said, you were right."

"That doesn't mean I wanted to be."

"You love being right." In fifth grade, Maya's anger management class forced her to make a list of things that brought her joy. Being right was number two. I was number eighteen.

She smiles and rests her hand on top of mine. "Not this time."

My fingers close around hers, and for a few seconds, I indulge in gratitude. While I wish we'd found our way back to each other without having my heart broken in the process, at least I have her at all. At some point, I'll tell her everything. Not today, maybe not even before I head back to California. But she's the only person I trust to tell.

"I'm sorry," I croak, the words scratching my throat on

their way out. "About everything, but especially what I said to you. You didn't deserve that."

"I'm the one who should be sorry." She laughs around a sniffle, wiping at the corners of her eyes with the back of her hand. "I've been . . . I don't know. Jealous, I guess?"

My brow furrows. "Of *me*?"

Maya's always been the cool one. The one with friends and flings and people who want to know what she's up to and what she thinks. I'm just her awkward two-minute-older brother who makes her look significantly cooler by comparison.

Her chuckle is as hoarse as my throat feels. "Yeah, you, dumbass," she teases, leaning over to flick me on the forehead. "Because you're brave. You moved to California without doubting yourself for a second while I just . . . panicked."

We'd never asked questions about Maya's reasoning behind choosing to stay home instead of heading to New York like she'd always planned. When she'd shrugged us off and said something about finances, we'd drawn our own conclusions. California isn't cheap, but CalArts at least offered me some type of financial aid, even if it was minuscule. Going to cosmetology school in the city meant finding an apartment— and you don't get scholarships for those. No matter how talented you are.

"New York was what I wanted. I knew that. But then I started thinking—what if I got there and I didn't like it? Or it didn't like *me*? What if all those fancy-ass New York kids with their seven-dollar lattes and four-thousand-dollars-a-month apartments thought I was annoying, or tacky, or . . . not good enough? What if I never fit in? And I wasted the last of Dad's savings on something that would've made me miserable."

Oof . . . Whoever said twins have a psychic bond may have been on to something. Neither of us spoke that fear out loud, and yet we've been hung up on the same one for months.

"I told myself I was staying home because I needed to. Because it was expensive, and it'd be weird for Dad to not have either of us around after losing Mami. I could still have my friends, my family, all the best parts of my life here, and that was fine. And I believed it too. Until you left."

Finally, she rolls onto her side and looks me dead in the eyes. Hers are clouded with tears.

"You were doing all the things I was afraid to do, and I was bitter, and frustrated, and scared. You got the fancy tablet and the top-tier school and the cool city, while I was home waiting for you to FaceTime me like you said you would. And then, when my phone didn't ring, I thought, maybe . . . I didn't fit into your life anymore either."

I go to protest, but she holds up a hand and continues.

"Then you came home and started talking about the mentorship, and you started spending all your time at the Seo-Cookes working on it, and it felt like you'd chosen them instead of us, instead of *me*."

"I didn't choose anything or anyone over you," I insist, squeezing her hand hard. Though I can see how she thought I did. "Honestly, California isn't anything like what I expected. It's lonely, and it's hard. And it feels like everyone is already so much better than me. . . . And I'm sorry for not just telling you that, but . . . I was scared. That if you saw me on FaceTime you'd know, and you'd tell Dad, and it would blow up, and someone would say I should come home. But I never should've let you think I didn't care about you."

"I'm sorry too." With a sniffle, she shakes her head and slips her hand out of mine. "I was bitter. About you leaving, about me staying. It was weird, not having you around anymore. I thought I'd get used to it eventually, work through being so angry all the time, like I did before . . . but this break felt so much like the old ones and . . . it freaked me out again. Not having this place anymore . . . not having you around."

"I'm always going to be around," I reassure her, wiping away one of the tears she didn't catch. I can't promise her the cabin, but I can promise her that. "You can't get rid of me that easily."

She nods as she rubs away the last of her tears with the back of her hand. "Think I can come with you to that pizza place when we visit for spring break? The one with all the toppings?"

"Oh God no." I wince at the thought. "I read the reviews and that place is definitely a no-go. Like, seven people have gotten sick after eating there." I bite back a grin. "But I think we can find something better."

The sound of her laugh relieves the pressure between my eyes, makes my heart swell with something other than sadness. Hugging with a half-asleep arm is awkward, but I lean into the embrace. My face winds up buried in her curls, and she smells so much like Mami, coconut conditioner and pineapple hair gel, that I hold her tighter.

From petty fights with the Seo-Cookes when we were kids

to losing the person we loved most, she has always been my silver lining.

"Forget about the games," she says after we untangle, tugging flyaway hairs free from her lip gloss. "No more snooping, no more cheating. We can crush them on our own merits."

A few weeks ago, I would've jumped at the chance to free myself of our unnecessarily high-stakes scheme. Tonight, I shake my head.

"No," I insist. Her brows knit in confusion. "I know how we can take them down."

CHAPTER TWENTY-ONE

On New Year's Day, Maya breaks out the megaphone again.

"Let's go, maggots! It's Lawgies time! ¡Levántate! ¡Levántate!" she shouts as she races through the cabin, banging on everyone's doors.

"Watch it, nena," Dad warns from the kitchen, plugging his ears when she turns on the megaphone's siren.

The wakeup call does the trick. Everyone in the cabin is up and somewhat coherent before the sun has fully risen, a Báez family first. Even more unusual: I was up before all of them.

"See, someone has the right idea," Maya praises once everyone piles into the kitchen, gesturing to where I'm already fully dressed and brewing coffee.

The dinner table is a mess of neon sweatbands, protein bars, and coffee-stained charts on our respective strengths and weaknesses. Once everyone is gathered and has a mug of coffee in hand, Maya pulls a box in from the living room, setting it down on the table with a clunk.

"I took the liberty of making us matching outfits." She holds a bright red T-shirt and matching sweatband up to her chest with a proud grin, BADASS BÁEZ written across both in bold, block letters.

"A very nice touch," Isabel praises, taking one of the shirts for herself.

"I thought the games don't start until noon?" Andy complains, still blinking the sleep out of his eyes. "It's not even eight. What're we supposed to do until then?"

Maya throws a T-shirt at his head. "Practice. Duh."

"But we've been practicing since we got here."

Maya downs the last of her coffee in one gulp. "And today's no exception."

"Before we go full Rambo," I begin, waiting until I have the room's attention to continue. "I have something I want to show everyone."

My heart flutters as I set my sketchbook down on the counter, flipped open to the finished portrait of Mami. "It's for my mentorship application." No one speaks up, most of them leaning in to get a better view. I hold my breath as they take it in, the first time I've ever shown them anything so personal.

It's not the same portrait as the one Julian saw that afternoon, though it is very similar. It's evolved into something much bigger—a complete scene instead of just a portrait. A combination of two ideas. Mami is still the focal point, wearing her favorite white sundress, orchids tucked into her curls. But instead of the ocean, she's somewhere more familiar. The edge of her hidden pier, one arm around Dad, with me in his lap. The other around Maya. Our cabin in the distance, visible through the gaps in the trees.

As angry as I still am with Julian, this was one thing he was right about. *This* is who I am as an artist. It only took a couple half-finished sketches and some spilled milk to figure that out. With the piece scanned and sent with the rest of my application, and a confirmation email from Cardarelli's assistant sitting in my inbox, I can finally breathe a little easier. I didn't need to submit by today, but I need all my focus.

The games have never felt so important, and Mami has never felt as present as she does here, in this cabin we renovated to be everything she wanted it to be.

Maya's hand finds mine, squeezing twice, an unspoken code we developed in middle school. I squeeze hers back when Dad scoops me up into a hug so tight it makes me cough. "It's beautiful, mijo," he whispers against my temple.

Today's not a day for crying, but I can't help the tears that well up when I wrap my arms around him.

"There's one more thing," I say before I can get too choked up to speak again. Pulling myself out of Dad's arms, I cross the kitchen to grab a tray out of the fridge, setting it down beside my sketchbook.

"I thought we could start a new tradition." My gaze flickers over to Isabel first, her hand over her mouth and her eyes glossy. "Tres leches cake on New Year's Day."

Dad barks out a laugh as he adjusts one of the cherries holding the smiling face together. Even Andy has cracked under the emotional pressure, two tears sliding down his cheeks. Isabel wipes her eyes before nodding.

"I think that's a great idea."

• • •

In comparison to our usual training routine, the morning is pretty tame. We can't go too hard either way, unless we want to wind up puking the modest slices of tres leches cake we helped ourselves to for breakfast. We saved the majority of it for later, but that amount of dairy can work a number on even the most lactose-tolerant stomach.

We start with some warm-up stretches together in the backyard before heading out for a relaxed jog around the lake to get our blood pumping. Maya even praises my form as we stretch down to touch our toes. By noon, we're energized with team spirit and two cups of coffee each.

Decked out in our matching T-shirts and sweatbands, we make our way to Allegheny Park to sign in and collect our team badges.

The park is as over the top as Liam's personality. The waterslide I'd spotted during my night out with Julian is three times bigger in person, looming so high above us, it looks like it's one with the clouds. There's the usual theme park smell—deep-fried everything and chlorine—mixed with a surprisingly floral scent. As if the entire park were covered in Glade Plug-ins. There's no way the Alleghenys will ever need Mr. Cooke and Spill-e; this place is immaculately clean all on its own.

"This is awesome," Andy whispers as we step through the

welcome gates and follow the path toward the check-in for the games.

Even Maya doesn't have anything snarky to say, keeping her mouth shut as she stomps ahead of us. Through her tinted sunglasses I can see her peeking at the slides, her eyes widening at the sheer size of the attractions here. As Julian said, it does feel like the ultimate sandbox. Waterslides with nerve-racking turns. A lazy river with a breathtaking view of the lake. Food stands and trucks for every cuisine you can think of.

It's magnificent and I hate it.

Much like at sign-ups, an unexpected crowd has already started to gather around.

Lake Andreas has come alive in the days leading up to the games. Literally. There are more people in town today than there have been all month. Old Bob's store had a line out the door yesterday. A flurry of new faces bustled in and out with arms full of groceries and snacks. This morning, a bright yellow sign on the souvenir shop proudly announced that they'd sold out of I GOT CRABS IN LAKE ANDREAS shirts. We even have a new set of neighbors—a family of four from Tampa who were more than happy with the deal they got on their mushroom cabin.

"Are all of these people competing?" Isabel asks as we struggle to stick together while navigating the crowd.

"They'd better not," Maya snips, glaring at every un-familiar face. "They don't get to show up at the last minute and blow our chances."

"Hey," Dad warns. "Cuídate, nena." He's had to say that a lot during this trip.

We're only halfway to the sign-in table when Old Bob

spots us. "And the stars of the show have arrived!" The crowd parts for him, breaking out into hushed whispers as he ushers us up to the front of the line.

"Quite a turnout you got this year," Dad says when a nearby woman starts taking pictures of us.

Old Bob beams while he hands us our entry badges. "We got a little creative with the marketing. My nephew's been making these, uh . . . What're they called, Janine?" he shouts over his shoulder to his wife, who's organizing entry badges.

"TikToks," she yells back.

"Right, TikToks," he says with a snap of his fingers. He reaches into his pocket, pulling out a crumpled poster. "Plus, we hung these up all over town. Folks ate 'em up."

The poster is very different from the initial flyer Old Bob had shown us. It's an illustration, depicting two teams, one red and one blue, competing in an intense game of tug-of-war. Front and center, between the two feuding families, are two boys. One red, one blue, holding hands. Beneath it, written in elegant script reads, *Lake Andreas: Where Anything Can Happen.*

Son of a bitch. They stole my face for a poster.

"Uh, very nice," Dad replies diplomatically.

"Is that us?" Andy points to the hulking strongman on the blue team, clearly a depiction of Henry.

Maya shakes her head, pointing to the tall boy on the red team. "No, *that's* us."

Andy pouts. "My arms are bigger than that."

Old Bob cackles as he takes the poster back, tucking it into his breast pocket. "Turns out the TikTok folks love a good rivalry." He nudges my arm with his elbow. "And a little star-crossed-lover action never hurts either."

Great, our family rivalry *and* my fake romance has an audience.

"That's very exciting, but we should go get ready for the first event." Dad grabs the last of our badges and pulls us away. While I haven't told anyone besides Maya about my fallout with Julian, it didn't take long for everyone to draw their own conclusions.

"Best of luck!" Old Bob calls out, waving his cane in the air. "Make us proud!"

The crowd gawks in awe as Dad bustles us toward the roped off parking lot where most of the events are being held, more of them whipping out their phones to snap photos of us. Going from seeing basically no one for three weeks to becoming a local celebrity overnight isn't helping our pregames jitters. We keep our eyes forward, following Dad until a shoulder knocks roughly into mine. I'm prepared to brush it off when a familiar flash of sandy-blond hair catches my eye. I turn on my heels, hoping that I was just seeing things, but no. The reality is as horrifying as my imagination.

"Good luck out there," Liam says with a sneer, an entry badge pinned to his T-shirt.

Of course Liam entered the games. As loose as the rules are, this seriously feels like cheating. How can the son of this year's sponsor be allowed to compete?

Behind Liam are three very confused-looking water park employees pinning entry badges to their shirts. Nothing in the rules ever said teams had to be made up of family members. Paying off his dad's employees must be Liam's way of getting around any potential conflicts of interest. Though this still seems like a serious violation.

Then again, I'm not surprised that Liam thinks he can be an exception.

"Don't need it, but thanks," I reply before rushing to catch up with the others. Liam winning could potentially work in our favor. The bet only said Mr. Cooke would get the cabin if *they* won. But I can't stomach the possibility of admitting defeat to someone like him.

It's probably a bad sign that I'm even entertaining the notion of losing.

After I catch up, Dad guides us behind a grilled cheese food truck, away from prying eyes.

"Well, that was unexpected," he says once we're out of earshot.

Maya takes a pack of safety pins from her backpack, handing one to each of us before working on pinning her badge to her T-shirt. "So long as they don't get in our way, they can take all the pictures they want."

The sound of a familiar cackle travels over to our hiding spot. Mr. Cooke slaps a hand on Liam's shoulder, too wrapped up with pleasantries to notice our presence. But the others do. All three of them—Henry, Stella, and Julian—freeze at the sight of us.

I tell myself I'm not going to look at Julian, and shocker, I don't listen.

It would hurt less if he wasn't looking at me, too, if his eyes weren't twice as stunning as I remembered. If I didn't have the tools to take him down sitting at the bottom of my backpack.

Julian takes a step toward me, but I'm tugged away before he can make it any farther.

With a scowl at the Seo-Cookes, Dad ushers us off in the opposite direction, but not before Maya can flip them off while Dad isn't watching. Andy quickly joins in, throwing in a stuck-out tongue for good measure. If my stomach wasn't trying to come out through my mouth, I might have joined them.

The worst part is that Julian still haunts my thoughts. I ripped the lazy doodles of him out of my sketchbook and buried them beneath the banana peels and rotten vegetables in the kitchen garbage can. New Nostalgia is wiped from my Spotify. My nose piercing isn't infected anymore, so the tea tree oil joined the sketches in the trash. I've severed everything that ties me to Julian, and yet I still don't feel any better.

Just because the proof of what we had is gone doesn't mean I'm ready to forget.

"All right, listen up," Dad announces, clapping his hands together to get our attention. "You guys have trained hard for this. And I'm very proud of all the work you've put in, regardless of what happens. But you'll have to make sure you stay alert." He stares pointedly at me. "We know they've played dirty before. Don't let any of them hurt you."

An unsettling burn trickles down my neck, between my shoulder blades. Eyes boring into me. I check to see if Julian is still there, waiting for me to face him, but they're gone. Even after all my efforts to forget him, I'm still searching for him in the crowd.

My jaw locks as I refocus, answering for the whole family. "We won't."

I won't. Never again.

CHAPTER TWENTY-TWO

The thing no one tells you about the games is that 90 percent of it is waiting around. Waiting for your chance to compete. Waiting for the next event to start.

Waiting to see how Dad does in the long jump.

"¡Vamos!" Dad shouts, letting out a battle cry before lunging as far as he can across the sand pit.

We wince at the hard thump of his landing. He's steady, but doubled over, muttering a string of *carajo*s under his breath. One of the few rules of the games is keeping things family friendly—aka no swearing. But there's no rule about cursing in Spanish.

Maya and I hold our breath as a volunteer scribbles down Dad's score. Six feet exactly, putting us firmly in the lead.

"Not bad, viejo," Isabel praises when Dad hobbles over to us, clutching his lower back.

"I'm getting too old for this." He slowly straightens, his spine audibly cracking.

Andy shudders. "Gross."

"That's middle age for you, bud," Dad replies with a wince.

With Dad upright again, we set our sights on the last contestant of the round—Mr. Cooke. He plays it calmer and cooler than Dad did, bouncing on the balls of his feet and exhaling sharply before he takes off. His leap through the air is smoother, more athletic.

The landing, though? Not so polished.

His ankle buckles under his weight before he's fully hit the ground, sending him flying face-first into the sand.

Fighting the urge to laugh at the sight of him absolutely eating shit is the real challenge.

"Guess I'm out of practice," Mr. Cooke announces once he's pulled himself onto his knees, his striped polo covered in sand.

Henry and Julian come to his aid, Henry hoisting him up while Julian wipes off his sunglasses. As entertaining as it was watching Mr. Cooke tumble like a five-year-old, all that matters is his score.

"Five feet eight inches," the volunteer announces. "Point goes to Team Five, the Báezes."

"I know that's right!" Maya shouts, and launches herself into Dad's arms.

We indulge in a round of hugs, pats on the back, and sips of water before hustling over to the next event. First place waits for no one.

We're off to a strong start, nabbing first place in both the logic puzzle challenge and the memorization code-breaking challenge. Starting with our specialty gives us an early lead, but our winning streak falters when it comes to the physical. The Seo-Cookes blow us out of the water, literally, during the kayak race. They're so far ahead of us that by the time Andy crosses the finish line, they are already downing Gatorades.

As expected, the newcomers don't take the competition nearly as seriously as we do. They laugh and giggle while hopping across the grass for the three-legged race, not even bothering to get up when they inevitably stumble. Most of them are satisfied with sitting out and watching us battle instead.

And then there's Liam.

Even without formal training, he's a force to be reckoned with. His team isn't half bad either. Whatever he's bribing his employee teammates with—PTO or straight-up cash—it's working. They land a few first- and second-place wins, narrowly edging us out of second place in the egg toss. We try not to psyche ourselves out too soon, focusing on doing our best without checking the scores.

Dad lets out a mighty cheer as the referee declares Andy the winner of the marshmallow-eating competition, with a record-setting total of eighteen marshmallows in two minutes. "Let's go! That's my boy!"

"For once your bottomless-pit stomach comes in handy." Maya shakes Andy's shoulder before heading off to the bulletin board where the schedule is posted to figure out where we need to head next.

"I don't feel so good," Andy mumbles, bracing himself on the emergency vomit bucket.

Isabel grimaces, kneeling down beside him and pressing her water bottle to his forehead. Andy's turning an unfortunate shade of green that makes my stomach churn too. If he's down for the count this close to the end of the day, we might be screwed.

Suddenly, Maya reappears beside us, dripping sweat and heaving for breath. "So, I don't want to freak anyone out." She pauses to brace her hands on her knees and take deep gulps of air. "But we need to win this next event."

I hand her my water bottle once she starts fanning herself. "Wasn't that always the goal?"

"No, we *have* to win." She kneels down beside Andy, holding up her phone. "I know I said we wouldn't check, but I couldn't help it. . . ."

It's a photo of the leaderboard. My curiosity gets the better of me, despite my gut instinct to look away. The Seo-Cookes are in first, with us and Liam's team tied for second. But the Seo-Cookes' lead is slim, just two points separating them from us.

"If we get anything less than first, we're done for. But if we do, and they get second—"

"We'll be tied," I finish for her, my stomach sinking as it slowly dawns on me that the 5K is the one thing standing between us and losing our cabin. And our fastest runner is turning green.

Across the field, Stella and Julian stand shoulder to shoulder, whispering intently, their expressions unreadable but borderline upset. Before I can pretend not to notice them, Julian's eyes meet mine. My cheeks burn as I quickly turn back around, ashamed of breaking the composure I'd been so proud of maintaining. It's easy to avoid Julian in the midst of a competition, but resisting the chance to sneak peeks during downtime is harder.

"You okay?" Maya asks while I stretch my arms out over my head to shake off any lingering thoughts of Julian.

She's asked me that same question dozens of times since I came home in tears yesterday. The answer remains the same, but it holds a different weight on my tongue.

"Yeah."

Even though it's not true, it feels less like a lie and more like a promise.

◆ ◆ ◆

When we'd first signed up for the Winter Games, having me run the last leg of the 5K seemed like a good plan. With Andy up first, followed by Maya, they'd be able to secure us a solid enough lead that even slowpokes like me and Dad should be able to clinch us a win. Now that we're here, I'm not so sure.

A handful of contestants must have dropped out after the last event, given the thinner crowd waiting at our designated mark in the woods just outside the park. Less competition is ideal, but having Stella positioned right beside me definitely isn't.

I start a fresh round of stretches while we wait, working some life back into my muscles. As nervous as I'm feeling, we don't have room for negativity. We *have* to win this, or we can kiss first place goodbye. No pressure. I'm totally calm and definitely not freaking out.

"Hey," Stella says as she approaches me.

Okay maybe I'm freaking out a little.

"Uh. Hi." I give her a once-over for weapons. It doesn't look like she has anything on her, but I brace myself for an attack anyway.

She doesn't respond at first, fidgeting uncomfortably and glancing at the other competitors. Three of them are chatting about their dinner plans and the other two, including Liam's teammate, are on their phones.

"I know this is probably a weird time to say this." She pauses, closing her eyes for a moment. "But I'm sorry."

Okay, they're *definitely* up to something. I check over my shoulder for any sign of Julian or Henry lingering in the trees. When I turn around, Stella's cheeks are dusted pink, her eyes downcast. I've never seen her look so . . . shy before.

"After Julian told us to call off our plans for the games, we freaked out. We'd just found that expired salami, and we had this great idea to plant a stink bomb under your porch, but it flopped at the last second. Bowing to you at the games felt like the last straw. We thought the chowder thing would be funny. Like old times. And we laughed at first, but then your sister started crying. . . . It doesn't feel the same now that we know about all the stuff Dad did."

"If you're so sorry, why aren't you apologizing to her?"

Her shoulders hunch as she shrinks in on herself, rubbing her hands along her arms. "Because I didn't think she'd let me."

She's right. Maya wouldn't let Stella get within five feet of her after everything that's happened. I'm not inclined to believe her, but there's something unusual about this quasi-apology. Not in a suspicious way, though. In a . . . genuine way. Stella's actually being expressive. She's got three inches of height on me but somehow seems so much smaller, her usual confidence dulled. Like Maya, she's never been afraid of using her piercing gaze to tear someone down. But now she can't even meet my eye.

"Julian told us about the robot. The one Dad took from you guys . . . We really didn't know. About that, or the bet he made either." Her tone is almost shameful, as if she's apologizing on her dad's behalf. "Dad's . . . a lot sometimes. All of the time." A hitch of her breath, and suddenly she's looking at me. "I'm sorry."

There are countless things she could be apologizing for, but it doesn't feel like I'm the one who should accept them.

"Julian is sorry too," she adds when I don't respond, looking down and kicking one of the rocks at her feet. "If having you around all the time when you were fake dating was annoying, it was nothing compared to you two actually together. He never shuts up about you."

The best thing to do would be to ignore Stella and focus on breathing exercises until Dad comes around the bend and hands me the baton. But . . .

"Really?" The minute the word comes out, I wince, wishing I could take it back.

She picks her head up, a small smile playing at the corners of her lips. "Yeah, it's super gross." For once, I don't detect a bite behind her voice. It's just a regular sarcastic joke, not a barbed insult or backhanded compliment. "This was the first time he's ever come to me about dating advice. I guess the Liam thing spooked him."

"He . . . what?"

"He wrote down all these things about you. Honestly, I thought it was kind of creepy until he told me about how Liam dumped him over stupid, petty stuff like not knowing his favorite snack. Still, Julian was pretty hopeless before he came to me, so you're welcome." Her smile widens, blossoming into a grin. "Except making you that cake. That was his idea."

My stomach flutters with a glimmer of hope. That maybe it was all a misunderstanding—that Julian really did stop scheming. But I hesitate, squashing that hope before it can grow into something dangerous. Maybe there was room for genuine interest in me somewhere in between the lies, but the list, the plotting against me. *That* was all Julian too. I was naïve enough to fall for a façade once. I can't afford to do it again.

"He really wants to talk to you," she adds.

My already sour mood worsens.

I shift my attention back to the race, stretching my leg out in front of me. "Well, I don't want to talk to him."

"I figured you'd say that." She stands in front of me, arms crossed. "I know I'm the last person you'll probably listen to, but can you please consider hearing him out?"

The audacity of this family never ceases to amaze me. "You're in my way."

A scream startles us before she can respond.

"They tripped me!" a voice cries out somewhere far behind us. The knot in the pit of my stomach tightens. It's Liam. "Those assholes freaking tripped me!"

I've done my best to push away the memory of Julian's

scribbled list of ways to sabotage me, but the first entry comes rushing back.

Trip them during the 5K.

They're still doing it. They're still cheating.

A smirk tugs at the edge of Stella's lips. Like she's proud of what they've done.

Am I next?

Through the trees, I can make out a shock of red, followed closely by a blur of blue. Dad and Julian. My body tenses, every muscle pulled taut as Dad comes into view, his shirt completely drenched. He has a narrow lead, but Julian is quickly gaining on him and who knows what they might have in store for us. For a split second, I lock eyes with Julian. Stella holds her ground beside me, not preparing to run. Preparing to block me. They're going to try and corner me, tackle me, or something. But I can't lose. I can't let Julian distract me again.

I hold my arm out as far as I can, taking off the second the baton touches my hand.

"¡Muévete, mijo! Go, go!" Dad shouts as I push right past Stella toward the finish line.

All at once, the world falls away. The trees blend into a blur of greens and browns, low-hanging branches and leaves whipping at my cheeks. My chest tightens, feeling impossibly small as my heart and lungs heave with every labored breath. The corners of my vision blur until the only thing I can make out is the path. Every inch of me burns, aches, begs me to give in. Flashes of practicing our smiles with Mami keeps me moving. Her scowl whenever we took anything less than first place pushes me through those last few feet.

We *have* to win.

I don't even realize I've crossed the finish line until I almost run into a table stacked with cups of Gatorade. Maya rushes to my side before I collide with the table, wrapping her arms around my waist.

"You did it, Dev!" she shouts directly into my ear.

Oh my God. Holy shit. *I did it.*

The minute she lets go of me, I fall to my knees, my arms barely keeping me upright. She quickly kneels beside me, trying to get me to sip Gatorade in between dry heaves. If I could, I'd lie down on the ground and fall asleep right there, letting the sun burn me to a crisp. But we still have one fight left and I have none in me. They still need me if we want to pull this off—we're close, but not out of the woods yet.

"Dude!" Andy exclaims, coming to join our huddle on the ground. He grips me by the shoulders, holding me up better than my own arms can. "That was *so* epic. I've never seen you run that fast before."

I open my mouth to reply, "Neither have I," but the minute I do, my body takes over. And I throw up.

CHAPTER TWENTY-THREE

It's a miracle I'm allowed to stay in the competition after vomiting all over the hydration station. Maybe it helped that everyone went absolutely wild after I crossed the finish line.

Well, almost everyone.

"They're cheating," Liam shouts the second he crosses the finish line, pointing at where I'm dry heaving over a trash can.

"We are not!" Maya takes charge of defending our honor, standing between me and Liam.

"Search their bags—you'll find something," Liam says to Old Bob. "Fishing wire. That's what they used to trip me."

A heave gets stuck in my throat. There may not be fishing wire in my bag, but there's definitely something else that'll get us kicked out of the competition.

Old Bob glances at us warily. "That doesn't seem necessary. Mr. All—"

"It *is* necessary," Liam sneers, getting so far up in Old Bob's face it makes my blood boil.

Old Bob looks torn, biting his lip, when another voice cuts through the crowd.

"That's rich coming from you," Stella calls out, arms crossed defiantly. "Why don't you check *his* bag?" she taunts with a raised brow.

The crowd breaks out into murmurs as the rest of us hold our breath. Whatever the Seo-Cookes have up their sleeves is more convoluted than ever.

"What're you—" Liam cuts off when Old Bob tentatively reaches for the Versace backpack slung across his shoulder. "Don't listen to her!" he snaps, the contents of his bag spilling out onto the grass as he wrenches it away from Old Bob.

Batons. Dozens of them.

The crowd gasps, and it takes everything in me not to join them.

"Those aren't mine!" Liam dives to pick up as many batons as he can, scanning them for something. Proof of his claim. "Someone put these in my bag, I swear!"

"Bro," Henry says, stepping up to join Stella with a look of disappointment. "Not cool."

I'm not saying I condone them cheating, but I've gotta say, it feels good as hell not to be a target for once.

Whatever Liam says next is drowned out by Old Bob blowing the whistle around his neck. "Mr. Allegheny, being in possession of spare batons is a clear violation of the rules of the games."

Liam's protests are ignored as two volunteers wearing staff shirts loop their arms through his. The remaining members of his team share confused looks before shrugging and walking off to a corn dog stand.

Watching Liam get escorted out of his own water park is the purest form of karma.

Stella's and Henry's gazes wander over to me once Liam's shouts are a distant echo. I don't say anything or give them a smile. Now that my stomach doesn't feel like a bag of microwaved popcorn, I head over to my family, where I'm safe.

The Seo-Cookes got rid of Liam. They can still get rid of us too.

• • •

The thirty-minute break between the 5K and our tie-breaker game of capture the flag is my saving grace. By the time we set up camp in the densest thicket of the woods next to the park, my body is thrumming with adrenaline. And caffeine. The two energy drinks I downed in under five minutes are definitely going to haunt me later, but for now I feel fan-freaking-tastic.

"You're sure you can handle this?" Maya whispers to me as we wait for the siren to signal the start of the game.

"You doubting me now?" I tease while bouncing from foot to foot.

She rests her hands on my shoulders, pushing lightly until I'm more anchored. "No, but you're running on three Red Bulls and pure rage, and from personal experience, that never ends well."

"*Two* Red Bulls."

She rolls her eyes and lets go of my shoulders. "Fine. But

remember, you don't have to do anything you don't want to do."

It's interesting how often people have said that to me this week, considering I've spent my entire winter break doing things I didn't want to do. Ironic, even, when the one time I did the thing I *wanted* to do I wound up here: heartbroken and as hell-bent on revenge as Maya was when we first arrived.

When the blare of a siren cuts through the woods, we take off. Maya and the others to the left side of the woods to set up a base camp for our flag and keep it safe, me in the opposite direction—to find where the enemy is hiding. My role is trickier, and thirty minutes ago, I might not have had the strength to pull it off—but I want to see this through.

The forest is dead silent, my steps sounding like miniature earthquakes. Time isn't on our side, so I tread as lightly as I can, moving quickly and quietly through the trees. I stop for every snapped branch and rustle of leaves, waiting for any signs of the competition. We're limited in how far into the woods we can go, and while I wouldn't put it past the Seo-Cookes to make finding their base as annoying as possible, they can't be very far. After about ten minutes of wandering around the edge of the woods, something catches my eye. First a shock of dark hair, and then a bright blue T-shirt. Found them.

Crouched behind a log, I reach into my backpack and pull out a crumpled plastic glove. I delicately unfurl our decoy flag, careful not to touch any of the poison ivy plastered to the back of it.

Armed with our poisonous decoy, I step out of hiding and

lay the trap. I shove the flag down into a nearby patch of dirt, doing a half-assed job of covering it up so it doesn't look *too* obviously like a trap. I dodge behind trees until I'm a safe distance away from the crime scene.

Tossing a sizable rock in the direction of the decoy flag sets it all in motion. The footsteps stop, then shift, the sounds of mud squelching and leaves crunching getting closer and closer. I hold my closed fist against my heart, begging it to calm down before it gives away my hiding spot. The figure comes into view, a few feet in front of the tree I'm hidden behind.

Of course, it's Julian. The universe couldn't send literally anyone else, could it?

He quickly spots the flag, stopping directly in front of it. I bite down on my tongue as I wait for him to grab it and promptly break out into hives. But he doesn't; he just stares at it. Shit, he knows we're up to something, doesn't he? They must've bugged the house. How else could they have known what we were planning?

Instead of grabbing the flag, he starts checking the area around it, searching for something. Or for one of us. I don't dare move a muscle as he comes toward my hiding spot. He's so close I can smell his lavender laundry detergent, the hint of cinnamon and nutmeg from his morning coffee. Or maybe I'm letting myself get too lost in my memories again. The universe does me one favor: He turns around. I don't let myself breathe a sigh of relief yet, not until I'm fully in the clear. With his back to me, I carefully peer out from behind the tree. He kicks at the ground in defeat, sighing as he squats down beside the flag.

It all happens in slow motion. His hand reaches for the flag, and my mind brings me back to the grocery store. To his outstretched hand helping me off the ground. To the way my heart sank the second I recognized him. To the flutter that hasn't gone away every time I look at him. Even when I wished it would. My heart takes over and my brain shuts down as I lunge straight for him, tackling him before he can touch the flag.

After everything, I still don't have it in me to hurt him.

As we roll into a pile of leaves, I kick the flag as far from us as I can. I'm prepared for a fight, ready to kick and scream if I have to, but except for a squeak of surprise and a bit of wriggling, Julian lets me take him down.

Pinning Julian's arms above his head isn't necessary when I've very clearly won this battle, but I do it anyway. The thrill of having some semblance of control over this situation, over *him*, sets my nerves on fire. I straddle his waist, keeping my hands closed around his wrists. Our chests heave in unison, our breath mingled together in the bit of space between us. Even with mud streaking his cheeks and sweat dripping down his forehead, he's still the most beautiful thing I've ever called mine.

I've thought about what I might say if I ran into Julian again before we headed home. A long and passionate speech leading with a "How dare you!" and ending with a slap to his stupid, perfect face. All those rehearsed words fall short when Julian smiles at me, bright and wonderful.

"Hi," he says as if nothing has changed.

I wish I could be eloquent, or better yet, witty, but I can only be myself. "There's poison ivy on the flag."

Julian's brow furrows as he pushes against my hold. "What?"

"I-it's a decoy," I stammer out, my brain begging me to shut up while I'm still ahead. "We thought if one of you fell for it and grabbed it, you'd be too hung up on the hives to hunt for our flag."

There's no *we*. After all the snooping over the past three weeks, it all came down to me. A plan that would possibly put one of them in danger if they fell for our trap like I thought they would. A selfish idea that filled me with the most vindictive and cruel sort of thrill, a thrill that never really sat right with me. Mami never would've wanted us to win this way, even if it meant losing the cabin. But I didn't care about how we won so long as we did.

I'd made such a big show of saying I had morals in this war we waged against the Seo-Cookes, only to throw them away because I was vengeful. If Julian could turn against me for the sake of a competition, then I could turn against him too.

But I'm not that person. And a part of me still hopes that deep down, he isn't either.

"Oh . . ." Julian stops resisting against my hold, looking past me at where the decoy flag has toppled into the grass. "So, shouldn't you have . . . *not* tackled me?"

"Add it to the never-ending list of stupid things I've done over the past month. If you want to touch the poison flag and break out into a rash, then be my guest."

Now that he's out of harm's way, I roll off him. He doesn't move, still splayed out on the ground.

"We can win without cheating," I say, more to myself than him. "You should try it sometime."

Finding the others will take time, and I'll need to come up with a gentle way to explain that I completely bombed the plan I'd been so intent on, so I take off in the direction I came. I've barely made it two feet when Julian's hand closes around my wrist.

"What is it with you and grabbing my wrist?" I snap.

"Thank you," he says at the same time, the soft cadence of his voice lost beneath the harshness of mine.

I hold my wrist to my chest, running my fingers along the tender skin until the warmth of his touch begins to fade. If we were still . . . whatever we were before, I'd say something cute like "That's what fake boyfriends are for." I'm not sure what I can say to him anymore.

"You're welcome." A civil response. Maybe that's all we can be now. Civil.

Because I'm weak, I give him a chance. I stay in place, arms crossed, waiting for him to tell me whatever it is he needs to say so badly. But he just stares at me. For a brief second, I wonder if he's going to kiss me. For an even briefer second, I *hope* he's going to kiss me. That's a dangerous line of thought, so I decide he's had enough time, and like I told him three weeks ago, I don't owe him anything.

"I told my dad," he calls out when I start walking away.

This is probably a trap, I tell myself. But that doesn't stop me from freezing. I don't turn around, scanning the perimeter for any of his siblings waiting to launch a sneak attack.

"Told him what?" I reply once I'm sure the coast is clear.

"Everything." His voice is closer, close enough that I can feel the words on the back of my neck. When I turn, he's there, too close and too earnest, but I don't run. "About Princeton, about what really happened with Liam."

I don't know if I should believe him, let alone how to respond. Logic says that this is part of his plan. Just because I figured out what he was up to doesn't mean he can't still see it through.

"How did he take it?" Neutral ground. My guard stays up.

"Better than I thought." He shrugs, the simple movement a startling reminder of how oddly close we are. It wouldn't take much to close the distance, just a tiny bit of courage. "Mom called him beforehand, after I told her I wanted to come clean. They talked for over an hour, and whatever she said made him willing to listen, for once."

This is the point where I should go. I've heard what he had to say, and while I'm glad he gets to live his truth, it doesn't change ours.

"I'm sorry," he says before I can decide either way. "For lying to you, for dragging you into this. And especially for hurting you. You don't have to forgive me, or ever talk to me again, but I couldn't let you leave without telling you that you're the most wonderful thing to happen to me in a really long time. And I'm sorry that I made you think you were anything less than that."

He says it so quickly it leaves him breathless. There are plenty of questions I could ask, routes I could take, and yet only one comes to mind.

"Did you tell him about us?" I ask, less than a whisper.

The question makes him smile, something that shouldn't still make my heart race. "Just the truth—that at first we were only pretending to be together because of Liam." I don't realize his hand is in mine until he's running his thumb along my knuckles. Did he reach out, or did I?

"Why not tell him the whole story?"

"Because the rest of it was real. And that part's just for us."

A thousand words sit on the tip of my tongue, but Julian has said the only ones that matter.

We meet halfway, his hand on my waist and my fingers in his hair. We kiss slow and fast, light and heavy, for every time I thought of him, but he wasn't there. Forgiveness, longing, apologies, written and whispered in the brush of our lips and tips of our fingers. When we open our eyes, it could all be over. He could knock me over and hold me down until his siblings secure the win. He could still stab me in the back like he'd planned to. For now, I hold him tight wherever I can, his shirt, his hair, nipping his lower lip with my teeth. I'm not ready to let him go yet.

Henry comes out of the woodwork, running over to Julian as quickly as he can. "Someone's coming," he announces, looking warily over his shoulder.

"Let's go, Romeo," Stella hisses, appearing from behind a nearby tree.

My stomach plummets as we pull apart. This is it, whatever they had planned. Julian senses my apprehension, tightening his grip around my waist. He's too strong for me to yank free, so he has me exactly where he wants me.

"Devin!" Maya calls out, followed by the sound of footsteps. I'm so glad she remembered my warning to come find me if I didn't make it back to base within fifteen minutes.

"Maya!" I shout back, hoping she'll know how to follow my voice.

My knee pivots, prepared to nail Julian right in the crotch, when he suddenly releases me. I stumble, tripping over a gnarled tree root and falling onto my ass. Everything but the treetops becomes a blur, stars and muted shapes clouding my vision. This is how I die, huh? Surrounded by the Seo-Cookes in the middle of the woods?

Can't say I didn't see that one coming.

A warmth covers me, a familiar smell overwhelming my senses. My body tenses beneath Julian's, his slotted so easily against mine. If I had any energy left, I'd push him away, but I accept my fate and let him press our linked fingers into the damp leaves.

"May the best man win," he whispers against my lips, and kisses me like I'm a prize to be won.

"Get off him! I have pepper spray!" Maya shouts, followed by the rattle of her shaking the can to life.

"Oh shit, she does." Henry springs into action, pulling Julian off me by the scruff of his shirt. Julian stumbles but manages to flash me one last smile before taking off into the trees with his siblings. They're gone faster than I can process, but before they disappear, I spot someone new waving to the three of them. Mr. Cooke, watching me for the briefest of seconds before vanishing into the trees.

Either I have a serious concussion, or we're going to see some pigs with wings any second now.

"Dev, are you okay?" Maya races toward me, tossing the can of pepper spray aside as she collapses onto the ground beside me.

I nod, propping myself up against the base of the tree. Once I'm up, I realize Julian pushed something into my hand before he took off.

"Did he hurt you?" Maya asks while brushing leaves and chunks of dirt off the back of my shirt.

I shake my head, slowly unfolding the crumpled ball of cloth. Maya freezes, lips parting in a silent gasp as I lay the bright blue cloth out in front of us.

TEAM 7: SEO-COOKE

"Did you . . ." Maya trails off, blinking up at me in awe.

My fingers run reverently along the name written in Victorian chicken scratch.

"We won."

CHAPTER TWENTY-FOUR

In under three hours, Maya manages to arrange the most raucous after-party Lake Andreas has ever seen.

Streamers and popped balloons litter our makeshift dance floor at Dixon's. If this year is about moving on from the past, this is the best place to start: with a ten-foot-long Meat Mayhem big enough to feed half of Lake Andreas. Our official family portrait serves as the centerpiece, displayed proudly behind the counter. Old Bob made an exception for the night, letting us hold on to it before it's sent off to its rightful place on the Wall of Champions in the visitors center. Turns out he made another exception, one most of us didn't know about. . . .

Old Bob removes the blanket covering the frame with a flourish and I almost choke on my Gatorade.

"How did they get this?!" I exclaim, racing up to the frame to confirm that I'm not just imagining things.

It's not the photo we'd posed for in front of Allegheny Park with Andy throwing up a peace sign and Maya sticking out her tongue. Instead, it's a framed copy of my application piece. Us with Mami on her secret pier.

"I asked if they'd be willing to bend the rules a little," Isabel says with a proud smile.

I whip around to face her. The others are too occupied with party setup to have noticed the portrait yet.

"But you and Andy aren't in it." Touched as I am, they were as much a part of the win as we were. And they're as much a part of this family too.

She shrugs, still admiring the portrait instead of looking at me. "We'll be in it next year."

My heart swells over the portrait, over her kindness, over the thought of us coming here again because we *can*. Words fall short, so I pull her in for a hug that says everything I can't.

"Thank you," I whisper into her shoulder. "For everything."

She responds by holding me close and running a hand through my hair the way Mami always would when she missed us. It takes all the energy in me not to cry as we untangle and take in my drawing one more time.

It'll fit in very nicely next to the twelve stiff, unsmiling Seo-Cooke portraits.

◆ ◆ ◆

Thanks to my twin, what the rest of us assumed would be a modest affair became a lake-wide event as big as the Winter Games themselves. All the locals and visitors who came up for the spectacle decide to stick around, eager to get a peek at Lake Andreas's newest Winter Games champions. Soon enough the sheriff comes along and closes down Fulton Drive, letting the party spill out onto the street when Dixon's becomes too packed and turning the other way when she catches me, Maya, and Andy sneaking sips of champagne.

Old Bob, Mario and Luigi, and the Martinezes work together to keep the food and drinks flowing throughout the night. A task made easier thanks to Dad's latest revived project—a motion-activated champagne dispenser. Well, it's more of a champagne sprayer at the moment, blasting spurts of Chandon at anyone who gets too close. But it's only a prototype, as he's made sure to remind everyone who's gotten soaked.

Our modest contribution of the last of our tres leches cake is quickly devoured, though we make sure to set aside a heaping serving for Old Bob and Janine.

We can't walk five feet without someone shouting "Congratulations!" in our ear or offering to buy us celebratory drinks. Local fame has its perks. Every few minutes we're being toasted to, drinking more than we probably should because victory champagne tastes *so* much better than enemy champagne.

Maya takes center stage, having changed out of her games attire into a red satin jumpsuit and matching wig so bright it could stop traffic. She takes every opportunity to recount the dramatic final moments of the games to anyone who'll listen. I don't bother telling her that Julian had pushed the flag into my hand. Not when it might make her think the win is cheap. She can believe what she wants. Her stories never quite stick to the truth anyway. Case in point, the pepper spray plays a much bigger role in her version of events.

Occasionally, she'll tap me in to tell my side of the events. I indulge her and play along, making the story seem more dramatic than it actually was. I leave out the part where Julian kissed me, though. That part's just for me.

There's no telling if the Seo-Cookes will show up, or if we'll be able to spot them in the huge crowd if they did. Same goes for Liam, who I doubt will make an appearance tonight. His dad didn't seem too pleased today. Your son getting caught cheating in front of potential clientele isn't a great look.

Fulton Drive becomes a mass of dancing bodies once Dad moves the stereo out front, taking over the role of DJ for the night. Isabel had been wary when he first hooked up his phone to the speakers, but it turns out everyone loves salsa music. Every few minutes, I take a lap, peeking over the tops of heads for any sign of the one person I want to see tonight.

"Stop being mopey and come dance with me!" Maya shouts over the beat of a Héctor Lavoe song. She tugs at the strap of my first-place medal, dragging me onto our make-shift dance floor. We miraculously make it over in one piece, stepping around spilled cups of champagne and abandoned paper plates. There's not much room, but I manage to twirl her at least once.

"He'll come," she whispers, resting her head on my shoulder.

"How do you know?" I tease, letting her take the lead.

At first, she doesn't respond, gripping my waist and dipping me dramatically. It's tipsy and messy and beautiful, like something straight out of a Lifetime movie.

"I'm a genius. I know things," she says once she's lifted me up.

Well, I can't argue with that. Instead, I return the favor and dip her as low to the ground as I can before spinning her again and again until she's tripping over herself and laughing so hard tears stream down her cheeks.

"Guys!" Andy shouts as he stumbles toward us, double-fisting cups of champagne, with most of it sprayed onto his shirt. "I love this place, and I love you two, and I never wanna leave," he slurs, confirming what we'd always suspected: He's a very affectionate drunk.

"Love you too." Maya throws her arms around him, hugging him as tight as her tiny body can. She leans back, attempting to hoist him into the air, but a slight misstep sends them tumbling to the ground in a pile of giggles and limbs. Their knees are skinned, and their elbows bruised, but we laugh it off, leaning on one another until they've stumbled back onto their feet.

I don't think much of the tap on my shoulder. There have been hands on me throughout the night. Usually, I'd snap at anyone who got that close to me without permission, but tonight I welcome everything. The praise, the congratulations, the joy. We're so well past tipsy I don't even recognize Stella and Henry at first, their somber faces blending in with the crowd.

"Oh . . . hi," I say once I realize who touched me.

Stella murmurs a greeting that I can't hear over the music. "We wanted to talk to Maya," she shouts this time, leaning in closer to me.

I see that Maya and Andy have started dancing, their arms flopping around. "You can try," I respond, stepping out of the way.

Stella bites her lip, gesturing for Henry to follow. As they brush past me, I notice the box of choco pies in Henry's hands and the bag of celebrity skincare products in Stella's. I could tell them that bribery won't get them very far, but they can learn that one for themselves. Besides, I'm sure Maya won't turn down food and free swag. I watch from a safe distance as the two of them approach her cautiously, heads hung. Andy heads off in the opposite direction, giving the three of them space. Once I'm sure they're not going to claw at each other, I step away, too, in search of a different Seo-Cooke.

Another two laps around the block and there's still no sign of Julian, but I spot someone just as intriguing.

Mr. Cooke lingers at the edge of the celebration, closer to the lake, for a full ten minutes before he finally makes a move. He's swapped out his usual business casual attire for linen pants paired with a guayabera, an ensemble even Dad can appreciate. His foot taps along to the beat of the music as everyone around him sways. No Latino can resist the allure of old-school salsa.

Once Celia Cruz's voice begins to fade, he heads into the crowd. A few feet away, Isabel leaves Dad with a parting kiss before heading toward the drinks table. I hold my breath as

I watch Mr. Cooke approach Dad, the tap on the shoulder almost startling Dad out of his board shorts. I'm too far away to hear what they're saying, but close enough to know the tension is as thick as a brick.

Whatever Mr. Cooke opens with, it's enough to get Dad to listen. His expression is unusually earnest, while Dad's is as puzzled as mine. The conversation stalls when Mr. Cooke hands over a piece of paper that makes Dad's mouth hang open—whether in shock, or outrage, I'm not sure.

Before I can find out more, a hand closes around my wrist. I smile, and let Julian drag me into the darkness.

"One day someone is going to kidnap me, and my Pavlovian response is going to be to kiss them," I say once I'm pressed up against the wall of a nearby alleyway.

Julian grins, raising an eyebrow. "You want to kiss me?"

I tap his left ear and give him a cheeky grin. "Selective hearing."

He presses a soft kiss to the inside of my wrist. The simple touch leaves goose bumps blossoming along my arms, but when he leans in for a proper kiss, I stop him with a hand to his chest.

As badly as I want to kiss him, he's not getting off that easy. "So, why are you late to the party?"

"Well, I *was* supposed to leave with everyone else, but I had to head home because . . ." He trails off, eyes wide with a new type of excitement as he roots through his tote bag. "I almost forgot to bring this."

My breath catches in my throat. Who would've thought a broken Roomba could make me want to cry?

I take Suck-o into my arms, delicately running a finger between its googly eyes. It's still covered in dents and scratches, but Julian wiped down the dust.

"It's about time this little guy goes home to his rightful owners," he says.

There are so many things I wish I could say, but they all fall short. So I keep it simple. "Thank you."

"That's what fake boyfriends are for." And then he winks. A perfect, effortless wink.

I shove him with my free hand. No one gets away with stealing my joke.

"There's more, though," Julian says, nodding his head at Suck-o. Confused, I turn it over and spot a small envelope, *Báez Family* written on it in unfamiliar handwriting. I quirk an eyebrow at Julian, but he mimes keeping his lips sealed.

The paper inside the envelope is difficult to decipher at first. It's written on company letterhead, a company I quickly realize is Cooke Corp. The first paragraph is mostly business jargon that I'll never understand, but the second paragraph makes the intent *very* clear.

"He's giving us shares in the company?" My voice is so high pitched I'm worried dogs will start showing up. "Y-you can't do that."

"We can, and we did. Or, well, Dad did. He's probably telling your dad about it right now." He jabs his thumb toward where I'd spotted Dad and Mr. Cooke. "It's the least we can do."

Someone desperately needs to pinch me before I decide to live in this daydream permanently. I don't know much about investments, but I know something like this would more than cover keeping the cabin in our name. It's just so far out of the realm of what we expected that it doesn't feel real, even with the proof in my shaking hand.

"It was his idea, actually," Julian continues, pointing to his dad's signature at the bottom of the page. "Ever since he and Mom talked, he's . . . changed. Or trying to. I don't really know what it means for us, but I think things are going to be different this year . . . good different."

There are so many things I could say, and yet all I can do is tremble and blurt out, "I can't believe we own part of a tech company."

Julian chuckles softly, the laughter dying down to a shy smile. "So, guess you're free of me now."

After everything, teasing is still my strong suit. "Yep. Been nice knowing you. Thanks for the Roomba."

The smirk gives him away, but he plays along. "Have a nice life."

I take a few seconds, waiting until he starts walking away to reach out and grab his wrist. He turns before I tug, his hand flying right to my waist. When I cradle his jaw, my thumb traces the edge of the scar on his lip I'd caused years ago, and I kiss him like it's an apology.

"Devin's Great California Adventure doesn't have as good of a ring to it," I say when we part. "Needs the Julian."

Julian's unfairly perfect smile is a bright spot in the darkness, still as stunning as the first day I really noticed him. When he kisses me, I see all our endless possibilities, each one sweeter than the last.

"C'mon," I whisper against his lips, grabbing the tote bag from his hand and tucking everything back in. Fingers linked, I start leading him toward the street. "I don't know if you noticed, but there's a party being thrown in my family's honor."

"So I've heard."

We make our way through the crowd, easily spotting the others at the center of a cluster of people, dancing and laughing together. Either the champagne has softened Maya, or Henry and Stella gave one damn good apology. Henry still seems on edge, tripping over himself as he tries to match Maya's lead. Stella's inhibitions are long gone as she lets Andy twirl her in circles, their cheeks flushed pink. I make my way to the center of the crowd, Julian's hand falling out of mine.

I hold my hand back out to him. "You coming?"

He does, stepping into our circle. Instead of taking my hand, though, he grabs my face with both of his and kisses me so hard I worry I'll lose my balance. But he doesn't let me fall.

I'd be perfectly happy if this was my forever—kissing Julian in the quiet town where we first met, surrounded by the people we love most. No school, no jobs, no mentorships. Just endless lazy afternoons. Lying in the Florida sun, night swims, and last-ditch attempts at bicycling lessons.

But I like our future more.

ACKNOWLEDGMENTS

Hot heck, you just finished my book! Or, if you're anything like me, you skipped straight to the acknowledgments because you're nosy—in which case, hello. I hope you read the book too.

I know you just (maybe) sat through hundreds of pages of my writing, but please bear with me for a few more pages. It took a whole lot of people to get to this point, and they deserve to be celebrated!

A book like this—about love in all its forms—could never have existed without my parents. I still haven't found the right words to thank you both for all of my possibilities, but this is a good place to start.

Mami, it would take another three hundred pages to tell you how lucky I am to call you my mom. You are the best person I know, and the world is a kinder, more beautiful place because of you. Thank you for protecting me from all the monstas.

Daddy, you taught me to love stories long before I started writing them. I wish you were here to see this one, but like the song says, "te llevo en mi corazón." Thank you for always telling me my dialogue could be better. I'd like to think it's improved.

One million and three thank-yous to my incomparable editors at Joy Revolution—Bria Ragin and Nicola and David Yoon. Bria, you are as kind as you are brilliant, and I'll forever be in awe of your editorial eye. David and Nicola, thank you for all you've done to bring such beautiful, joyful stories into the world. It's an honor beyond my wildest dreams to be a part of this family.

Thank you to the entire team at RHCB—especially Wendy Loggia, Beverly Horowitz, and Barbara Marcus—for letting me bring this book into the world. Thank you to Colleen Fellingham, Tamar Schwartz, Stephanie Bay, Cindy Durand, and Shameiza Ally for all your help in bringing this book to life.

Jon Reyes and Angela Kim, thank you so much for your care in helping shape these characters and their stories.

Casey Moses designed the cover of my dreams, Cannaday Chapman's illustration brought it to life, and Ken Crossland made these pages feel like a real book. I'm blown away by your talents.

My superstar agent, Uwe Stender, was the first publishing professional to believe in me and this story, and I'm extremely lucky to have someone so phenomenal championing my work. Thank you, Uwe, for all you've done for me and Devin and Julian. Someday we'll have tres leches cake together!

Thank you to Justine Pucella Winans—my wonderful and hilarious mentor—for helping me shape that messy third-person draft into the story it is today! The way I approach storytelling has been forever changed by your guidance, and I'm eternally grateful to you for believing in me. And for all the Jasper pics. And for showing me the best taco spot in LA.

Alex, Helena, and Leila, this journey wouldn't have been the same without our BTS listening parties and champagne Zooms. I love you three endlessly. Fuck it we ball!

Priv Nation, thank you for being a part of this journey since the very beginning and for all the games of Mafia. GCMJLAASW . . . FC. Special thank-you to Alex Arias for being the kindest soul I've ever had the joy of knowing and letting me borrow our shared brain cell long enough to write this book.

Ye Olde Penthouse LLC—Elisabeth, Jess, Mary Kate, and Rachel, who are the greatest roommates you could ever have—thank you for supporting this dream since Salice 709.

Siena, my dear friend and first ever roomie, thank you for sharing your choco pies.

Trang Thanh Tran and Taleen Voskuni, whose amazing debuts are out by the time you're reading this—I'm so grateful we get to be on this road together.

To the amazing friends who read this story in its various forms—Mary Feely, Bryn Roxburg, Sophia DeRise, Jenna Miller, Hayden Sharpe, Kade Dishmon, Kait Stevens, Sydney Langford, and my first-ever beta, Adri Rodriguez—thank you for laughing at my jokes in their roughest form!

Chanelle, the OG, has been on this ride since the first grade. Thank you for all the adventures and for always coming to hang at your summer home in Prague.

Tim and Jon, the best D&D squad. We planted a dog face, and we have most certainly grown a dog tree.

Thank you to my team at MTV (and former MTV-er Anna) for being so supportive and letting me use Butter in a promo. You've made so many of my dreams come true.

Thank you to BTS, because I can.

My family has encouraged me to be a writer since elementary school, and I hope you all know how much it means to me that I've always had you in my corner. To my tíos, Alex, Booboo, and Raul; my titís, Debbie, Marilyn, and Sandra; and Doreen, the best madrina in the world—thank you for everything. We're the best family around. Anai and Jonathan, our summer antics are a novel all on their own. Someday I'll write it.

Abuela, su fuerza es una inspiración, y te quiero por toda mi vida, con todo mi corazón.

Isabel, soy la persona que soy hoy porque tenía usted en mi vida. Siempre soy tu reina.

Thank you to the Myrick Magidson family for your endless support, love, and tomato sandwiches. And for letting me steal Suck-o.

Dr. Porridge, you only showed up after I finished writing this book, but you make my life so much brighter that I had to include you. Even though you are a dog and will never be able to read this. I'm sorry I'm writing this right now instead of petting you.

And last, but not least, Duncan. My best friend, my partner in all things. I couldn't have done this without you. Guess you made it to the acknowledgments after all.

ABOUT THE AUTHOR

Elle Gonzalez Rose is a producer and author from New York who's better at writing love stories about short, queer Boricuas than she is at writing bios. Her dog thinks she's okay. *Caught in a Bad Fauxmance* is her debut novel—Elle's, not the dog's.

ellegonzalezrose.com

Underlined

Where Books Are Life

your favorite **books**

your favorite **authors**

all in one place

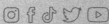